ONLY THE BEGINNING

ONLY YOU, #4

ELLE THORPE

WWW.ELLETHORPE.COM

For my beautiful sister, Michela. Here's something to read during 2am baby duty.

1

BIANCA

"*F*uck, you have great tits."

I checked my watch. Wow. What a compliment, and not even ten minutes into the date. I fought to keep from rolling my eyes, and instead, smiled tightly at the dickhead sitting across the table from me.

He was a handsome dickhead, with his dirty-blond hair and chiselled jaw. His collared white shirt clung to a muscular frame, tanned skin on display where he'd left several buttons undone. Not just several. Half his shirt, really. I could see the tops of his abs. He obviously thought it was sexy, and maybe his shit come-on lines, if that was what that had been, worked on some people. Maybe he just flashed that fake white smile, told women their tits were great, and they threw their underwear at him.

Vomit.

"You wanna get outta here?" he asked, voice smooth as silk.

"What?" I stuttered. Was he serious? Our waiter had barely had time to take our entree order. "What about dinner?"

He shrugged, and then one eye kind of half closed, and he went back to smirking at me.

I stifled a laugh. Was that supposed to be a sexy wink? It

looked more like an eye twitch. Suddenly, I regretted every single one of my life choices that had led to this moment.

"Sure, we can eat. If you really want."

What I really wanted was a drink. And to yell at my best friend for making me come on a ridiculous Tinder date anyway. I should have known better than to take advice from someone who had been with her husband for ten years and had probably never even downloaded a hookup app.

"Excuse me for a moment." I picked up my bag and carried it to the bathrooms, pulling out my phone while I locked the stall door behind me. At least it was nice in here. The tiles were black marble, or at least imitation marble, and the fittings glinted silver under chrome lights. Sitting on the closed lid of the toilet, I called Reese.

"I hate you," I moaned when she answered.

"What did I do?"

"You made me come on this stupid date! The guy's opening line was to tell me my tits were great, and he's already giving me the come-on. He's probably going to ask me for anal before we even get to dessert at this rate."

Reese snorted on her laugh. But I was serious, so it didn't seem all that funny. "I should have never come."

That sobered her. "Why not? You keep telling me there's nothing between you and Ri—"

"Don't say his name!" I cut her off, imagining one hand on her hip and a frown creasing the space between her eyebrows.

She sighed. "B, he's one of our best friends. His name is going to come up."

"No, he's one of your best friends."

"Come on, you know that's not true. He cares about you, and you care about him, in some weird, demented sort of way. Not that anyone else would know it with the way you two go at each other like pit bulls in a dogfight."

I sighed. She was right. But I wished she'd stop. She was only making things worse. Every time his name was said out loud, all it did was make me think about the last time we'd been together. And all the times before that.

"You're thinking about him, aren't you? B, you gotta stop this. You and Riley—"

"Aaaah!"

She was rolling her eyes for sure.

"Fine. You and the man who shall not be named, you can't keep doing whatever the hell you've been doing for the past ten years. Just tell him you love him and live happily ever after already."

Jeez, she was over the top. And I was supposed to be the actress. Maybe I should get her a job on my show. "You said it yourself, Reese. All we do is fight."

"And fuck."

My cheeks heated at the thought. Yes. We fucked. A lot.

"We don't work. We can barely be in the same room as each other without a screaming match breaking out. Yeah, there's chemistry there. There always has been. We scratch an itch for each other from time to time. But chemistry isn't the grounds for a relationship."

There was a moment of silence, then, "I know."

"Are you pouting?" I asked with a laugh. I knew our friends wanted Riley and me to get our shit together, but it was never going to happen. There was nothing between us. Nothing but history. And history should stay in the past. "Look, I'm ditching this date."

"No, wait. Stop. You know I'm Team Riley but I'm also Team Bianca. Tell me, once and for all, there's really nothing there between you two, and I will never mention it again."

Ugh, the woman was exasperating sometimes. "There's nothing between us," I said truthfully. "I mean it, Reese. I need you to have my back. You know I have no willpower around him. I need a boyfriend. I wouldn't still be having casual sex with him if I had someone else. That's why you made me come here, remember?"

"Right. No more sleeping with Riley. I shall never speak of the two of you again. Now get back out there and give that guy a proper chance. Maybe he was just nervous."

I doubted the dickhead had ever been nervous. And I also doubted Reese would never speak of Riley and me again. I'd told her just last week that I was done giving in to my basic urges, which was why I'd agreed to come on a Tinder date. Riley and I hadn't dated in ten years. It was time to put whatever we were to each other to bed. To start acting like grown adults. Not horny twenty-somethings who hated each other but couldn't keep their hands to themselves.

But goddammit. Was the dickhead waiting for me in the restaurant really the answer? Riley and I might have spent years arguing, but he'd never leered at me the way Dickhead had.

"Okay, I'm going back to deal with Prince Not So Charming." I laughed, though it sounded fake even to my own ears.

I said goodbye to Reese and pushed open the bathroom door. I'd been in there for ages and I semi hoped my date might have given up and gone home. I slid my bag strap up on my shoulder, flicked my hair back off my face, and lifted my head.

And froze. My gaze collided with familiar brown eyes, and heat swept through my body like a wildfire. I swore quietly under my breath.

Riley.

This was exactly why he was the man who should not be named. Because everything about him, his name, his beautiful face, his smouldering gaze—everything about him scrambled my senses. I'd never been able to think straight around him. There had always been something between us. Something so damn strong it had a force of its own. Something strong enough that it had withstood ten years.

I faltered. Images of the last time we'd been together flashed in front of my eyes. His lips on my neck. My legs wrapped around his back. His cock buried deep inside me and my orgasm roaring through my core.

Fuck.

I had to stop this. My date was waiting for me. And, with a start, I noticed Riley was on a date of his own. The realisation hit me like a punch to the stomach. The woman across from him chatted happily, not seeming to notice that he'd been staring at me since I'd walked out of the bathroom. Jealousy flared in my chest. It wasn't like we kept each other updated on our lives, but surely Reese would have told me if he was seeing someone. Her husband was his best friend after all. She had to have known...

I couldn't stop staring, his eyes holding me to the spot. The air between us crackled with an energy so tangible I could practically see it. I shook my head slightly. *Get a grip.* He wasn't mine. He hadn't been mine in so long, I had no right to be jealous. Dragging my gaze away from him, I pulled back my shoulders and made my way to my table.

I knew he was watching me. And despite knowing I shouldn't, I liked it.

2

RILEY

"*D*o you know her?"

I whipped my head back to focus on my date. Cora. The woman from the office of the construction company I worked for. I didn't go in there much, just a few times a month to drop off paperwork. But she always flirted with me, and she was gorgeous, with long auburn hair and big green eyes. She'd lined them in black tonight, and her lips were plump and red. She was a flat-out siren, really. Just...not the siren I wanted.

"Uh. No," I lied. "Sorry. She just looks like someone I know."

"Isn't it funny when that happens? When I was in high school..."

Her voice faded into the noise of the restaurant, and I smiled, nodded and occasionally made encouraging sounds when she paused for breath. She was a talker. But that was fine, because I wasn't.

Cora filled me in on her entire high school experience while I fought every muscle in my body. Every instinct screamed that Bianca was close by. I curled my fingers around the tabletop, digging my fingers into the hard wood, struggling to keep myself out of her magnetic pull. It was an almost painful feeling by now. Being in the same room as her but not touching her. It was the same physical ache that hadn't let up for even a minute since she'd broken my heart ten years ago. Fuck.

Cora excused herself to go to the bathroom, a welcome relief, and I reached for my phone, listening to the voicemail message Low had sent me earlier in the week.

"Listen, bro. Reese would kill me if she knew I was telling you this. But Bianca was over here last night, and, well...she told Reese she doesn't want to do the fighting hate-sex thing you two have been doing anymore. She said it's holding her back, and I'm sorry, man, but I think she's right. She's holding you back, too. Have you even dated at all in the past decade? You're going to end up one of those old men who sits on his porch and yells at the neighbourhood kids if you keep this up. Just...I don't know. Branch out. Leave B alone. You guys have been there, done that. It didn't work. I know it's not my business, but maybe it's time to accept that. See you at football on Saturday."

I stabbed the cancel button. I'd listened to the message probably fifty times the day he'd sent it. At first, I'd been pissed off and ready to storm over there and tell him exactly where to shove his shit advice. What did he know about Bianca and me? We were...complicated.

But the more I'd listened, the more my anger had dissipated. Nothing he'd said was a lie. Every time I saw her, we somehow ended up in an argument, or we ended up not talking at all and just started ripping clothes off. There was no middle ground. Nothing solid to build on. Just the glimmering memory of something magical that had turned sour.

A loud scrape of a chair caught my attention, and I took the opportunity to swivel backwards, my gaze landing on Bianca's lithe frame. She was shaking her head at her date, her expression full of irritation. I picked up my wine glass, forcing myself to take a sip and remain seated. I didn't like the way he was leering at her. He said something back to her, then she threw her hands in the air and stormed away from him.

I frowned, though pleased she was ending her date. The guy was a complete tool. Who did he think he was anyway? He looked like an over-tanned, washed-up Hollywood wannabe who was past his prime. But I didn't like that she was upset. I followed her with my eyes until she disappeared around a corner into the depths of the restaurant and I lost sight of her. My gaze narrowed on the over-buffed jerk she'd been out with. He didn't try to go after her. Just pulled her plate of food across the table and started eating. I let out a long breath, trying to calm the protective urge to go after her and make sure she was okay. If Low's message was true, and I had no reason to doubt him, Bianca didn't want me around. I'd half-heartedly tried this before. Avoiding her. I'd tried it many times, actually. But she was like a drug I couldn't quit. And she seemed to feel the same about me. Every time I'd managed to leave her alone, inevitably, she'd turn up somewhere I was, and we'd fall back into our same old routine. We weren't together. We hadn't been since we were barely older than teenagers. And yet we couldn't seem to get out of each other's bubbles.

Cora leant in and raked her fingernails gently across my forearm. I hadn't even noticed her return. She had her breasts pushed so high they practically spilled from her dress. What the fuck was wrong with me? Sitting here, pining away over a woman I'd never been able to have. A woman who clearly didn't want me, not for anything more than to argue or have sex with, when there was a perfectly viable alternative right in front of me. One who was giving me every signal in the book that she was a green light.

"Listen, Riley," Cora said, her voice sultry. She looked up at me through lowered lashes and licked her tongue over her lips. It was supposed to be a seductive move but did nothing for me.

"I'm not going to beat around the bush. I don't need this to be some epic romance."

I paused. "Okay."

"You understand what I'm saying?"

Oh, I understood. I just wasn't sure I wanted to do anything about it.

But then I heard Low's voice in my ear. *"Leave B alone. You're holding her back."* Tension threaded through my back. That was the last thing I'd ever wanted. I never wanted to be someone who held her back. She was a star in an inky-black sky. If she wasn't allowed to shine, the nights would be dark.

I nodded to Cora. "I understand." *Fucking hell. Grow a pair, Riley.* I was single. Cora was single. She wanted this. And maybe it was what I needed. I hadn't slept with anyone but Bianca for most of my adult life. I'd put her on a pedestal. Staying faithful to a woman I wasn't even in a relationship with. It was fucking ridiculous.

I held my hand out to Cora, and she gave me a million-dollar smile. Then I led her to the door, like I took women home every day. Other single men in their thirties did this? Didn't they? Screw it. I was doing it. I could do a night of casual sex with someone other than Bianca. Pussy was pussy. A tight wet hole to get off in.

Even as I thought it, I knew I was full of shit. I couldn't pull that sort of attitude off. But I continued the internal pep talk anyway. *Change is as good as a holiday. You have to move on with someone else eventually. Get back in the saddle.* All the clichéd metaphors I could think of.

I held open the restaurant door, then put my hand on the small of Cora's back as I walked her to her car.

"My place?" she purred, pushing herself against my chest in the dimly lit car park.

She was warm and soft where I was hard, and it was on the

tip of my tongue to say yes, when a shiny red convertible parked in the next row over caught my eye.

Bianca's convertible.

I stepped back, running my fingers through my hair. Hadn't she left? But if her car was still here, then maybe she was, too. And so was that jerk she'd been on a date with. Unease settled over me. She hadn't wanted to be near that guy. *I* didn't want her near that guy.

All thoughts of going home to have meaningless sex with Cora disintegrated. I had to find Bianca. Just to make sure she was okay. Even though we fought all the time, she was still my friend. Sort of. At the least, Low and Reese would have my head if I told them I'd just left when she could have been in a dangerous situation.

I opened the door for Cora, and she got in. "Follow me home?"

I shook my head. "Maybe next time." I was an asshole. I knew I was giving her mixed signals. I expected her to spit fire at me, but to my surprise she just shrugged.

"You know how to reach me if you change your mind." She drove away with a small wave.

"You're a fucking idiot," I muttered to myself as I watched her headlights disappear into the darkness. And I was. Cora was amazing. And maybe I'd really regret letting her go when I woke up with a raging case of blue balls tomorrow morning.

But there was no denying that if Bianca needed me, I was going to drop everything for her and run.

I always had. And I always would.

3

BIANCA

I liked tequila. Who knew? Not me, until I'd sat down in the darkened corner of the restaurant bar and ordered a double shot. And then another. The first shot had burned its way down my throat, but the pleasant warmth it left in its wake had me chasing more of it. By the bottom of the third shot, I was pleasantly buzzed. Which was exactly where I wanted to be. Because dating sucked. Tinder sucked. And guys with piercing brown eyes who shall not be named? Well, they sucked, too.

My date had been a disaster. When he'd asked if I thought one of my costars was up for a threesome, I'd left. I'd considered just going straight home, but... Riley.

He was still there on his date, and I hated that I was being so ridiculous, but I had to know if he was going home with her. The thought of him doing all the things he usually did to me, to someone else...it made me feel sick. It was like a train wreck I couldn't look away from. So instead of leaving, I'd hidden in the restaurant bar, slamming back shots and studying the door with the laser-like focus of a hawk. I couldn't see his table, but there was only one exit point. They'd have to leave eventually.

And when they finally did, my heart sank. The woman he was with moved like a panther, all sleek lines and long limbs. Her hourglass figure was perfection in a tight dress, and even I knew she'd be dynamite in bed. Sexual confidence just oozed from her. Riley opened the restaurant door, his hand resting on the bare skin of her back, ushering her through. My heart took another beating as he walked her to her car and she pressed herself against him.

I turned away. I couldn't watch anymore. I couldn't watch him lean down and press his mouth to hers. Because I knew exactly what his kisses felt like. They were earth-shattering. Full of a passion and desire, and I'd felt each and every one of them to my toes. I'd promised myself, and Reese, that I'd stop this ridiculous charade with Riley, but the thought of never getting one of his kisses again left me hollow inside.

I threw back another shot and my head swayed. Shit. How many had I had? Too many to drive, that was for sure. Oh well. I'd just stay here drinking by myself until they closed the bar down. It wasn't like I had anywhere better to be.

"Bianca?"

Damn. His voice in my head sounded exactly like it did in real life. Deep and gravelly. So sexy.

"Bianca," he said again.

With a start, I realised there was a hand on my arm and the voice wasn't in my head, but next to my ear. My eyes snapped open.

Why did he have to be so hot? His hair was a little longer than normal. Not quite as long as it had been when we'd dated, though. He'd had a sort of punk-rock style back then, but it had evolved over the years. He was still all jeans and band t-shirts. But he'd lost the eyebrow ring at some point and cut his locks. His dark-brown eyes had once been so carefree, but now they seemed worried. Frown lines creased his forehead, and without thinking, I reached up and smoothed them away. The pads of my thumbs tingled as they came in contact with his skin.

"You came back," I whispered. "What happened to your date?"

He sighed and sat next to me. I knew I shouldn't, and if I'd been sober, I probably wouldn't have, but I inched closer to his warmth. Our arms rested side by side. Not quite touching.

"I saw your car in the parking lot. That jerk you were on a date with is here somewhere. I didn't want him giving you a hard time."

"Oh." Dammit. "I ruined your date, didn't I? You'd probably be having hot sex with her right now if you hadn't seen my car, huh?" My stomach rolled, the thought of him in someone else's bed making me ill. I mean, I was sure he slept with women besides me. We had no formal arrangements. We weren't even fuck buddies. We were just exes who still had mutual friends. Which meant we inevitably ran into each other from time to time. And most of those times, we either ended up in an argument, or we ended up having sex.

He dipped his head to search my face. "You didn't ruin anything, B. You couldn't."

His words soothed my tormented soul, and I leaned my head on his shoulder so the room would stop spinning. He put his arm around my shoulders, and I snuggled in closer to his chest, instantly relaxed. We always had fitted together so well.

Why couldn't it always be like this?

"Why can't we just be two people who met right here, right now? Why do we have to have all the baggage?"

I tilted my head up, letting my lips brush his neck. A tiny tremor ran through him.

"What would you say if we were just meeting for the first time?"

I straightened, fighting the dizziness, and gave him my best smile while extending a hand for him to shake. He stared at it for a moment, then his lips curled up, and he took it. His big hand enveloped mine as we shook.

"I'm BB," I said chirpily.

He raised an eyebrow. "You'd go with BB instead of Bianca?"

I shrugged. "Probably. Until I got to know you better." BB was the stage name I'd used ever since I'd first started acting. To most of the Australian population, I was BB James. Aussie starlet, lead actress on an evening soapie. To my friends and family —to Riley—I was Bianca or just B.

"Nice to meet you then, BB," he said in an overexaggerated fashion. "I'm Riley. I build houses for a living. And I have a fifteen-year-old daughter named Sadie. She's beautiful, and smart—gets straight A's at school. She's amazing. Being her dad is the best thing in the world."

I knew about his daughter, of course, but I feigned surprise. "Fifteen-year-old daughter, huh? Wow, that must make you pretty old." I fought the smile when he rolled his eyes.

"I was sixteen when her mother fell pregnant."

"Ah, I see," I said, carrying on the charade. "Hot, *young,* single dad then, are you?"

He leaned in a fraction. "You think I'm hot?"

"You know I do." I wasn't sure if we were still playing the game or not. My heart thumped, and my gaze dipped to his mouth

"Dammit, Bianca," he said in a strangled voice. "You gotta stop looking at me like that."

"Like what?" I whispered, moving closer so our lips were only inches apart.

"Like you want me to kiss you."

"I do, though."

He groaned, his arm circling me. "You're drunk."

"I don't care." I wrapped my arms around his neck and

kissed his lips. He froze beneath my touch, but that didn't deter me. I knew what he liked. I nipped at his lips, running my tongue along the seam, urging him to open for me.

"Fuck me," he whispered against my mouth. With a move so swift I didn't notice, or maybe he was slow, but my tequila-riddled brain was slower, he bundled me into his arms and stormed across the restaurant towards his jeep.

I giggled. "So, caveman. Where are we going?"

"I'm taking you home."

I grinned. About time.

4

RILEY

A long blonde strand of hair fell across Bianca's sleeping face. She'd curled up on the passenger seat of my jeep and dozed off before I'd even been able to get to the driver's side. I'd known that would happen. I knew her well enough to know she was a complete lightweight when it came to alcohol. She was tiny, and she hadn't eaten her meal. I was surprised she'd lasted as long as she had, considering the handful of empty shot glasses on the table when I'd gotten there.

I'd refused to kiss her back. Not because I didn't want to. Because, fuck knows, I always wanted to kiss her. I'd kiss every inch of her a thousand times over if she'd just let me. But it wasn't what she needed. She'd been right when she'd told Reese we couldn't keep doing what we were doing. That we were bad for each other. I had to respect that, even when she was too drunk to remember. She didn't really want me in that moment. I was just safe—and familiar.

I took the half a dozen streets from the restaurant to Bianca's apartment, entering the code that let me into the garage, and parked the jeep in her spot. She didn't stir as I lifted her from the seat and grabbed the jacket and handbag she'd tossed onto the floor. "Hey, Jerry," I said to the security guard reading a book in the lobby.

He glanced up, lifting a hand in greeting then frowned at Bianca bundled up in my arms. "She okay?"

I nodded. "Tequila."

He chuckled. "Yeah, it'll do that to ya."

He went back to his book, and I took the lift to Bianca's top-floor apartment. Inside, I kicked my shoes off and padded across the pristine space before depositing her gently on the bed. I straightened, and it hit me in the gut again, just how beautiful she was. She'd stopped my heart the minute I'd met her, and age had done nothing but increase my attraction to her. She was my perfect woman with her curves in all the right places.

Tugging up a blanket, I tucked it around her, pausing as her eyelids fluttered open. They were slightly bloodshot and panicked, but when her gaze landed on me, she quieted.

"What are you doing?"

"Tucking you into bed. I brought you home."

"For sex."

I shook my head, fighting back a laugh at the disoriented expression on her face. "No, sweetheart. I brought you home to sleep off the copious amounts of alcohol you drank tonight."

I expected her to just sink back into the mattress, but she didn't. She crawled to her knees then across the bed. She knelt in front of me and lifted her shirt. Whoa.

"B..." I warned.

She wasn't listening. She reached back and unclasped her bra, pulling it away, letting her breasts fall free. I'd seen her bare skin so many times, but this didn't feel right. She was too drunk. And after what she'd said to Reese less than a week ago, I just couldn't see her like this.

I turned away.

Picking up her shirt, I held it out to her. "Please, B." My voice was hoarse. God. I knew how good she felt. I knew how her taste changed slightly, right before she orgasmed. And if I lived to be a million years old, I'd still never never get enough of it.

But not like this.

There was a long pause then she yanked the shirt out of my grasp. The sheets shuffled as she moved around, putting clothes back on. "Just go, Riley," she said quietly.

The hurt in her voice cut through me. But what the hell was I supposed to do? I couldn't make love to her again, not after she'd been so committed to wanting something different. I couldn't do that, just because she was drunk and horny. It wasn't right.

I pivoted and stared at the tiny ball she'd formed with her body, a blanket tucked right up to her chin, her back to me. I forced the words from my mouth. "Goodnight."

She didn't answer. I closed her bedroom door softly behind me, placed her bag, jacket, and keys, neatly on the kitchen bench, and tugged on my shoes. Then I left her apartment, being careful to make sure it locked behind me.

She probably wouldn't remember any of this in the morning. But I would.

5

BIANCA

I dropped the top on my convertible once I left the city limits, even though the late winter air was still brisk. My sorry, hungover ass needed the fresh air washing over my face. It helped clear my head, and I sucked in greedy lungfuls while I coasted the familiar roads to my parents' house. This was my Saturday morning ritual. I'd made this trip every Saturday morning since I'd moved to the city. I hadn't missed one.

Sometimes, like today, it was the last thing I felt like doing. But I went anyway. A hangover and the lingering embarrassment from last night certainly wasn't a good enough reason not to go. It was the one thing I had promised my mother when I'd left home at nineteen. I'd known she'd worry herself into an early grave if she didn't see me regularly. And I didn't want to add to the already long list of worrying images that consumed her thoughts night and day. I loved her too much, and I hated to see her suffering the way she did.

I still vaguely remembered the way she'd been before.

And my heart broke for her and the way her life had been turned upside down. So if my coming home for breakfast once a week helped her in some tiny way, then I was going to do it.

I just hoped she hadn't watched my show this week.

The handbrake clicked as I lifted it up, and I parked my car in the driveway of the little suburban home I'd grown up in. It was still exactly the same as I remembered. Not a thing out of place, everything blending in perfectly with the other houses on the street, not drawing any attention to the people that lived inside. Just the way my mother liked it.

I waved a hand in greeting when I saw her peep through the heavy curtains, and the front door swung open before I even reached the steps. She didn't come out to greet me, though, the way she had when I was a kid coming home from school. She'd been a bit better back then, in the first few years after we'd moved to Australia. I'd only been six, but I remembered her greeting me on the driveway after the school bus had dropped me off.

But she'd gotten worse over the years. And I knew she wouldn't leave the depths of her house now. Not even for me.

"Hi, baby," she said quietly, tucking me into her arms once I'd stepped through the doorway. She held me tight, then pulled back and ran her gaze over me, as if assuring herself I was okay. All in one piece.

Healthy.

Breathing.

She frowned. "You don't look well. Are you sick?"

I shook my head. "I'm fine." I didn't want to tell her I'd just written myself off last night. That wouldn't go down well with her. She'd work herself up into a state, and it would ruin the morning.

She studied me doubtfully, but I moved past her and dumped my keys and bag on the kitchen bench, then kissed my father on the cheek. He glanced up from where he was flipping bacon on the stovetop, took in my probably dishevelled appearance, and winked at me.

"Big night?" he whispered.

I nodded, and we shared a small smile.

"Sit down, kiddo. Breakfast will be ready in a minute."

I dragged a stool from beneath the breakfast bar where we always ate and watched Dad's back as he expertly moved around the kitchen. Mum did most of the cooking normally, since she was home all the time, and it gave her something to do. But Dad was always in charge of Saturday morning fry-ups. They were his specialty, and I ate super healthy all week just so I could indulge on the weekends.

Mum sat next to me. "I watched the show this week."

I fought back a cringe and instead plastered a smile on my face. "You did? What did you think of Elaina's new storyline?"

She turned her light-blue eyes on me. She was still a beautiful woman, even in her sixties. An elegant, timeless beauty the magazines had called her once upon a time. Her skin was still pale and smooth, with only small lines around her eyes and forehead betraying her age. My father made her sit in patches of sun during the day, but the fact she rarely left the house meant the sun hadn't aged her the way it did most women.

"You were wonderful, sweetheart. You always are. Elaina is a great role."

I nodded and picked up my fork to stab at a piece of bacon my father had placed in front of me. There was a but coming, I could feel it.

"But that little girl you have on your show. The one who plays Layla?"

Yep, there it was. I knew as soon as I'd read the script that my mother would be upset we were bringing in another child actor. I didn't dare tell her that the girl playing Layla was actually two children. Identical twins, Audrey and Emily. I glanced over at my father, and he gave me an apologetic shrug. I pressed my lips firmly together to keep from telling him off. I'd called and warned him not to let Mum watch the show this week.

"It should be illegal," she said stiffly. Her fingers trembled as she picked up her fork. "It's dangerous. Especially in this day and age. The whole world will know who and where they are at all times of the day. They'll have photographers watching them and following them. It's irresponsible parenting, that's what it is."

Mum's breaths came in short pants, quickening until my heart thumped, my worry for her overwhelming everything else.

"Isn't there anything you can do, Bianca?" she pleaded. "Speak to the director or something? Those little girls don't know what they're getting into. I just want to shake their parents. Shake some sense into them and tell them exactly what can happen if—"

Her fork clattered against her plate, and she pulled her trembling hands into her lap, hunching her shoulders as she curled in on herself.

"Oh, Mum," I said, circling my arm around her shoulders. All I could do was hold her while she shook. This was why I'd told Dad not to let her watch the show. I'd known Emily and Audrey's baby-doll faces and golden blonde curls would be triggering for her.

I looked to Dad helplessly, but he was staring sadly at my mother, resignation in his eyes. He'd given up on her getting better a long time ago, I knew that. He did his best to care for her, getting her doctor to come to the house and check her medications, but I knew he thought she was too deeply scarred for it to really be of much help. What she really needed was a therapist. And I'd tried. God knows I'd tried so many times, but she refused to speak of her past. She didn't trust anyone outside my dad and me. She was convinced any therapist she spoke to would sell her story to the tabloids.

And I couldn't blame her. I'd only been a child when our lives had all changed in the blink of an eye. But I still had memories from that day that haunted me. We'd lost so much, but my mother most of all. Because she'd lost herself, too.

"They could be hurt, Bianca. Please. You need to do something. Hollywood is no place for little girls."

I tugged her closer and rested my head on her shoulder. I didn't bother correcting her, telling her that this wasn't Hollywood. I knew she wasn't talking about my show anymore, or Emily and Audrey. She'd slipped into her own, dark memories. And I knew from all the other times this had happened, that it would be some time before we got her back. And all we could do in the meantime was hold her and hope that she was strong enough to pull herself out.

Hollywood had left my mother scarred and broken. I knew it killed her every day that I was acting. And I hated that. I truly did. But I was selfish. The lure of acting had drawn me in like a siren, and I couldn't resist it. Acting fed my soul. And that came with a guilt I had learned to live with. But there was one thing on which I agreed with my mother. Children didn't belong in this industry. This lifestyle chewed people up and spat them out.

6

BIANCA

"*I* love baby showers," Reese announced later that afternoon, her gaze travelling around the outdoor area we'd just spent the last two hours decorating.

I'd driven straight from my parents' place to Reese's where we were hosting a baby shower for our other bestie, Elodie. We'd strung white lanterns around the yard and set up tables with fresh flower centrepieces. Jamison, Elodie's husband, and Low had been put to work in the kitchen, making platters of food for the guests who would be arriving soon.

I squinted at her through my pounding headache. Comforting my mother, then decorating in the sun for hours hadn't helped my hangover any. "You do?" I glanced over at Elodie who wore an expression I was sure matched mine. Reese had become oddly sappy since getting married. "All the stupid games, and the predictions and watching someone open a billionty gifts. Not to mention then listening to them *oooh* and *aaah* over each of them. You love all that?" I questioned her but then kind of wished I hadn't. I was just making my headache worse by talking.

The baby shower was the last thing I wanted to do right now, but Elodie and Jamison were important to me. Jamison and I had worked together at a bar a million years ago, along with Low, Reese, and the man who shall not be named. Elodie had joined our little circle of friends when she'd begun dating Jamison, and the six of us had been tight. For a while. Until things went south with Riley and me. But despite that, and despite us all moving on from bartending into our careers, we'd remained friends. So I couldn't be a no-show today. These people were as much my family as my parents were, and I wasn't going to miss a special day for them. So I'd dosed up on paracetamol and energy drinks, and dragged my ass to coo over onesies and eat my weight in baby-themed cupcakes.

"There'll be none of that baby shower ridiculousness here today," Elodie announced, placing her hands on her swollen belly. "This is just an excuse to have a barbecue. The guys are all staying."

I paused. "They are?"

Shit. That meant...

"Riley's here," Jamison yelled to Elodie from inside the house. "He's going to get the meat started."

Reese and Elodie both turned to look at me.

"What?" I had to force the word out. I hadn't told them about last night. I hadn't even really let myself think about it. It was all too mortifying to be real.

"Are you cool? Or are you still having adverse reactions to hearing his name?"

Ha. Adverse reactions. If only they knew exactly how opposite to adverse my reactions had been last night when I'd practically thrown myself at the man.

I waved a hand around in the air like I was totally chill. On the inside, I was running away screaming. But I was an actress. I could fake it. "It's fine."

Riley stepped through the back door onto the patio, and

Reese and Elodie both called out greetings to him. I couldn't do it, though. I wanted to show my friends that I was sticking to my word. That I was ending this ongoing drama between Riley and me, but speaking to him after last night just wasn't an option. So instead, I turned away and busied myself with some white balloons and pretended I hadn't noticed his entrance.

I'd noticed, though. Because I always noticed him, no matter where we were. It was that stupid, seemingly inbuilt connection that sounded alarms in my brain and sent shockwaves through my body every time he was around. Sometimes I didn't even need to see him.

I just knew.

Like now. Even with my back to him, I knew he was watching me. I could feel his heated gaze, burning the skin at the back of my neck.

Elodie and Jamison's guests soon began filling the space, and I was grateful because it was easier to hide in a crowd. I sat with Elodie's mother for a while and chatted, while her crazy mane of silver hair bobbed around in the pleasant afternoon breeze. And then I found Nathan, Elodie's eldest son, and asked him about school and his friends. He was fifteen, though, so that conversation was as short-lived as you might expect. He took the first opportunity to ditch me, and I couldn't blame him. I wouldn't have wanted to hang out with my parents' friends when I was fifteen either.

"Bianca," Riley said from behind me.

I spun around. Shit. I'd lost track of where he was and hadn't even seen him coming. My face burned, remembering the way I'd asked him for sex last night and how he'd shut me down.

I was pathetic. Telling all my friends I was done with him, that there'd never been anything between us, then practically jumping in his lap the very next time I saw him. And it wasn't fair on him either, sending him such mixed messages.

I couldn't stand here and talk to him like nothing had happened. Or worse. We'd pretend to talk nicely for a few minutes, then inevitably, one of us would pick a fight and we'd end up in an argument. I couldn't do that. Not today and after the morning I'd had with my mother.

"Hey, sorry, Elodie asked me to get some more ice. I have to go," I lied. I pulled away from him, threading my way through the crowd and around the side of the house to where my car was parked. I was fumbling with the keys, stabbing at the unlock button, when he caught up to me, his big hand curling around my wrist.

"Don't run," he said quietly in my ear.

My damn traitorous knees went weak, and I had to force them to hold my weight. "I'm not," I said indignantly. His fingers still covered the pulse point in my wrist, and I wondered if he could feel exactly how fast my heart was beating.

"About last night—"

"I don't want to talk about last night."

"Why?"

"Why?" I pulled my hand away from him, hoping that if he wasn't touching me, I could get my thoughts into some sort of coherent order. It didn't work, though, because his broad body crowded in on me, forcing me backwards until I was trapped between him and my car. I knew without a doubt he'd move and let me pass if I really wanted him to. But we both knew what this was. We both knew I liked having him this close, even if it meant I couldn't think straight. "Last night was embarrassing. You completely rejected me."

He stepped back an inch. "What? I didn't reject you at all. You were blind drunk. I'm surprised you even remember."

Irritation crept in, drowning out my lust. "It's me, Riley. We've been screwing around for years. I'm not some random woman you picked up in a bar. You flat-out rejected me."

"I was being a gentleman."

Or, he left to go find his date and fuck her. That was what this whole thing boiled down to, wasn't it? I couldn't get the image of Riley and that woman from last night out of my head. His fingers touching the bare skin of her back. Him smiling at her as he'd pushed open the restaurant door for her. And the way, she'd been all over him in the car park. He'd taken me home because I was drunk and he felt sorry for me. And I'd thrown myself at him like a fool, only to be put aside with a pitying look.

Ugh. I knew I was overreacting. Beneath all the yelling we did, he cared about me. If nothing else, he knew how to be a friend, and he'd been watching out for me. And I was grateful, because I really had drunk way too much. But after he'd left, I'd spent all night imagining him having sex with someone else. Someone else raking her nails down his skin. Someone else writhing beneath him while he drove his cock deep between her legs. I hadn't slept, while my jealous mind played image after image of him with another woman, each and every thought making me sicker than the last.

I shook my head. I needed to get away from him. I needed some space from him. Some time to think. I couldn't do that when he was standing so damn close. I jabbed the unlock button on my car again, and this time, I opened the door. Just like I knew he would, he stepped back and let me, but his frustration was evident in the way he thrust his fingers through his hair.

"B. Just talk to me!"

I couldn't. We didn't talk. If we talked, I might blurt out the truth. "I have to go get ice," I replied lamely.

His dark gaze locked with mine, and I tried to ignore the hurt I saw there. This. This is exactly why I'd told Reese I was giving him up. We weren't good for each other. One of us always ended up hurting the other. We'd never been able to get our shit together. I needed a clean break. And so did he.

He just nodded. And I pulled the door closed before driving off.

I didn't get the ice. And I didn't return to the party.

It was better for everyone, especially Riley, if I stayed away.

7

RILEY

*I*t had been my ex's weekend with my daughter, Sadie, so I hadn't seen her in over a week. And that sucked. I hated the weekends she didn't come stay with me. I called her all the time, and for fifteen, she was pretty good about answering. But as I often did after one of my solo weekends, I dropped by her mother's house on my way to work, just because I missed her.

Eliza, Sadie's mother, opened the door and kissed me on the cheek in greeting. She didn't seem at all surprised that I was on her doorstep at eight a.m. on a Monday morning. "Hey. She's upstairs, but I've got to go. Remind her to take her sport gear, will you? I know she deliberately forgets it on Mondays so she doesn't have to participate." A tiny smile lifted the corner of her mouth. "I used to do exactly the same thing in high school, so I get it, but also, I'm her mother, and it's a required subject. Make sure she has it packed, Riley."

I gave her a mock salute which she didn't see as she was too busy bellowing down the hallway for her husband, Simon, to hurry up. He jogged around the corner, straightening his tie, and gave me a nod as he passed. The door slammed shut behind them, and I was left in the empty hallway alone.

Eliza and I hadn't always been on such good terms. She'd fallen pregnant at fifteen after a summer fling. I'd known nothing about her pregnancy until she came back in my life five years later with a five-year-old who wanted to call me Daddy. I'd fallen in love with Sadie right then and there, but it had taken me a long time to forgive or to trust her mother again.

I bounded up the stairs, pausing at Sadie's closed bedroom door, and knocked out the complicated pattern I'd used every time I wanted to enter her room since she was a little kid. She was too old for games like that now, of course. But I still always did it, out of habit.

The door swung open. "Dad!" she yelped, grabbing my arm and dragging me inside. Then she checked the hallway in both directions.

I sat on her bed and laughed as she closed the door behind her, leaning against it dramatically.

"Something is up with Mum," she declared.

I tilted my head. "What does that mean? If you got in trouble with her, don't ask me to bail you out. You know your mum and I are a joint force on things like that."

She shook her head. "I haven't done anything. Swear. They're planning something."

"To take over the world perhaps?" I couldn't hide my amusement. She looked so serious.

She groaned and threw a pillow at me. But then she sat next to me, and I realised she was truly worried about something. And that sobered me.

"Dad, I'm serious. Can you ask her?"

"You're going to have to give me something more than that. What's been going on? And why haven't you asked her?"

She threw up her hands. "I did! She said everything was fine."

I put my arm around her shoulders and pulled her to my side, kissing the top of her head. "Then I'm sure it is. Stop worrying."

She nodded, and I stood, but when I glanced back at her, she was nibbling her thumbnail and staring blankly at her bedroom door.

"Sadie."

"Mmm?" she replied, but she was so distracted by whatever it was her over active imagination had conjured up that I didn't think she'd really heard me.

"Look at me." I waited for her to turn her big brown eyes on me. "Everything is fine. And I need to get to work. But the next time I see your mum, I will ask her what's going on."

Her eyes brightened, and my heart swelled. I hated seeing her upset.

"And then you'll tell me, right? Whatever it is, you'll tell me?"

I rolled my eyes. "When have I ever been able to keep anything from you? We're a team."

She stood and wrapped her arms around me, and I held her tight. She was only a head shorter than me now, but she was still that big-eyed little girl who'd waltzed into my life ten years ago and taken it by storm. And I loved every damn thing about her. I just wished I got to see her more.

"I've got to go to work," I said stiffly, pulling away before I could get sappy. She wouldn't appreciate that. "Bye, baby girl. Don't forget your sports uniform."

I left her to moan about how much she hated exercise and chuckled my way down the stairs to the front door. Strolling across the front lawn to my jeep, I tried to ignore the seed of worry that Sadie had planted in my head. Eliza and I had become a good team over the years, and she always kept me in the loop. I'd know if something was wrong. Until I knew otherwise, I'd just assume there was no drama brewing. Lord knew I'd had enough of that with Bianca over the weekend.

I slid into the driver's seat, resting my hands on the wheel. If I was truthful, part of the reason I'd wanted to see Sadie this morning was because I needed a break from thinking about Bianca. I hated the way she'd left the baby shower on Saturday, and it had played over in my mind all day Sunday while I'd tried, unsuccessfully, to watch football. I knew from experience that I'd be replaying our argument over and over until the next time I saw her. It happened every time. I dropped my head down onto my hands and groaned. Why couldn't things ever just be simple with us? If she had been any other woman, I would have labelled her too much work and run for the hills. But it was Bianca. And I had never been able to just let her go. Not fully.

Sadie held half my heart, but Bianca owned the rest.

And that was fucked up because I obviously didn't own hers. Not even a little piece of it.

I needed therapy.

I shoved the keys into the ignition and cranked them, but the engine let out a pitiful cough, and then silence.

"You've got to be kidding me," I grumbled under my breath. Shoving myself off the seat, I got out, popped the hood, then wondered why I'd even bothered. I didn't know jack shit about cars. And, I realised with a sinking feeling, I didn't have the spare cash to call roadside assistance. Shit. It would have to sit here until I could get someone out to look at it. I fumbled in my pocket, finding my phone, and brought up Jamison's number. He might not have left for the law practice he worked at, and maybe he could give me a lift. His house wasn't far from Eliza's.

He picked up on the first ring, and I quickly explained the situation to him.

"Shit, Ri. Sorry, I'm already in the city. I've got court today."

"Ah, damn. Never mind. I'll call an Uber."

"No, don't. I'll call Elodie. She'll have already dropped Sophie at daycare and she'll just be out walking—"

"No, don't, Jam. It's fine. I'll—"

"Already calling her. Uber's get expensive, man. And if your jeep is off the road, that's going to cost you, too. Let us help." He hung up before I could get another word in.

My face heated. I knew he meant well, but it was embarrassing, knowing your friends all earnt more money than you. Jamison had gone into law. Reese and Low both worked at Low's family racecourse. And Bianca had a lead actress salary, so who knew how much she earned. But I was sure they all earned enough to pay for their cars if they broke down. Not that they would, because they all drove new models. Unlike my beat-up, twelve-year-old jeep.

I wandered back inside the house to wait for Elodie. My salary wasn't bad. But I was paying a Sydney mortgage on one wage, and that was tough. But I'd wanted that house so desperately. I'd wanted a home for Sadie. When she'd been little, I'd lived with a string of roommates, with her sleeping in a twin bed across the room from me. It wasn't right. She'd deserved a room of her own. And I'd given her that. If it meant my pride took a beating when I didn't have the cash to pay for an Uber, then so be it. Sadie was more important than my pride. She was more important than anything.

8

BIANCA

*S*weat dripped down my back, despite the cool winter breeze that blew over my bare skin, forcing me to jog on the spot to keep warm. I glanced over at Elodie who leaned heavily against a tree, her workout shirt stretched tight over her rounded stomach. She rubbed her back and took long, deep breaths. I bit my lip as I studied her. The stopwatch app on my phone declared it had only been a few minutes since we'd last stopped, and that made me nervous. Very, very nervous. I might not have known anything about babies, but I knew enough from Hollywood movies to know that contractions a few minutes apart meant a baby was on its way. And Elodie looked more than ready to pop.

"El? You okay?" I asked tentatively.

She straightened her posture and smiled at me, which did little to settle the nerves building in my belly.

"I'm great. Let's keep going. We still need to do another lap. Sorry I'm so slow today."

Our regular Monday morning walk being slower than usual was the least of my concerns. "Do you think that's a good idea? We're right near the car. Maybe one lap is enough today."

She laughed. "B, I'm fine. I swear. Your face is hilarious. These are just Braxton Hicks contractions. They're not a big deal. I had them for weeks before Sophie was born. And walking is good. It helps get everything dilating and effacing. It'll make my eventual labour easier and quicker."

I had my doubts but what did I know? She'd had two kids already. I didn't even hold other people's babies. She was the boss. "Okay then. But you tell me if they get any worse, and I'll have you at that hospital in no time. Red lights and speed limits be damned."

She shook her head. "You're so dramatic. Always the actress."

We started up our walk again, but we'd barely covered ten meters when Elodie's phone began playing *Love Shack*.

She sighed as she fished it from the waistband of her workout pants. "It's Jamison. He's been calling me every hour, on the hour, to make sure I'm not in labour. Like I'd forget to ring him If I was."

She answered the call as another pain caught her, and handed the phone to me.

"Hey, Jam," I said to Elodie's husband.

"Bianca?" he asked, his voice immediately concerned. "What's happening? Where's Elodie?"

"She's here, but she's having those Braxton thingos."

"Oh, right. Yeah, she had those for ages when she was pregnant with Sophie. They're no big deal."

"So she said." They still looked like a big deal to me.

Elodie was upright and smiling again, so I handed the phone back. She listened for a moment before glancing over at me with a worried expression on her face.

"What?" I mouthed.

She shook her head and waved me off as she said to Jamison, "Okay, no worries. Yeah, I love you, too. See you tonight."

She lowered the phone, and I raised an eyebrow in question.

"Jamison needs me to...uh, pick up something. So we will have to cut our walk short after all."

Relief loosened muscles I didn't realise I'd been tensing. "Good." I fished my car key from my workout armband. "Your fake contractions make me nervous. Where are we going?"

"South Street."

I held her door open for her and waited while she gingerly lowered herself in. Then I climbed into the driver's side of my convertible.

South Street was only a few blocks away, so it was only minutes later when I asked Elodie for the house number. "What are we picking up anyway?" I asked, cruising the street, looking for number eighty-seven. We rounded a bend in the long road, and a familiar black jeep came into view. My heart sped up. It was parked right out front of our destination.

I knew that jeep. Intimately. I knew there was a rip in the front passenger seat. I knew there was a pine-tree-shaped air freshener hanging from the rearview mirror that had been there so long it had no smell left. And I knew the back seat was just big enough to have sex on. I knew, because I'd spent a lot of time naked on it, doing just that.

"Seriously?" I hissed to Elodie, pulling up next to it. "What are we doing here?"

She held up her hands in surrender. "Don't shoot the pregnant lady. His car won't start, and he needs a lift to work."

My eyes widened as I glared past the jeep at the house. "Whose place is this? Are we picking him up from a hookup?" Oh my god. It was that woman's house. The one from his date on Friday night. It had to be.

Elodie shrugged. "I've no idea. He called Jamison for a lift, but Jam has a court case in half an hour and couldn't do it. He knew we would be walking around here so— What are you doing!"

I'd put the car in drive and was taking off the handbrake. "Leaving! You know how we are, El! We can't even be in the same room without trying to kill each other."

"You didn't seem to have any problems with that at the wedding a few weeks back."

I cringed. She was referring to the time Riley and I had gotten down and dirty in a tent at Low and Reese's wedding. She didn't even know about the disaster that was this past weekend. Thank God. That would have just been feeding her ammunition to use against my protests.

"Yeah, well, that was a mistake." Just like every other time we'd hooked up over the past ten years.

Elodie steeled me with a look that I was sure she'd perfected over the years on her two eldest kids. It made me want to shrivel into my seat.

"I know there's more history between the two of you than any of us will ever know, but he's our friend, Bianca. And he's stuck. He'd do it for you."

"Unlikely," I huffed, though I knew that was unfair. He probably would have picked me up, but he would have been just as childish about it.

Elodie rolled her eyes and picked up her phone, shooting off a message to tell Riley we were here. A moment later, the front door opened, and Riley came out carrying his phone and wallet. Despite my protests, my heart skipped a beat, just like it did every time I saw him. I didn't know what it was about him, but he had an effect on me that no other man ever had. Because trust me, I'd tried to find it elsewhere.

He wasn't overly tall, a little under six foot, but his shoulders were broad, and his tight white t-shirt left nothing to the imagination. My mouth dried. I knew exactly how chiselled he was beneath that shirt, the daily grind of the construction work he did evident in every muscle. He paused when he saw my car, then walked stiffly across the lawn, as if he were forcing his feet to move.

Shit. He had to be pissed after the way I'd left things at the baby shower. There was only two ways for this to go down. It would either be epically awkward. Or we'd end up in a screaming match. It was the only way with the two of us. Unless we were having sex. That seemed to be the only time we were in sync.

Elodie rolled down the window. "I know what you're going to say," she said to him in her no-nonsense mum voice. "Bianca's already tried it. Get in."

Riley opened his mouth, no doubt to argue, but Elodie hit the button that rolled the window up, leaving Riley no option but to open the back door. As soon as he did, his scent—his cologne mixed with something that was uniquely him—filled my nose, and my stomach flipped. I'd always loved that cologne. Whenever I walked by someone else wearing it, I immediately thought of Riley. I couldn't help it. I breathed him in while trying to ignore the butterflies that rioted in my stomach. They were no longer fluttering about in worry over Elodie. These butterflies had Riley's name stamped all over them.

I refused to make eye contact with him as he slid into his seat, pointedly staring out the windscreen, waiting for him to get his seat belt on.

Elodie rubbed her belly and groaned as another Braxton Hicks contraction hit her, and in the rearview mirror, Riley's head snapped up. He scooted to the middle so he could see between the two front seats and took in Elodie's pained face. His eyebrows pulled together in concern.

"What's wrong? Are you hurt? Is it the baby?"

Elodie was too busy sucking in lungfuls of air to answer him.

So I answered on her behalf. "She's having contractions. But it's okay. They're just the practice ones."

"Why is she in so much pain then?"

"She's okay."

"She's obviously not."

Irritation prickled at me, even though I'd said exactly the same thing a few minutes before. Dammit, I'd meant it when I said I needed space from him. I didn't want to be stuck in this car with him! "She's fine."

"She looks like she needs a doctor."

Irritation turned to anger as I twisted to face him. "Do you ever listen? She told me she's fine. She's had two babies before this. How many have you had? No offence, Riley, but I'll take her opinion over yours any day."

Riley winced, and I immediately realised that had been a low blow. I knew how much it had hurt him that Eliza had kept Sadie from him for so long. I opened my mouth to apologize, but a shield came down over his dark eyes.

"Fine. Of course, you know everything. If she has this baby in the car, that's on you."

What? How would that be on me? My slight feelings of guilt disappeared. My gaze bored into him, locking with his like a magnet. "She knows her own body, Riley. If she says she's not in labour then she's not. Just mind your own business."

Riley's face went red, and he pressed his lips together. I knew that look. It was the look he got right before he exploded. My blood thrummed through my veins, welcoming the fight. I knew how insane we were. I complained about us fighting all the time, but something inside me obviously fed on it. It fed him, too. I knew it did. Every argument only fuelled the fire that had always been present between us. It had never quite gone out, and after ten years, I wasn't sure it ever would. And I had no idea if that was a good or a bad thing.

"You're unbelievable, you know that? She's my friend, too.

I'm allowed to be concerned about her." His voice got louder with every word as he continued on his rant.

I was just as loud when I yelled back, "Oh, here we go again. Neither of us own our friends, Riley, we've had this argument before. If you hate it so much when I'm around, why—"

Elodie groaned long and loud, cutting me off. Riley and I both whipped our heads in her direction and stared. There was something distinctively un-practice-like about that noise. As the contraction subsided, she gasped, her eyes going wide.

"My water just broke."

9

RILEY

*E*lodie's gaze darted between Bianca and me, her eyes so panicked the whites were visible the whole way around. "Can one of you say something, please?" she asked.

Bianca's jaw was on the floor, but I managed to choke out, "Your water did what? Here? What do we do now?"

Elodie looked to Bianca apologetically. "I'm so sorry, your car seat is ruined."

That seemed to snap Bianca out of her trance, which was good because I felt like time was standing still.

Elodie moaned, another contraction hitting her, and Bianca put the car into drive, slamming her foot down on the accelerator.

We sped through the streets, and I tried to mutter supportive and encouraging phrases, but even with Elodie in labour, it was Bianca who kept drawing my attention. It was always the same. Her very presence short-circuited something in my brain until all I could concentrate on was her.

It was a shame I was the last person she wanted in her car.

"Aaaaah!" Elodie yelled, drawing my attention back to her as she clutched the 'holy shit!' bar with one hand and her belly with the other.

I slid forward on the seat and grabbed Elodie's arm, adrenaline coursing through me. "What? Is it coming already?" Oh my god, I wasn't prepared for this. I hadn't been there for Sadie's birth. I didn't know what to do. I was already picturing delivering this baby on the side of the road, and that thought freaked me right the fuck out. I couldn't do that. "Bianca, drive faster," I urged.

"I'm already doing ten over!"

Elodie shook her head. "No, no, it's just the contraction combined with the bumping car—"

"Bianca, watch the bumps," I yelled.

She shot a death look over her shoulder. "Do you think I'm deliberately hitting them?"

I rolled my eyes. Any tenderness between us at the bar on Friday night had been completely forgotten.

I found Elodie's hand and squeezed it. "I'll call Jamison and get him to meet us at the hospital."

She nodded, but another contraction gripped her, and she dropped my hand. I dialled Jamison's number.

Straight to voicemail. "Shit!"

"Call again. He's in court," Bianca said, her fingers locked tight around the steering wheel. Her gaze alternated between the road and shooting worried glances at Elodie.

I nodded and dialled again, relief coursing through me when he answered. "Elodie's having the baby," I gasped before he could even say hello. I probably sounded as if I were the one having contractions. I was oddly out of breath.

Elodie's guttural moan ripped through the car again. Hadn't she just had a contraction? She shouldn't be having another one yet, should she?

"She is?" Jamison asked. "Where are you?" There was a shuffling of papers and voices in the background.

"Bianca and I are with her, we're taking her to the hospital. You need to hurry."

"I'm leaving now. But stop stressing. Her labour with Sophie took hours."

Elodie moaned again, and I took in her panting and shifting on the front seat.

"I don't think you have hours, Jam. Hurry."

Bianca gave me a questioning look as I ended the call, and I shrugged. It didn't matter, because Bianca was pulling up to the emergency entrance. Before she'd even lifted the handbrake, I was out of the car and at Elodie's door.

Elodie stared at me with big brown eyes. "Where is he? I can't do this without him."

I gave her my most reassuring smile. "You won't have to, he'll be here soon. Can you walk? I can carry you if you can't."

"Or maybe I'll just get a wheelchair, hero," Bianca quipped.

I glared, but it landed on her back. She was already running towards the entrance. She returned in under a minute and held the chair steady while we helped Elodie into it. Then we ran for the electronic doors.

"Slow down!" Elodie yelled, gripping the armrests so hard her knuckles turned white.

"Sorry! Sorry!" Bianca and I said in unison, slightly slowing our panicked pace from sprinting to just running.

I felt better now that we were at the hospital and I knew the baby wasn't going to be born on the side of the road, but the noises coming from Elodie and the fact Jamison wasn't here was not good.

We skidded into the delivery suite's waiting room, and Bianca pushed the buzzer on the locked doors.

Elodie clutched her hands to her belly, her body tensing, while I hissed to Bianca, "Press it again!"

"I've pressed it three times, Riley, I can't make them unlock the door. Quit ordering me around."

"I'm not!" God, she was infuriating sometimes. "Why are you always on my case?"

"Ugghhh you two are the worst birth partners ever! Can you just shut the fuck up with your fighting for three seconds and think about something other than yourselves? All the people in this room don't give a shit about your squabbling. And neither do I. So shut up or leave me alone. I'd rather have this baby by myself than listen to the two of you for another moment."

Bianca and I stared at Elodie in shock. Mild-mannered Elodie, who never swore, never had a bad word to say about anyone. Beautiful, sweet Elodie who had just called us on our shit in front of a waiting room full of people.

Over the top of Elodie's hunched back, my gaze met Bianca's, and I shook my head slightly. She nodded. We didn't need words to communicate. It was written on her face. Put this aside and work together. Elodie needed us more than we needed to argue. I felt like an asshole.

The doors finally opened to admit us, and we were met by a middle-aged nurse. "What do we have here?" she asked with an easy-going smile.

"Baby coming," I panted.

The nurse smiled kindly at me. "Your first baby, is it?"

Bianca scoffed as I shook my head. "I'm not the father. Just the friend."

From the wheelchair, Elodie shifted and looked up at the nurse. "There's so much pressure. I need to push."

Holy shit. Where was Jamison?

The nurse nodded then shifted her focus back to me. And then at Bianca. "Take her straight into delivery room two. It's just there, on your right. I'll meet you there in a moment and we'll see where we're at."

Bianca and I both nodded and hurried into the room the nurse had pointed out.

I closed the door behind us and wheeled Elodie into the middle of the small space. It was sparsely furnished—a bed in the centre, a leather recliner by a small, high window, and a door which presumably led to a bathroom.

"You doing okay there, El?" Bianca asked, kneeling in front of her.

I did the same thing. Elodie seemed paler than normal, a fine sheen of sweat sticking to her skin. She'd shifted to the very edge of the wheelchair and was tugging at her pants. "I think I can feel the head," she gasped.

The blood drained from my face.

"I need to get these off. I need you to look."

"I can't—" Bianca's panicked gaze met mine, and I grabbed her hand. Despite the situation, my skin tingled the minute I touched her. I made my gaze as steady as possible.

"I'm going to go get the nurse. You help her, okay?"

Something changed in her eyes, and she nodded, turning to help Elodie with her pants as I opened the door to the hallway. And crashed straight into Jamison.

Thank you, Lord.

"Where is she? In there?" he cried.

I nodded, then clapped him on the back, a little of the pressure I'd felt since I'd heard Elodie's first moan easing. "Your kid is in a hurry, mate. Get in there. I'm going to find the nurse."

He nodded, pushing past me, and I grabbed the nearest professional, ignored her protests, and dragged her into the room with me. Jamison and Bianca had managed to get a gown on Elodie and had helped her to the bed. They stood either side of her, gripping her hands while Elodie pushed. I hovered in the doorway, unsure of what to do. The nurse got down the business end and sat back with a laugh. A laugh! This didn't seem like the time for laughing.

"We have a head! You're doing great, Mum, all by yourself. You don't even need me. Just keep doing what you're doing, and I'll catch. One more big push, and you'll meet your baby."

Something welled up inside me. I'd missed all this with my Sadie. Missed her first moments. Her first years. I'd missed so damn much.

My gaze fixated on Bianca, watching the way she murmured soothing words to Elodie, despite her face being ashen. Bianca hated kids, but she loved her friends with all her heart. Well, not me. Obviously. But Elodie and Jamison for sure. Despite myself, I was impressed with her. She was normally such a diva, with her assistants and paparazzi following her and her glamour model boyfriends. But right here, right now, she was far from BB the actress. Here she looked a lot like the girl I used to tend bar with.

Like no time had passed, memories assaulted me. Her tying on her bar apron, pulling her long blonde hair up into a pony-tail and exposing her neck. The times I'd cornered her in the kitchen before our shift started, stealing kisses until somebody busted us. Going home with her after shift and spending hours in bed, the way you did when you were young and couldn't keep your hands off each other.

A cry pierced the air, startling me from my Bianca bubble and the nurse held up a squirming, gunk-covered baby. Holy hell, there was blood and white stuff all over it. It was enough to turn my stomach, but then I took in the relief, mixed with joy and instant love on Jamison's and Elodie's faces, and had to choke back a lump in my throat. Well, shit. It was kind of beautiful. In a disgusting sort of way.

"It's a boy," Jamison said, choking on a sob, his gaze full of admiration for the woman who'd just birthed his son. He leant in and kissed her so tenderly as the nurse placed the little one in Elodie's arms.

The baby immediately quieted, and the room went silent as he stared up at them. Bianca backed away and came to stand by my side, watching the trio share their first moments.

"We really fucked that up," I said quietly, guilt eating away at me. "She shouldn't have had to yell at us."

"I know."

"What happened to us, B? We were a good team. Once upon a time."

"That was a long time ago, Riley." Her voice was soft as she added, "Times change."

Didn't I know it.

10

RILEY

It was late by the time Bianca and I walked side by side through the hospital corridors on our way to retrieve her car. People bustled around us, their shoes squeaking on the scuffed linoleum floors, though I barely noticed. I was still completely overwhelmed by everything that had happened with Elodie, but Bianca's fingers were mere inches from mine, and the need to reach out and touch her crowded my thoughts. I just wanted to take my fingers, thread them through hers, and feel the soft skin of her palm against mine. It would be so easy. She was so close, and the simple gesture would ease a part of me that always ached.

But I knew it wouldn't be welcome. So instead I tried to focus on putting one foot in front of the other. I'd get my stuff from her car, then I'd get an Uber home, which was what I should have done this morning. Exactly what I would have done if I'd known Bianca had been with Elodie. The adrenaline had worn off and left me suddenly exhausted. I was ready to go home, have a shower, and crash out with some takeaway in front of the TV for the evening.

At the end of the corridor, the entrance to the parking lot

loomed, and I quickened my pace. I needed fresh air. Being this close to Bianca was never easy for me, which was why I avoided being alone with her in the first place. It had been different on Friday night. She'd been drunk and let her guard down. It happened when we slept together, too. I got to see the real her. The Bianca who I remembered from all those years ago. But with her walls up, I never knew what to expect, so I walked on eggshells.

"I'll just grab my wallet and stuff from your car then I'll order an Uber," I said to her.

She stiffened at my side, then shrugged. "If that's what you want."

I nodded. It was. The thought of sitting in her car, just the two of us, alone, with no Elodie as a buffer would be too awkward. We'd just end up in a screaming match. Or we'd have sex, *and then* we'd end up in a screaming match.

The automatic doors whooshed open, and a wall of noise hit us like a smack in the face.

"Shit," Bianca hissed next to me, inching closer.

I blinked in the bright sunlight, bringing an arm up to shield my eyes, and tried to work out what the hell was going on. A crowd of people surrounded us, all yelling, jostling, fighting to get closer. There were so many of them crowding in that my chest immediately tightened, my heartrate picking up. Instinctively, I reached for Bianca, circling my arm around her petite shoulders, and pulled her to my side, ignoring the jolt that slammed through me as soon as my skin touched hers. I felt, more than saw her glance up at me, but there was no time to respond before a guy with a heavy-duty camera jumped in front of us, forcing us to stop.

"BB!" he yelled. "BB! Look this way." He didn't even bother holding his camera to his eye, but the blinding flash attached to it went off several times.

I wanted to rip it from his pudgy hands and smash it on the concrete beneath our feet.

"BB! What are you doing here? We heard there was an overdose. Was it you? Do you care to comment?"

Bianca pulled away from me, stopping, and I looked down at her in confusion. What the fuck was she doing? I needed to get us to the safety of the car before one of the thirty guys surrounding us crushed her. There was nothing of her. If these parasites pressed in on us, she could be seriously hurt. Dammit, was this what she put up with every day? My stomach churned. She needed a bodyguard, keeping these people at bay.

She tugged her hair from the messy ponytail she'd been sporting and ran her fingers through the long, golden strands. Then she plastered on a huge smile.

And just like that, the last traces of Bianca, the girl I'd once been in love with, disappeared, leaving only BB, the actress. The woman I couldn't get close to, no matter how hard I tried.

A laugh that sounded nothing like her own fell from her lips. "Do I look like I've overdosed, guys? Come on now."

"We've all heard the drug rumours, though, BB. You can't blame us for assuming."

She shrugged. "You guys know they aren't true either. My friend had a baby. That's it. Just regular, run-of-the-mill childbirth."

"When are you going to have a baby, BB? Is this guy a potential baby daddy? What's his name?"

My mouth dropped open as the attention turned on me. A microphone was thrust into my face, and flashes went off again, black dots floating in front of my eyes. The crowd surged, and Bianca held her hands up in a calming gesture.

"Come on, guys, don't push. I'll answer any questions you have, the jostling isn't necessary..."

But her words fell on deaf ears. The photographers and

reporters all continued trying to get closer to her, shoulder barging each other, not caring if they stepped on feet or knocked people over. With every second that passed, I had less and less breathing room, and my anger spiked. How many up-skirt shots had these guys stolen from her? How many times had I asked her about a bruise on her body and fumed when she'd confessed it was thanks to an overly eager jerk with a camera?

"Bianca, come on," I said in her ear, but she just smiled and continued answering a question about her TV show until a burly-looking guy, solid and well over six feet, grabbed her arm, thrusting a microphone into her face. She winced, covering it quickly with her fake-ass smile, but I saw it.

And I saw red.

Without thinking about it, I drew my arm back and swung a punch that smashed into the guy's cheek bone. Pain vibrated up my arm, but I ignored it as the guy stumbled back.

"Hey!" he yelled.

I didn't care. Let him come at me. Blood pounded in my ears, and I was riled up. I would have been happy to take him on. He had no damn right to touch her. He'd hurt her.

"You don't fucking touch her." I grabbed Bianca around the waist and got us moving towards her car again.

"Riley!"

But I wasn't listening. I pushed and shoved people out of the way, with single-minded focus. I had to get her out of there. These people were vultures. They didn't care if they hurt her. She was tiny. They'd mow her down, all for the sake of the gossip mags and internet headlines. I stormed my way through until eventually they moved and I could get her door open.

Once she was in, I threw myself into the back seat, hitting the lock button as I went. For a long moment, Bianca just sat there, her fingers clutching the steering wheel until her knuckles blanched white. My breath came in short, erratic bursts as I tried to calm down. The paparazzi hadn't let up. They banged on the windows and yelled her name. Flashes from their cameras continued to blind us.

"What are you doing? Drive!" If she didn't go now, they'd surround the car. What was she waiting for?

She shook her head, turned the car on, and put it in drive. We were out on the road before the vice on my chest loosened a little, and I felt like I could breathe. I ran my gaze over her profile, again and again, checking her for injuries, reassuring myself she was fine.

"You shouldn't have done that," she said coldly.

And just like that, the vice was back, threatening to cut me in half.

---

*B*ianca

My blood boiled, but I knew that wasn't why my skin felt so heated. I could still feel the warmth from being pressed into Riley's side as he herded me to the car. And one part of me just wanted to hold on to that sensation. Hold on to the way it felt to have his strong arm around me. Hold on to the way he always made me feel safe.

God knows, I hated the ridiculous media packs that followed me around. My stomach had dropped through the floor as soon as the hospital doors had opened and they'd rushed us. The panic I'd felt in that moment had been crushing, and that scared me. Because panic like that was crippling. I saw the proof of that every day with my mother. And I didn't want that to be my life. So yeah, one half of me had wanted to reach out to Riley, let him wrap me in his arms and bury my face in his neck.

But the other half of me was raging mad. And that was the

half that won out, now that we were away from the crush of people.

"I don't need you to babysit me, Riley," I snapped as I navigated the city streets. "I'm plenty capable of handling the paparazzi." And I was. Just because I was scared on the inside, didn't mean I hadn't learned how to deal with them. I'd been doing this a long time. As long as I didn't let the fear and panic overtake me, I was fine. I *was* fine.

In the rearview mirror, his eyes narrowed into slits. "You've got to be kidding? You are not seriously angry at me right now?"

"Of course I am! I'm not some damsel in distress!" Ugh. He made me so mad when he acted like my boyfriend. "You punched a guy in the face. What if he presses charges? That, back there, is my job. I've managed it just fine for ten years. If you suddenly want a career as my bodyguard, talk to my manager."

I beeped the horn at the car in front of me when they took longer than necessary at a stop light, then instantly felt bad. It wasn't the car in front of me that was pissing me off. It was the guy behind me. Did he seriously think I didn't know how to do my job? Would I walk onto his construction site and start bossing him around?

"Unbelievable. That guy was hurting you. What did you want me to do, shake his bloody hand and congratulate him? They were out of control."

The glimmering anger in his eyes shocked me, but I shook my head. He had no idea. That group of paps was nothing compared to some media swarms I'd been pulled out of in the past.

For the past ten years I'd been the darling of Australian television. I'd caught a lucky break at twenty-two and landed a role in a popular evening drama. The role, that was supposed to only be a three-episode arc, somehow became my full-time job. It was all I'd known for the past ten years. And I loved it. That job was my whole life. The cast and crew were my family, and there were very few places I preferred to be than on set. But that didn't mean it hadn't cost me plenty over the years.

I pulled my car into the parking garage of my apartment building and yanked up the handbrake. Riley and I opened our doors and got out of the car, both of us slamming them behind us. I leant back on the cool metal and folded my arms across my chest, watching him pace up and down. His body radiated tension. He was coiled so tight I knew he was going to snap at any minute. My god. The man was such a stress head. But it was also kind of amazing, the way he looked out for me. No one else in my life did that in quite the same way he did. I softened a little.

"I knew what I was doing, Riley. Nothing was going to happen."

He whirled on me, the intensity in his gaze shocking me as he crowded into my space, planting both hands on the car, either side of my body. I didn't flinch. I just stared him down. The part of me that had softened grew irritated again. He wanted an argument. He needed the release. Maybe I did, too. And this was what we did best, him and I. We fought.

"Nothing was going to happen? What if those guys had pushed so hard you fell and were trampled?" His eyes blazed into mine, and my breath caught. He was so close. He had a handful of freckles across his nose that I'd once given names to, one morning when we'd lain in bed, wrapped in each other's arms. Did he remember that? Did he think back on those mornings and nights where all we'd needed was each other?

Our lips hovered inches apart, his scent engulfing me until it was all I could think about. Something in his gaze softened just the tiniest bit, and his gaze dropped to my lips. Fuck. What was his question? I racked my brain, trying to remember, but I couldn't think.

"Uggghhhhhhh, fuck!" he bit out before his lips slammed down on mine.

I didn't hesitate for a second. I pulled him close, wrapping my arms around his neck and digging my fingers into his hair. His body ground me into the side of my car, his erection all too evident against my belly. Fuck indeed.

His lips moved over mine, hot and demanding, his tongue circling in the practiced rhythm we'd developed over so many years of making out. But somehow, it still always felt like the first time. It never felt old with him. I still got that feeling in my chest and the butterflies in my stomach. He devoured my mouth until an ache deep within me opened up and I broke away panting. His eyes were focussed hard on me, and I knew he was checking to see if I wanted more.

He always checked. He never assumed.

It was one of the things I would have loved about him if I wasn't so busy fighting with him and pushing him away all the time. But all he would have seen in my gaze was pure, unadulterated wanting. He yanked open the door, nudging me down on the back seat, and I struggled to get my athletic pants off while searching for his mouth again.

His lips landed on my neck, his body covering mine, and the two of us both struggled to get our clothes down far enough to get what we both wanted. My hips jerked towards him as if they had a mind of their own, and I groaned when the warm skin of his cock nudged against my opening. Trusting that he'd stop this if he wasn't up to date on his STD tests, I spread my legs wider, my core throbbing with need.

"You good?" he murmured into my neck, "I want—"

"I'm good." Or I would be in a minute.

He reached down and guided himself to my entrance,

inching in, giving me time to adjust to his width. But I didn't need it. Wetness pooled between my legs, and my core ached. I wanted him. And I wanted him now. I circled my legs around his ass and pulled him to me, both of us crying out as he sank all the way inside, in one long, hot stroke. My eyes rolled back in my head when he found his rhythm, his hips thrusting in and out. God, I'd missed this. It had only been a few weeks since we'd last hooked up at the wedding, but it felt like a lifetime. He shifted off me slightly so he could reach between us and find my clit, a practised move he knew I liked.

Best thing about a ten-year fuck buddy? His ability to get me off quicker than I ever could. Down and dirty in the back seat of a car? No problem. He knew exactly how to work my body.

I groaned at the pressure building inside me. His hot gaze bounced between my face, checking my reactions then straying to the place our bodies were joined. I writhed beneath him, so turned on by him watching, at the feel of his body in and around me. At the way he made me feel like the only woman in the world, even if we were just having a quickie in the back seat of the car. When I cried out my release, he silenced me with his kisses. He followed me over the edge, body shaking, my name a shout on his lips before he collapsed down on top of me.

I pressed my lips to his neck, inhaling and memorising the moment. Burning it into my memory, because in a second, he'd climb off me. He'd do his pants up, bite his lip, and shake his head, a mess of confusion, longing, and need still written into his expression. And then he'd leave. And I'd let him go. Just like always. But there was always this moment. The one minute we had where maybe, just for a moment, we both forgot about how different we were, and why we'd never been able to make this thing between us work.

11

RILEY

I didn't want to move. I didn't care that we were in Bianca's garage, on the tiny back seat of her car or that I had a cramp in my calf. With Bianca's lips pressed to my neck, my cock still throbbing inside her, her walls still clamping down on me from her orgasm, there was no place else I wanted to be. I never knew how long it would be before we'd fall back into bed together, and every time I assumed it would be the last. Because one day, it would be. It was only a matter of time before she found some guy who could give her everything she wanted, and that would be it. That would be the end of us. For good.

The thought hit me like a ton of bricks. It hurt every time I walked away from her, but today as I pulled out of her and sat up, the thought of letting her go again cut me to my very soul.

I yanked on the workpants I was still wearing from this morning and did up the fly before running my hands through my hair. I watched her as she scrambled to the other side of the seat and pulled on her yoga pants. She was barely on the other side of the car, but it felt so damn far away.

"I'm sick of this, B," I said quietly.

She paused to meet my gaze, but she only held it for a

moment. Then she whipped her head around and renewed her efforts at getting dressed, straightening herself up with vigour. She yanked her shirt so sharply one of the seams tore.

"It's not like I forced you, Riley. And you've never minded any other time. If you don't want to do this, then don't."

She reached for the door handle, trying to escape the confines of the car and the awkward post-sex conversation. Normally, I would have let her go. We sucked at the talking bit. We were great in bed. She was by far the best sex I'd ever had, not that I had a lot to compare it with, but every time we came together it blew my mind. It was everything else we'd never been able to work out. But after watching Jamison and Elodie and the way they looked at each other as they'd held their newborn baby, something inside me had cracked wide open. I was thirty-two years old. What the fuck was I doing with my life? I hadn't had a serious relationship in years. People had tried to set me up, and sometimes I'd even gone on dates, but nothing had ever come of it. And I knew why.

I grabbed her arm. "That's not what I meant."

She relaxed a little and sat back on the seat next to me. "What then?"

"Aren't you sick of this, too? All we do is fight and fuck."

She shrugged. "It's what we do. It's what works."

"I don't want to do it anymore."

She flinched but tried to cover by pulling her arm away. "You've met someone?"

"What? No!" I grabbed her hand again and threaded my fingers between hers, even though it felt strange to do so. We didn't touch. Not like this. Not when we weren't screwing. "I'm just too old for this shit. I want more. I don't want to just screw you and then watch you walk away. I want to take you out. Do this thing right."

She sighed. "We already tried that. It didn't work."

"We tried when we were twenty-two. I'm not the same person I was then. Are you?"

Her eyebrows drew together, and my fingers itched to reach out and smooth the frown from her forehead.

"So...what then? You want to date?"

Was that what I wanted? No, I wanted a whole lot more than just a date. But baby steps. "Yeah. I do. At the very least, can we be friends who fuck instead of enemies?"

She was silent for a moment as she searched my face. "Riley, there's so much stuff I haven't told you. So much water under the bridge. I don't see how we can overcome that if I'm being honest."

Her words hurt, but this was the closest she'd ever come to agreeing to something more, and I didn't want to let it slip through my fingers. "Fresh slate then. We start over. From today. Our pasts don't exist. We're meeting right now for the first time." It didn't matter what had happened in the past. We didn't have to rehash old hurts. Not if we could just move forward together.

"Just like we did on Friday night? How many times can two people first meet?" Her voice sounded dubious, but a tiny smile lifted the corner of her mouth, and that was all I needed.

"Please. Give it a try?" Then I stuck my hand out. "I'm Riley."

The moments ticked by in agonising slowness, until she reached out to take my hand.

"Bianca."

Hope filled my chest. It was as close to a new beginning as we were going to get.

12

BIANCA

Seven a.m. starts sucked. Though it could have been worse I supposed. The catering company was here at this time, so I could at least get a cup of coffee. Some mornings, we had five a.m. starts, and those truly were a nightmare. Nobody around here was very pleasant to work with before coffee. Myself included.

I poured a mug full of steaming liquid and inhaled, letting the warmth and the pleasant smell of roasted coffee beans fill my lungs. I closed my eyes for a moment and reminded myself of how damn lucky I was to have this job, and to have had it for as long as I had. It was maybe not the role of a lifetime, by Hollywood standards, but I'd never had ambitions that big. I loved the Australian television scene, and unlike most of the starlets I worked with, I had no desire to move up the food chain. I had everything I wanted right here. Sort of.

A loud *thunk* startled me, and my eyes flew open as I spun to find the source of the noise.

A set assistant tapped the stack of envelopes he'd just dumped on the table. "Yours," he said to me.

"What are they?"

"No idea. I had to sign for them. Came in yesterday when you were off. Jackson is going to have your head over that, by the way. We had to reschedule the whole day."

Ugh. I did feel bad about that, but it wasn't like I could have just left Elodie to go off to work. "I know. I'm sorry. I had a good excuse. I swear."

He shrugged, heading for the door. "Tell Jackson, not me."

I winced. Jackson, our director, hated anyone putting out his schedule. But since I never did, I knew he'd forgive me for one day. Even if he did pretend to pout about it for an hour first.

I eyed the stack of envelopes and picked them up right as my phone rang. Dropping them back on the table with a sigh, I rummaged through my bag.

"BB!" my manager, Tangie, said with entirely too much energy for this time of morning. "Did you get the scripts I sent over yesterday?"

Well, that explained the envelopes. "Just got them then. Why are there so many?"

"Because your Logie Award nomination has made my job a breeze! I got you auditions for three upcoming projects. You'd be great for all of them, of course. But Ridge Leone specifically asked after you, and if you got the part in his movie it would do big things for your career, honey. Really big things."

I cradled the phone between my ear and shoulder while I ripped the ends off the envelopes and pulled the scripts out, shuffling through them while Tangie chirped on about the virtues of Ridge Leone's projects. I frowned as I flipped through his script. "These are all Sydney-based productions, though, right?"

"Of course!" Tangie answered smoothly. "You said you didn't want overseas stuff, and I heard you. Though I really wish you'd reconsider. There's at least half a dozen huge movies casting right now for next season..."

I shook my head even though she couldn't see me. "Australia only, Tangie. I agreed to do a movie while *Ocean Bay* is on hiatus, but that's it."

Tangie sighed loudly into the phone. "You're entirely too loyal to that show. It's holding you back."

"It's not holding me back if it's exactly where I want to be," I replied firmly. We'd had this argument multiple times before. I looked around the familiar building that I'd been pouring my coffee in for the past ten years. This building, my trailer, our sets...this was as much my home as the expensive apartment I owned by the beach.

"Fine, fine. Just go over the scripts and learn your lines, because the auditions are at the end of the week. You'll kill it. Let me know how you go."

"Will do," I answered before cancelling the call. I picked up the stack of scripts again, balanced my coffee and phone on top, and took exactly one step towards the door when my phone rang again.

"Bloody hell," I muttered, placing everything back down on the table and flipping my phone over so I could see the display. Surprise caught me off guard when it was Riley's name flashing. He never called me. My finger froze over the accept button as our conversation in the car yesterday came back to me. We'd had those conversations before. Where we'd be caught up in the moment, and one of us would suggest we try again. Try for something more. But then in the cold hard light of day, away from the crazy attraction we'd always had, we came to our senses. So why the hell was he calling me? This wasn't what we did. And it made me nervous.

"Riley?"

"Yeah. Hey."

There was an awkward silence. It drew out, and I had no

idea how to fill it so I just waited. And tried to calm the butterflies in my belly. Had he been serious yesterday?

"Do you have a newspaper?" he asked eventually.

I let out a breath. Okay. That wasn't what I'd been hoping for. "Um, no? Because I'm not eighty? I read the news on my phone, like everyone else."

He chuckled. "Damn."

"Why?"

"I just...never mind."

Intrigued, I didn't want to let it go. "Wait." I walked over to where Danny, one of our regular caterers, was prepping bacon and egg rolls.

He smiled up at me as I approached, his eyes crinkling in the corners. "Morning, Miss BB."

"Morning. You don't happen to have a copy of today's paper, do you?"

He nodded, tilting his head towards the counter behind him where there was an abandoned coffee cup and a newspaper. "I was reading it just before I started my shift," he explained.

"Mind if I borrow it for a moment?"

He shook his head and I retrieved it from the kitchen counter before I turned my attention back to Riley. "Okay, so I have the paper."

"Turn to page thirty-six,"

I flicked through the pages with no idea where this was going but I wanted to find out. "The Live events page?"

"That's the one. Now close your eyes."

"Why?"

"Just do it."

"Fine. My eyes are closed. But I don't know why you made me get a newspaper if I was just going to close my eyes and not read it."

"If you were quiet for more than three seconds, I could tell you."

I wanted to retort but bit my lip.

"It's killing you not to have the last word, isn't it?" He laughed into the phone, and if he hadn't sounded so damn sexy, I would have hung up on him.

"Are your eyes closed?"

"Yes," I replied, my voice soft.

"Then point to a spot on the page."

I did as I was told.

"Now open your eyes and tell me where we're going tonight."

My eyes flew open. Where we were going tonight? Was he asking me out? Whoa. That definitely wasn't part of our regular routine. We were never alone, unless we were having sex.

I looked down at the spot on the newspaper my finger was touching and read the words out loud. "Live Music. Eight p.m. till late. Main act, Rip Chord."

"Pick you up at seven then?"

A burst of excitement blew away the butterflies in my stomach. The feeling took me by surprise. Were we seriously going to try this again, after all these years? It would be awkward as hell, but I couldn't deny that I wanted to. I wanted to with every fibre of my being. But he hadn't dated me since I'd begun acting. He didn't know how his life would change. Not just his life either, but Sadie's. Had he thought that through? That by dating me, his daughter would become a person of interest in the sick games the media played? I barely knew the girl, but I knew how much she meant to Riley. I didn't want to do anything that might jeopardise her safety or the relationship she had with him.

"Riley, I don't know about this. My world is...complicated. And public. And you and Sadie—"

"Sadie and I are my responsibility. Not yours. It's one date, B. Give me that. Please."

Please. Damn, that word on his lips would have had me agreeing to anything.

I opened my mouth to tell him yes, I could give him that, even though it was selfish to draw him into a world I knew he wouldn't be happy in. But a new worry cut off my tongue. I wrestled with the thought, trying to ignore it, but then knowing I couldn't, I fought to meld it into something I could actually voice.

"What if they're awful?" I chewed my bottom lip. "The band, I mean," I tacked on in a rush. It was the best I could do, given he was waiting for my answer. But what I really meant was, what if we're awful? What if we end up in another screaming match? I'd always had the possibility of us being together hanging over my heart, and I liked it. It was that, *well, maybe one day it will happen* feeling. A possibility. But if we tried, and we failed? Then that was it. There was nothing more for us after that. I'd have to close the door on the only man who had been a regular part of my life for what felt like forever.

But Riley's voice was strong and confident when it came across the line, like he didn't have a doubt in the world.

"What if they're great?"

13

BIANCA

The music, though I hesitated to call it that, coming from the beer garden of the pub made me cringe. The sound system screeched, the lead singer wailed, and by the looks of the crowded bar area, there was no one outside listening. More like, we were all inside trying to buy enough alcohol to make these guys sound decent.

"Are my ears bleeding?" I asked Riley as we stood side by side at the bar. I turned my head slightly so he could see my profile. "Seriously, you need to check."

He chuckled, and I smiled in spite of myself, while settling to lean against the bar top. The band being abysmal was probably a sign that this whole evening was going to tank. We'd managed not to argue yet, but we'd only been here a few minutes. Give it time.

Riley ordered us some drinks, and we wandered the crowd before spotting a tiny booth in a back corner. We placed our drinks down and squeezed in, and I tried to cover my surprise when he moved so close our arms brushed. My skin sparked.

"How was work?" he asked casually, taking a sip of his drink.

Was he really as calm, cool, and collected as he looked? Or

was he just hiding his nerves well? Maybe his level of investment was lower than mine and that was why he wasn't freaking out like I was. Maybe he hadn't thought through the repercussions of this date going badly like I had. He was a guy after all. He probably hadn't thought beyond his next beer.

"Good. Busy. We had to shoot extra scenes to start making up for yesterday. And my manager sent me a bunch of scripts to go over for auditions next week."

"Any good ones?"

I nodded enthusiastically. "Yeah, actually there was. Ridge Leone's new script is kind of amazing. I spent all day reading it."

He frowned. "Ridge Leone...why does his name sound familiar?"

My mouth dropped open. "Maybe because he directed and produced that movie *Walk it Home*?"

Riley shook his head slightly.

"It was the biggest movie of last year, Riley. You had to have heard of it?"

He shrugged. "I did say he sounded familiar."

The man obviously lived under a rock. "Well, he's super-hot right now. And I really want this part. It would be perfect for me, and Tangie said it would fit into my *Ocean Bay* schedule. I can't believe they're filming it in Australia."

He broke out in an easy grin that made my heart flip. God, he was handsome. His dark-brown hair was always a little too long, a little shaggy and messed up. He hadn't shaved for a few days, the stubble across his jaw accentuating how strong it was. And I couldn't even look at his dimple without wriggling in my seat. He'd always done it for me, and age hadn't changed that. He'd added some tattoos over the years, but other than that, looks wise, he was still the same man I'd fallen for ten years ago. Just an older, more filled out, sexier version.

His hand covered mine, and I had to fight to keep my concentration. The feel of his skin was distracting.

"You'll get it, no sweat," he said. "You're a great actress."

I quirked an eyebrow. "You watch *Ocean Bay*?"

He turned away, but not before I saw a blush stain his cheeks.

"Nah. But you know, Reese and Low and Jam and Elodie all go on about how good you are in it."

He didn't fool me for a second.

"I call bullshit. You totally watch it." I laughed. "Which bit do you like best? The overblown drama? The lusty kissing scenes that never go any further because of the seven p.m. timeslot? The long runs on the beach that were likely inspired by *Baywatch*?" I nudged him playfully and was pleased when he nudged me back.

"Shut up. Fine. I watch it. Sometimes. But it's only to see you."

I stilled. "Really?"

He lifted his eyes so his gaze met mine. "Yeah. Really."

I let my head drop and tried to stifle the smile that threatened to give away how pleased I was by that statement.

The music outside changed, and the deep baritone voice that spoke into the microphone was entirely different to the nasally, whiny-sounding one that had been there moments earlier. "Hey, you guys, we're Rip Chord, and we're going to play some covers for you tonight, as well as some of our original stuff. We hope you like it."

"Couldn't be any worse than the last guys," I muttered.

"Truth," Riley replied as the first notes of Rip Chord's opening song, a slow rock cover, came through the speaker.

I recognised it instantly and closed my eyes, the lead singer's sultry voice filling the air.

"You like this song," Riley stated more than asked.

I didn't open my eyes. Just nodded and swayed along with the beat.

"Come dance with me then."

I opened one eye. "You dance? Since when?"

"Since right now when I saw that look on your face."

The corner of my mouth lifted, and when he held his hand out to me, I took it, allowing him to guide me from my seat. He didn't let go, and I stared at our interlinked fingers as he led me through the crowd. We reached the dance floor which had suddenly filled with bodies now that the ear bleeders had left the building, and he pulled me into his arms. I stared up at him, linking my fingers around his neck and swaying to the beat. At first, we were out of time with the song, but dancing with him was exactly like having sex with him. We found our rhythm quickly, and then it was amazing. His fingers rested gently on my lower back, every now and then the fabric of my dress moving just enough that his skin glanced over mine, sending tingles of awareness across my entire body.

"It's been a long time since we've done this," I whispered. I couldn't even remember the last time. We'd been at plenty of events where we could have—weddings, christenings, barbecues. We both loved our small circle of friends dearly and spent a lot of time with them, but normally we sat at opposite sides of the room, glaring at each other.

"Too long," he whispered. His breath tickled my neck, a tremble beginning as I nodded.

"It's nice. This not fighting."

"I agree. But I have to confess something."

I pulled back, searching his brown-eyed gaze questioningly. "What?"

He tugged me to his chest again, his lips brushing against me as he spoke into my ear. "It feels strange to have you in my arms but not be trying to get you naked." His voice was husky. "I'm fighting the urge to take you into the bathrooms and fuck you senseless."

The mental image of him leaning me over the bathroom sink shot straight to my core. That was exactly what we would have normally done. We probably would have been out with our friends, gotten in some petty argument, then gone somewhere and fucked until we were too breathless to yell anymore. A pulse began to throb between my legs at the thought of getting naked with him. Had it really only been last night that we'd gotten it on in the garage of my building? Goddamn him. He always had this effect on me. I could be blazing mad at him, but with just one look I'd be wet and tearing off his clothes. But that never really got us anywhere, did it?

I shook my head slowly. "We shouldn't. If this is truly going to be a fresh start, then we need to treat it that way. We can't just keep doing what we've been doing. We already know that doesn't work."

He sighed, his warm breath brushing over my cheek. "I know. And I agree. We should take this slow. But did you have to wear that dress? I dream about you in that dress, you know."

My nipples tightened. "Really? What else am I doing in your dreams?"

He groaned and ground himself against me, and I giggled, when I noticed his erection.

"Stop. Please," he begged.

Please again. Every time he said that... But he was right. We needed to stop or we both knew where this would end up. "Okay, I'm sorry. This isn't easy for me either, you know." If he had any idea how damp my underwear was right now, he'd get that.

Thankfully, the song changed to a more upbeat cover, and we moved away from each other. A woman tapped me on the shoulder and shyly asked for a selfie. I agreed quickly, glad for the space between Riley and me, because although my head knew that taking it slow was the right thing to do, my hormones had other ideas. The woman thanked me, and Riley grabbed my hand, spinning me round, making me laugh before his gaze focussed on something over my shoulder, and he stopped completely.

"What?" I asked, turning in the direction he was looking.

"Nothing, that's just my ex over there with her husband. Can you hang on a second? I need to ask her something about Sadie."

I forced a smile. "Sure. Of course. Go."

"I'll be right back."

"I'll be here."

I forced my focus to the stage, watching as the lead singer strummed his guitar and sang into the microphone, but I couldn't help glancing over my shoulder at where Riley was shaking hands with his ex's new partner.

Riley must have said something funny because the couple both broke into laughter. I turned back around, feeling like I was intruding on their family time. And if I was being truthful, I didn't want to see him with her. It was ridiculous, because the woman was a newlywed, and even now she sat on her husband's lap, their fingers interlinked. But I'd given him up once before for her, when she'd come back into his life with a five-year-old he knew nothing about. And deep down, I harboured some resentment about that.

So instead I gazed up at the lead singer and sang along with him. He caught my eye, did a double-take when he recognised me, then mouthed 'holy shit!' before he turned back to his mic. I couldn't help but laugh. Even after ten years, it still surprised me when people recognised me. It was even more of a shock when they were actually excited to meet me.

A warm hand touched the bare skin on the back of my neck, and I shivered, spinning to face Riley.

"Sorry," he said, close to my ear.

I shook my head. Riley and I never spoke about his daughter or his ex during our hookups. I mean, why would we? We didn't talk about much of anything really. And I'd been avoiding the topic tonight, knowing it had been one of the contributing factors to our ongoing tensions. But the topic had to be addressed at some point.

"How is Sadie?" I asked. "How old is she now?"

"Fifteen. She's good. For the most part. Super smart. Though the teenage attitude can be a killer."

I smiled. "I'll bet. So strange to think of her as fifteen. I haven't seen her since she was a little girl. She was only five back when we were dating..."

"Yeah. She's definitely not five anymore." Riley smiled, but his posture had stiffened at the mention of the first time we'd dated, and I wished I hadn't brought it up. We'd been having fun. I didn't want that to end yet by discussing our past.

I knew we'd have to eventually. But not yet.

14

BIANCA

I never realised the term 'thunderous applause' could apply to an audience of three people. But as I finished my audition, the clapping from the director and the two producers was overwhelming. Their claps and exclamations over how great my audition had been echoed around the large, sparsely furnished room. And I rode the wave. I loved acting. From the very first TV commercial I'd done as a child, I'd always known it was my calling. I got a rush from slipping into a character's shoes and losing myself in the moment. I wanted the opportunity to do it for the rest of my life. And that was partly why my dreams weren't too big. I loved the stability that *Ocean Bay* provided me. A steady, weekly paycheck. A chance to do what I loved on a daily basis. Movie acting was different. It was a few months of shooting, then double or triple that in waiting while they put it all together. Then longer again before it actually released. Things moved faster in television. It was much more fulfilling.

Ridge Leone crossed the small space and took my hand between his, shaking it enthusiastically. "That was incredible. I knew you'd be perfect for the role of Josie. She's great, huh?"

"She is. I adore her." And that was the honest truth. I loved *Ocean Bay*, but it was typical soapie acting. This movie Ridge was producing was something entirely different. And it would fill my upcoming hiatus beautifully.

I loved to work. So I always tried to do a movie in my off months from the TV show. Normally I chose little indie films, with no budget, and worked just for the love of it rather than the measly paycheck. But this movie was something different. It had big names attached to it, and it still blew me away that I was even being considered.

"Tangie told you this audition was just a formality, right?" Ridge asked as he released my hand.

I gave him a questioning look.

"If you want it, the part is yours. I'll send an official offer over to your team and I hope you'll accept."

Excitement stole my breath. Was he serious? A bubble of fangirly screams rose up in my throat, but I swallowed them down and tried to fight the urge to hug him. Instead, I nodded, not trusting myself to speak.

Ridge clapped me on the back and guided me towards the door. "I'm thrilled to have you on board. LA is so beautiful at this time of year. Not as hot as Sydney. Perfect shooting weather."

My smile faltered. "I thought this project was filming in Sydney?"

Ridge's laugh boomed. "What gave you that idea? No, honey. We're doing worldwide casting, but the movie will shoot in LA. Is that a problem for you?"

"Of course not," I lied, while internally plotting how best to painfully murder my manager.

Ridge walked me out into the bright sunlight. "We'll be in touch. Thanks for coming in, BB."

I climbed into my car, waited for Ridge to return to the

building, then dialled Tangie's number. She squealed into my ear before I could even say anything.

"They already called! They're sending over an offer! You aced it, babe! Oh my word. This will mean big things for you, BB!"

"Or it will mean nothing more than you being fired," I yelled, cutting off her gushing. She fell silent on the other end, but I wasn't done. "I told you I didn't want any overseas projects! I specifically asked you if this movie shot in Australia, and you flat-out lied. Give me one good reason I shouldn't fire you right now?"

"Because you love this script and you want this part?"

My blood cooled a little. Damn her, she was right. But that in turn made me even more cranky. "You're right. I do. So now I'm even more pissed because you made me want it and I can't have it. I don't want to spend months overseas, Tangie! All my family and friends are here. I hate the LA scene. It's so bloody phony. I don't fit in there. It's bad enough when I have to go for a few days of promo. I can't live there for three months. I'll die of smog inhalation."

"It's no worse than Sydney. Smog inhalation is not a reason to turn down the part. You're going to have to come up with an excuse better than that one."

I smiled in spite of myself. She'd been my manager for ten years, and we had more than just a professional relationship. She was my friend. Which was probably why she'd pulled a stunt like this. She thought she could get away with it. And she was right. I knew she always had my best interests at heart, but she'd never been able to understand my desire to stay here. I'd never told her the real reasons I couldn't leave. I'd never told her about my mother. And I'd never told her about Riley.

She sighed. "Look, it'll take them weeks to get a contract

together. We have some time. Just don't make me turn it down yet. Let's just see what happens."

"Turn it down, Tangie. I'm not taking it," I said firmly.

"Ugh!" she huffed. "You're the most painful client ever. I should fire you."

"But you won't." I laughed.

"Fine. But only because you're up for a gold Logie, and that's good for business. Speaking of which, you know the ceremony is next week. Should I ring Jerome? I know his manager will be up for the two of you going together. And you two have gotten along in the past, right?"

I rolled my eyes. Jerome was a B-grade actor from another local soap. We'd filled in as dates for each other in the past, all organised by our managers for publicity. I didn't date, and he dated the type his manager didn't want him seen with, so we were always available for each other. It had worked out nicely in the past. He was a bit egotistical but after a few drinks he could actually be fun. I opened my mouth to confirm, a force of habit, but then the thought of Riley in a tux crossed my mind, and my mouth dried. I didn't want to go to the awards with Jerome. Not when there was even the slightest possibility I could go with Riley. Was it too soon to ask? We'd only had one date. Which had been a great night despite the awkward conversation about his ex and his daughter. We'd gotten past that, and we'd managed not to fight or have angry hate-sex afterwards either. He hadn't even kissed me when he'd dropped me off. He'd been pure gentleman.

It had been sweet. If frustrating.

I wanted to ask him to come with me but didn't want to scare him off either. The way he'd handled, or rather hadn't handled, the paparazzi outside the hospital concerned me. That tiny group had been nothing compared to walking a red carpet at one of the biggest award nights Australia had. Tangie would flip.

She'd already had to sort out the mess he'd created by punching that photographer. Predictably, he'd started throwing around threats of suing. Tangie had promised him an exclusive tip-off, and he'd quietened down. But she wouldn't be happy about me going with Riley after all that. I respected that we'd made a bit of a mess for her, but the thought of going with Jerome made me cringe.

"Don't call Jerome. I'll organise my own date."

I hung up the phone before she could ask me who I was going to take.

15

RILEY

The beer in my hand was getting warm, but I continued to pick at the label instead of drinking. Like I did most evenings, I sat on the front steps of the little three-bedroom townhouse I'd bought when Sadie was ten, watching the occasional car drive by or kids walking their dogs. It was a nice, family neighbourhood, outside the city. Jamison and Elodie had a place in the same suburb, as did my ex.

I knocked on the wood of the step I'd repaired the day I'd gotten the keys to the house. It had been rotted through, and I wouldn't let her come over until I'd fixed it. When she'd finally arrived, I'd stood back and watched her run up these stairs, her tiny sneaker-encased feet pounding on the new board, and felt the satisfaction that came with knowing I was providing a safe place for my daughter to live.

Then I'd run up the stairs after her, trailing her as she'd run from room to room, squealing her excitement. This house had helped us cement our status as a family of two. No more couch surfing. No more roommates. This was a permanent home where she could have her own room and have friends come to play. And where I'd gotten to know all the quirks that made her amazing. It left me with pretty much no disposable income, but it was worth every cent to know she felt at home here with me. And I lived for the days I had custody of her.

But now that was all going to change. I just knew it. Something had been up with Eliza when I'd bumped into her at the pub last night, and the fact she'd messaged me this morning to ask for a family meeting confirmed it. I'd blown off Sadie's concerns about her mother being up to something, but now I couldn't deny it. Something was definitely wrong, and it was all I could think about. We had a big construction project on at work, and a deadline we didn't have a hope in meeting, but even the frenzied pace of the job site hadn't kept me from worrying about it.

I looked up as a car pulled into my driveway and my heart kicked when I recognised Bianca's convertible. Abandoning my beer, I strode across the yard and was by her car before she could even turn off the ignition. I opened the door for her, and she climbed out, the late afternoon sunlight bouncing off the golden waves that flowed down her back. Her blue eyes locked with mine, and it was all I could do to keep myself from gathering her to my chest and kissing her pretty pink lips until they were swollen and begging for more.

But I was used to wanting Bianca and not doing anything about it. I had ten years of experience in that department. In fact, I had so much experience I could have written a manual. One hundred and one ways to distract yourself from the woman who owned your goddamn heart but didn't know it. Spoiler alert —my top tips included a lot of jacking off in the shower.

My cock thickened and I tried to clear my mind. She'd been right when she'd said we needed to take it slow. We already knew that the physical side of us worked. It was everything else we had to work out. And getting naked was only going to distract us from the real things we needed to focus on.

But still, I leant in and brushed my lips across her cheek, her soft warm skin against my mouth doing nothing to help the erection situation. She smelled faintly of perfume, something sweet and feminine that suited her to a T. I wanted to bury my nose in the crook of her neck and breathe her in but I knew that wasn't exactly 'take it slow' behaviour.

So instead, I pulled away and gave her a slow smile. "What are you doing here? Not that I'm complaining."

She shook herself, like maybe I'd had some effect on her, too. But then she recovered and grinned at me. "I brought you something."

"You did?" I leant on the car door.

She held up one finger in a 'wait' motion before she reached over the centre console and grabbed a large flat box from the passenger seat. It was tied with a golden ribbon.

She passed it to me, her smile going shy.

I squinted at the box, then shook it, making her laugh. "What is it? Early Christmas present?"

"Open it and find out."

I undid the ribbon and lifted the lid. Inside lay a crisp new tuxedo with a folded note on top. I quirked an eyebrow. "What's this for?" I asked, running my fingertips over the soft material of the suit. Then quirked an eyebrow at her. "Wait, are you *Pretty Woman*-ing me?"

She laughed as I unfolded the note, but her laughter sounded nervous. "I guess I am. Do you like it?"

I let her question go unanswered while I read the note out loud. It simply said, *Be my Logies date?*

I put the note back in the box and closed the lid. "The Logies? Isn't that strictly stars only? No dates allowed?"

She shook her head, then shrugged. "Not if you're up for the gold."

My mouth dropped open. "You're up for gold?"

"So my manager says."

I let out a long, low whistle before I reached out and took her hand, lacing her fingers between mine. "That's amazing, B. But..." But I wouldn't fit in. I was a carpenter, with calloused hands and dirt smeared across my face ninety percent of the day. I'd never worn a tux in my life. I picked up the sleeve, touching the silky material. Then placed it back down neatly. I'd look ridiculous. I didn't know how to socialise with those people. What if I embarrassed her? My face went hot. I couldn't think of anything worse. It was different, back when we'd first dated. We'd both been bartending while we tried to work out what we wanted to do with the rest of our lives. My life had gone one way, while hers had gone so far in the other direction we'd completely lost sight of each other.

"I really want you to come. You wanted to date...I'm asking you on a date." Her eyebrows drew together. "God, I feel like I'm asking you to the year ten formal dance. I'm so nervous I want to throw up."

My lips pulled up at the edges a little, but shit. This was suddenly getting real. Every moment of Bianca's life was so public. Mine was anything but. I lived alone, apart from when Sadie was here. I had a steady job at a construction site. I was practically a hermit compared to her. "There'll be a lot of people there, won't there? Cameras and reporters?"

I hadn't done a very good job of dealing with either last time.

She hesitated, then nodded. "I want to be honest. It'll make the media at the hospital the other day look like child's play." She dropped my hand and stepped back. "You don't have to say yes. I know...I know my life is a lot for anyone to take on." She studied me for a long moment. "You know what, I'm sorry. This is too much, too soon. I don't know what I was thinking. There's a guy from another show that can be my date—"

"No." The words shot from my mouth before I even considered what I was saying. I'd had to sit at home and watch her do these red-carpet events for years, always on the arm of some guy so good-looking it made even me want to drop to my knees in front of them. I couldn't count the nights I'd watched some TV jerk put his hands on her bare back or her neck, or the times I'd seen his arm graze her breast. I'd sat in my living room, watching them on the TV, unable to drag my gaze away with frustration coursing through my veins. But all those other times I'd been powerless to stop it.

This time wasn't like those other times.

"I'll go," I said, taking her hand and kissing her palm. Fuck, I was an idiot. Of course I'd go, if that was what she wanted. "I'll bring my autograph book."

She let out a little squeal of delight and launched herself at me. I wrapped my arms around her waist and inhaled her scent the way I'd wanted to since she'd first appeared in my driveway. Then prayed to God I wouldn't screw it up.

16

RILEY

I knocked on Eliza and Simon's door at exactly seven p.m., then shoved my hands deep in my pockets while I waited for someone to open it. I tapped my boot against their doormat, trying to fight off the nerves that rolled in my gut. There had to be something wrong. Eliza and I might have been on good terms, but they never just invited me over for dinner. And we'd never had a 'family' meeting.

The door opened, and Sadie's new stepdad filled the frame. We were similar heights and builds, but he was fair, with sandy-blond hair and light skin, while I was dark and tanned from spending all day outside. He stuck his hand out for me to shake, and I took it. He was a nice guy. We'd met on numerous occasions over the years, at Sadie's birthdays and school events, and I liked him. He loved Sadie and her mum, and that was good enough for me.

"Hey, come in. Eliza's down in the kitchen."

I nodded and followed behind him. "Where's Sadie?"

"She's at Imogen's," Eliza called as the hall opened up into their spacious kitchen and dining area.

I hovered on the spot awkwardly, not really knowing why I was here if Sadie wasn't.

Eliza waved towards the dining room table. "Go sit."

I nodded curtly and moved to pull back one of the wooden chairs. I sat uncomfortably, but that had nothing to do with the hard seat. Simon dropped into the chair across from me, and Eliza the chair next to him. I suddenly felt like I was at a job interview.

"Why am I here?" I blurted, then hoped it didn't sound rude. "I mean, Sadie isn't even here, and the three of us don't really just hang out so..."

Eliza folded her hands on the table. "We have a proposition for you."

"Okay..." They were making me so damn nervous my palms were sweating. I wished she'd just spit out whatever was going on. I picked up the jug of water sitting on the table and poured myself a glass, trying not to let them see my hand shaking. I took a sip.

"We want to have a threesome. With you."

The glass slipped from my fingers and bounced on the wooden table, sloshing water everywhere. "Shit!" I scrambled to pick it up, grabbing for a napkin to clean up the spill while avoiding Eliza's eyes. A threesome? That was why they'd asked me over here and gotten rid of Sadie for the night? What the hell was I supposed to say? The last thing I wanted to do was have a threesome with my ex and her new husband. Had they lost their freaking minds?

"Eliza," Simon warned, his tone exasperated.

I snapped my head up to see Eliza wiping tears from the corners of her eyes.

"Riley, chill. I'm joking. I couldn't help it. You looked so serious. You should see your face." She broke off into peals of laughter, and I scowled. But as I settled back into my chair and folded my arms across my chest, I realised I didn't feel nervous anymore. So at least there was that.

"Why am I really here then?"

She sobered. "Simon's been offered a job. In Bathurst. We're moving."

My heart sank. Bathurst was almost three hours away. "What about Sadie?" I pushed back my chair and stood. "Come on, Eliza, that's not fair. You can't just up and take my daughter away from me without so much as a discussion." She'd done that once before, when she found out she was pregnant and didn't tell me. I'd eventually forgiven her for that, but I wasn't about to stand by and lose another five years of my daughter's life. "No."

She sighed and pointed to the chair I'd abandoned. "Calm your farm. Sit down. This, right now, is the discussion. I said *we're* moving. I didn't say anything about Sadie."

"What the hell does that mean? She lives with you all but two days a fortnight."

"And that's what we need to discuss. We've already spoken to her about it. And...well, let's just say she wasn't very happy about the idea of moving to the country, away from all her friends. I'd expected that. And truthfully, this is a very big opportunity for Simon, and I'll find work there, but there's less out there for Sadie. Less options for university and for an eventual job. She'd be limited."

My mind was ticking over a hundred miles a minute. I thought I knew where they were going with this, but I needed them to spell it out for me because I didn't dare hope.

"Sadie wants to come live with you, full time. And although the thought of living away from her kills me, I can understand. And I want this life for her. I want her to have options. She's settled and happy, and I don't want to disrupt that. We need to go, but she doesn't. Not if you agree for her to live with you full time."

My mouth dropped open, but I abruptly shut it as a grin spread across my face. And then I jumped from my chair, strode around the table, and pulled Eliza into a bear hug.

"Oof," she grunted, pushing at my chest. "Get off, you lug." But she was laughing. "So I guess that's a yes?"

I gave her a look. "Of course it's a yes. She can move in tonight." I couldn't stop grinning. It felt like Christmas day and my birthday all rolled into one. I hated saying goodbye to Sadie after my weekends with her. Now I wouldn't have to. "This is the best news ever."

Eliza rolled her eyes. "Geez, Riley, thanks. Glad you're so keen to get rid of us."

"You know what I mean."

She nodded. "I know. Now listen, she's excited about living with you, but I still get her at least once a month. We'll meet halfway for me to pick her up until she can drive. And you have to make sure she FaceTimes me every day. And don't let her go all emo teenager. And watch her with that kid, Nathan."

I scrunched up my face. "Jamison and Elodie's kid?" Nathan was Elodie's son with her first husband. I knew Nathan and Sadie went to school together, but I'd never realised they were even friends.

She nodded. "She has a crush on him. Haven't you noticed?"

I shook my head, and she patted me on the back.

"Welcome to the world of full-time parenting a teenage girl, Riley. You're going to love it."

---

*M*y jeep spluttered into the driveway of Sadie's friend Imogen's house, but I was too high to let it worry me. A guy from my worksite had done a patch-up job on the engine and got it going again, but he'd warned me it wouldn't last. I made a mental note to talk to the bank about getting a car loan. Sadie would need to be driven to all her after school activities and to friends' houses, and it wouldn't be long before she'd be driving, too. She wasn't driving the jeep. I'd find a way to make the repayments on something newer. Something safer for her. Something that didn't need to be clutch started once a week.

I beeped the horn then got out of the car to lean against the bonnet while I waited for Sadie to come down. I waved to Imogen's mother who'd peeked out from behind the curtains to see who was making a racket in her driveway. She waved back when she recognised me and let the curtain fall back. Eventually, the front door of the two-storey house flew open, and then there she was, running towards me, her long hair flying out behind her.

She skidded to a stop a few feet away. "Did Mum talk to you?"

I nodded, trying to keep a poker face. "Mmmm hmmmm."

Her eyes went big. "And?"

"What do you mean and? And of course, I said yes."

She let out a squeal and launched herself into my arms. I laughed and hugged her back, lifting her off her feet. When I put her back down, though, I frowned at her. "You didn't really think I'd say no, did you?"

She shrugged as she tugged her school bag up on her shoulder and made her way to the passenger side of the jeep. I followed suit and got in the driver's side. I shoved the key in the ignition while she buckled herself in and frowned when the engine struggled to turn over.

"Dad, this car is a hunk of junk," Sadie announced.

I glanced over at her. "I know. But don't change the subject. I'm concerned that you even considered the idea that I wouldn't say yes to you living with me full time."

She rolled her eyes. "Don't be dramatic. I just thought you might not want me cramping your style. You know. With the ladies." She wriggled her eyebrows.

I coughed to hide my surprise, then recovered enough to say, "You're the most important lady in my life, kiddo."

She smiled, but I realised it wasn't one hundred percent the truth. I suddenly wanted to tell her about Bianca. Because Bianca was important to me, too. Very important. Was it too soon to tell Sadie about her? But no, I had to, didn't I? If I was going to be Bianca's Logies date, I had to tell Sadie now. She and her friends all loved that stuff, they'd be watching for sure. And if Bianca was up for the gold, then there was a good chance my ugly mug would be on screen at some point. My mouth went dry.

"Sadie, I need to talk to you about something."

She twisted in her seat, and I navigated the jeep around a corner before I continued. God, how did I talk to a fifteen-year-old about this? I never brought home women. There were no women, other than Bianca. I didn't date. And even when I tried, the one date I had gone on had ended up with me taking Bianca home.

"Got a girlfriend I don't know about, Dad?" she asked with a knowing smirk.

My face grew hot. How the hell did she—

"Ha! You so do! Who is she?"

"Uh, her name's Bianca, but she's not my girlfriend. She's just—"

"Your fuck buddy?"

"Sadie!" I said sharply. Jesus! "Don't let your mother hear you talk like that. Actually, just—don't talk like that."

She rolled her eyes again.

"Bianca and I are just seeing each other. I don't know where it's going yet."

"But you looooove her," Sadie replied in a singsong voice. Goddammit. How did I end up being the one who was embarrassed in this conversation? Shouldn't it have been the other way around?

"I don't love her."

Lies, a voice in my head shouted.

Seemed I wasn't doing a very good job about convincing Sadie either. She just laughed at me. "Sure you don't, Dad. It's written all over your face. So what does she do? What's she like? When do I get to meet her?" Sadie shot out questions on rapid fire while I tried to keep up.

"Uh, well, you've actually already met her. When you were a kid. It's been a long time, though, you might not remember."

She scrunched up her face, then shrugged.

"Didn't think so. She's an actress."

Her eyes lit up. "Really? Can she introduce me to Chris Hemsworth?"

I ignored that last bit, because my daughter wanting to meet a man old enough to be her father was disturbing. "Really. She's on that show you like, *Ocean Bay*? She plays Elaina."

There was a long silence where Sadie's mouth dropped open, then a screech that made me jump so bad I had to yank the wheel back to avoid crashing into the gutter.

"You're dating BB James?" she screamed, practically blowing out my eardrum. She bounced up and down on the seat, waving her arms around and grabbed at my shirt until I batted her hands away. "OMG, you're in love with BB James. She's going to be my step mum, and we're going to live in a mansion and—"

"Whoa. None of that is happening. Slow your roll, kiddo." Then I gave her a side grin. "I am going to be her date to the Logies, though."

I couldn't help but laugh as new screams of excitement

echoed around the car. Well, at least I didn't have to worry about her hating my girlfriend.

Girlfriend. Damn, I liked the way that sounded. I wanted that. So much. I knew asking Bianca to make this thing between us official was totally jumping the gun, but I wanted it. I wanted *her*. Maybe, after the Logies, if that all went well, I could ask her. Warmth curled around me at the thought. Yeah, I was going to do it. I'd make things official with Bianca and I'd have my daughter living with me full time.

The two dreams I'd silently harboured for years would both come true. And I'd be the luckiest son of a bitch alive.

17

BIANCA

The rhythmic thumping of my feet as they hit the tarred road soothed my frayed nerves. Which was the whole reason I'd decided to run in the first place. I needed the ache in my lungs and the burn in my muscles to distract me from the butterflies that swarmed in my stomach.

The Logies were mere hours away, and Tangie had sent me over a jam-packed schedule for the day, including an interview, a facial, hair, and makeup. They'd all be descending on my apartment any time now, but I found my feet taking me farther and farther away from all of that. And instead I made a turn I didn't take as often as I should.

I pushed myself harder, flying by the rows of headstones and neatly manicured lawns. A tiny stream trickled nearby, and I slowed my pace once I passed it, searching for the right memorial garden.

Disgust for myself rose. I should know where her garden was. It should be ingrained in my memory.

I hunched over, peering at each plaque until I finally found the one I was looking for. There was a bunch of flowers, slightly wilted, sitting in a plastic disposable cemetery vase. My father had to have left them. It was only him, my mother, and I who knew about this garden, and my mother couldn't leave the house. Not even to put flowers on her own daughter's grave.

Her remains weren't beneath the dirt here. They lay in a grave across the other side of the world, but when my parents had first moved to Australia, when my mother had been...better, they'd wanted a place they could go to remember my sister.

There wasn't a soul around at this early hour of the morning, but I sat quietly next to the rocks that marked the boundaries of the garden and trailed my fingers over the nameplate. *Brittany Ann James* the golden-plated letters spelt out. *Much loved daughter of Sam and Trish James, big sister to Bianca. Always loved, always missed.*

I sighed. "Hey, sis," I said softly. "I'm sorry I haven't visited in a while. Doesn't mean I don't think of you all the time." And I did. I'd been a child when my sister had died but I still remembered so much about her. Her photos lined the halls of my parents' house, a shrine of sorts to the child they'd lost. Brittany had been my idol as a kid. Four years older than me and brighter than sunshine. I still missed her, every day. I still wondered what it would have been like to grow up with her, and where we'd be now and how different my life might have turned out. How different my mother's life might have been.

"The Logies are tonight," I said with a small smile. "I'm up for the gold. I bet you would have won ten of these by now if you were still here."

That wasn't really true, though. If she'd still been here, I doubted we would have ever moved from LA. Maybe we would have been winning Oscars instead.

My sister had been an amazing child actress. I sometimes watched old episodes of the TV show we'd been on as kids, and was blown away by the talent I hadn't recognised in her at the time. I'd been too young to know a star when I saw one. She'd just been the older sister I desperately wanted to be like. Now, there was no doubt in my mind that she would have been great. But she'd never had the chance.

I sat there for a long time, with just my memories for company. I didn't try to stop them as they washed over me. Some were happy—the times we'd spent riding our bikes around the neighbourhood, like regular kids, and the Christmas mornings where we'd worn matching pyjamas and ripped paper off presents together. But they were shadowed by the memories of the night she'd died. The screams. The blood. The sirens. Time had dulled the pain, but they were memories I couldn't forget. I didn't want to. Not even the bad ones, because forgetting meant forgetting her.

I straightened the flowers in the vase, then kissed my finger-tips and pressed them to the B on her name. One B for Bianca, one B for Brittany. That was how I'd come up with my stage name. It seemed fitting. Because she was always going to be a part of me.

Before I walked away, I whispered, "If I win tonight, this one is for you."

18

BIANCA

*T*he black leather seats of the air-conditioned limo were smooth beneath my palms as I slid across, farther into the darkness of the interior. I was grateful that the privacy screen was up, because my dress had a thigh high split that made getting into the limo without flashing anyone a difficult task. Tangie was going to Hell for insisting I wear this dress. It showed off so much more skin that I was used to, but she'd been adamant that all eyes would be on me tonight and I had to wear something knockout. This dress definitely fit the bill.

I could admit, though, that when my stylist had finished tugging me into it, I'd liked what I'd seen in the mirror. The material flowed with my curves and cut deep at the front, showing off pushed-up cleavage. I'd had to be taped in, and I just prayed it would all hold together. I didn't want to be in the morning papers for a nip slip.

Unfortunately, sweating the tape off was a real possibility. My palms were damp as I peered through the window of the limo and cruised the city streets heading for Riley's suburb. My heart pounded at the thought of spending the night with him. I didn't want to scare him off by introducing him to the public too soon, but the fact I was going to one of these events with someone I actually liked made the whole process seem so much more exciting. Normally, award shows were pure work. But tonight, I felt like a fairy princess who got to go to the ball with her prince charming.

My mouth dried when the limo stopped in front of Riley's house. He was already waiting out the front, standing in the tuxedo I'd bought for him, holding a single white rose. Shit. He was the hottest man I'd ever seen. He always had been, but he'd aged some, slight lines around his eyes now, that had never been there before. But they only made me want him more. I'd never been able to resist him, which was why I'd spent years trying to avoid him.

He shifted his weight from foot to foot and pulled at his collar. I knew he was uncomfortable about coming tonight, which made my heart fill that little bit more. He was doing this for me. He was getting nothing out of it. He had no ulterior motive, like my usual dates did. He didn't want to meet some director or casting agent. He didn't want to hobnob with the rich and famous. He didn't want an invite to the afterparty.

He opened the door, his gaze locking with mine, punching the air from my lungs.

He just wanted me.

He slid across the seat, closing the door behind him. "Hey," he said quietly, handing me the rose.

I took it from him, marvelling at this sweet side of him I hadn't known existed. I hadn't expected a flower.

"Hey, yourself," I replied before holding the rose under my nose and inhaling its perfume.

He watched me with a quiet gaze that was hypnotising. I couldn't look away. No man should look that good in a tuxedo. It fit him perfectly, his broad shoulders filling the jacket. He had his hair slicked back, and his crisp white shirt complemented his deep tan. I shamelessly let my gaze travel over him, until he reached over and grasped my chin, forcing me to gaze into his eyes. They were full of amusement, but beneath that, something hotter lingered.

"You keep staring at me like that, and we aren't going to make it to the party."

If I wasn't so busy being lost in his eyes, I would have laughed at him calling the biggest event on the Australian TV calendar 'a party'.

"Maybe I suddenly don't want to go," I whispered, inching closer to him and letting my hand rest on his thigh.

His muscle contracted then relaxed.

"Fine by me. We can just stay right here all night if you like. The driver can cruise the city while we...do other things back here." His finger trailed along my bare thigh, inching higher and making me clench my legs together. My nipples tightened and I fought back a moan.

Not needing any more encouragement, his fingers slipped beneath the fabric of my dress, heading for the apex of my thighs, and even though I knew we shouldn't—we would be at the red carpet in less than ten minutes—I let my knees fall apart, just enough.

His eyes flared as he leaned in, his breath misting over mine, and claimed my mouth. His kiss was hot and possessive. Branding as he pushed his tongue inside, and I welcomed him there. I loved the way he kissed. We were so in sync. It was like he could read my mind. He knew exactly what I wanted, sometimes even before I did. My bones turned to liquid when he grazed his fingertips over my bare pussy.

He pulled his hand back with a groan of frustration.

"What?" I asked, panting. That tiny touch had done nothing but raise my heartrate. I wanted him there, between my legs, his fingers working my most sensitive places.

"No underwear?"

"Not possible in a dress like this."

He groaned again, burying his handsome face in his hands. "How am I supposed to get through the next six hours, knowing you're bare and wet beneath that dress?"

I closed my eyes for a moment. Because, god, it would be so easy to blow this whole thing off and just lose myself in this man. But I couldn't do that. We were less than a few kilometres from a crowd full of people and reporters with cameras, and it would be career suicide. BB James, caught going to third base in the back of a limo. No, that couldn't happen. Tangie would never forgive me, and neither would the head honchos at *Ocean Bay*. My squeaky-clean reputation was something the network had always counted on, and my Logie nomination was top-notch publicity for the show. I owed it to them, and to the rest of the people who worked on the show, to do this thing. There would be plenty of time later, for Riley and me to be alone. So instead of pulling down his zipper and climbing on his cock, I pulled myself together.

Riley's disappointment as I straightened my dress was almost comical. I smirked at him. "You're going to have to deal, buddy." I pointed out the tinted glass window behind him. "Because we're just about there."

"Better tell the driver to go around the block a few times until I get myself under control."

I couldn't help but laugh. But I still felt his kisses on my lips and his fingertips between my thighs. He wasn't the only one who would be struggling to keep their hands to themselves until the next time we were alone.

I took a deep breath, peering out the window while Riley adjusted himself. Crowds lined the street, hoping for an early glimpse of the stars, though I knew the tint on these windows was dark enough that we couldn't be seen. I spotted a couple of posters with my name, and I smiled. Most of my fans were older ladies who loved their soaps, but there were a lot of hot, young guys on the show who often got around in nothing more than board shorts so we had a younger following as well. Even if the fans did mostly scream for the boys, they liked me okay, too. And I was happy to play second fiddle.

Riley let out a low wolf-whistle. "This is all a big deal, huh?"

I nodded.

"Sadie is watching."

Whoa. "She is? So you…"

"Told her about us? Sort of. I told her I was your date for the night. She wants to know if you can hook her up with Chris Hemsworth."

I laughed but had a million questions swirling through my mind. He'd told his daughter about us? What did that mean? I had no idea what the two of us even were to each other. I tried to form the questions, but they wouldn't leave my lips. Instead, I went with the safe route. "I hate to break it to her, but I think Chris Hemsworth is married."

The limo pulled to a stop, and the driver dropped the partition an inch. "You're up, Miss James. Good luck," my driver said cheerfully.

"Thank you, Harrison. See you after the show."

He flashed me a thumbs-up, then raised the privacy screen again.

I found Riley's hand and squeezed it. "Ready?"

He leant in and brushed his lips over mine, the kiss soft, sweet, and lingering. All worries completely flew out of my head. Now wasn't the time.

He took a deep breath. "Now I am."

Someone opened the door, and Riley got out. From behind barricades, the mass of fans cheered, and Riley turned back to me, holding out his hand for me to take. I thought I heard him mumble "Holy shit!" under his breath but I couldn't tell for sure because the crowd was loud.

"They like you," I said to him with a laugh, exiting the car and standing while throwing them a casual wave.

But Riley pulled me back to the semi sense of privacy created by his back and the limo's open door.

"I don't care if they like me," he said near my ear. "I only care whether you do."

Thank God I was holding on to the doorframe, because I probably would have swooned. My eyes closed as his breath brushed over my neck, and I had to force them open again before I gave away to thousands of people exactly how turned on I was right now.

"I—"

"This way please, Miss James," a sharply dressed man with a clipboard and an earpiece said loudly, ushering us away from the crowd towards the long strip of red carpet, lined on both sides by cameras and reporters.

A cameraman yelled something about my tits, but I ignored him, not giving him the satisfaction of a reaction. We followed the organiser obediently, and I took Riley's arm. There was a stiffness in his frame that hadn't been there a minute ago.

"Listen," I said between flashing smiles to cameras. "They're probably going to ask you questions. But don't worry, you don't have to say anything. I'll handle it."

He nodded, but his body didn't relax. And when I glanced up at him, his face was like stone. My stomach sank. He looked like he was in physical pain.

That wasn't what I wanted. I wanted the two of us to have a magical night. I wanted to be that Disney princess who got to go to the ball and be swept off her feet by her Prince Charming.

But judging from the expression on Riley's face, asking him to be my date might have been my worst idea yet.

19

RILEY

$\mathcal{T}$here were people everywhere. It wasn't a crowd. It was a sea of screaming fans as far as I could see in both directions. Security guards in tuxedos lined the barricades that kept people off the red carpet, so logically I knew we had plenty of room. But I still felt as if walls were pressing in on me. I knew Bianca was a big star in this country. But I'd never expected anything like this. This was insane.

A security guard directed us to a backdrop that displayed the award show's logo, and I stood, shell-shocked, while Bianca tossed her hair over her shoulder and posed for the group of photographers. Cameras flashed and clicked, and people yelled for her attention. I blinked and tried to smile, but I knew it probably came across as more of a grimace. I was so uncomfortable. Not only in this suit but with all these people staring at us. What if I fucked this up? She'd said I didn't have to speak, but I didn't just want to be her arm candy. We'd be here until midnight at least, so I had to speak to somebody at some point. But what if I said something stupid and embarrassed her? I was a carpenter. I knew tools and wood. And guys who swore and drank beer after hours. The people milling around us, with their pristine nails and hair, had probably never lifted a hammer in their lives. What the hell was I going to talk about for the next six hours? If they started discussing casting calls and stage directions or any of the other showbiz stuff I knew nothing about, I'd just be standing there like a chump. I didn't fit in here at all, and as soon as I opened my mouth, they'd realise that.

We shuffled along the red carpet some more, and Bianca led me around, greeting people as she went. She introduced me to them all, and each time I tried to force something other than a polite "hello" from my lips. But it wouldn't come.

"You okay?" Bianca asked, placing her hand in mine.

"Of course," I lied.

She didn't look like she believed me.

"There's one more section of reporters up ahead before we get to the doors."

I nodded. I could see the entrance to the building the show was taking place in and I yearned to make a run for it.

Bianca pulled me to a stop beside her as half a dozen reporters shoved microphones in our faces.

"BB!" a woman yelled, even though we were standing less than a meter from her.

I took a step back.

"How does it feel to be the favourite for tonight's gold Logie?"

"I'm not the favourite!" Bianca laughed. "I'm just honoured to be nominated. It's an exceptional group of actors to be associated with."

"And who's your date?" another reporter yelled.

Why the hell were they shouting? The reporters all turned to me.

"What's your name? Are you two dating? Is it serious?"

I stiffened. Is it serious? Wow. Like that was anybody's business. I opened my mouth to reply, but Bianca beat me to it.

"No, we aren't dating, he's just a friend."

I snapped my mouth closed. Bianca continued answering questions with practiced ease, but all I could hear was her telling them we were just friends. Friends? We'd been a lot of things, but we'd never been friends. We hadn't even been friends with benefits. We'd just been...benefits. Was friends where she honestly thought we were? I knew it hadn't been long since we'd first decided to try to make this thing between us work, but I hadn't stopped thinking about her all week. I'd often thought of her, even before we'd agreed to call a truce, but that had increased tenfold since our first date. And now I felt like a bloody fool.

Eventually, Bianca wrapped up her PR, and we walked into the lobby of the building.

"That went well, don't you think? For your first red carpet?" Bianca's big blue eyes looked up at me, full of excitement.

I nodded. But, to be honest, I had no idea. About anything.

20

BIANCA

*T*wo things I'd learned in the last three hours. One—the actress seated next to me had no boundaries. She also never shut up. And two—Riley hated award ceremonies with the fire of a thousand burning suns.

"So, then they cancelled my bikini wax, and Justin had to go muff diving with that whole downstairs situation..."

I closed my eyes and tried to remember that I'd once been a barely twenty starlet myself. Though I was pretty sure I'd never been an over sharer the way Sienna was. I smiled politely and turned back to Riley who was glowering at a plate of uneaten food, stabbing at it with a knife like he wanted to murder someone.

I let out a long breath. "Hey." I placed my hand over his. "What did that meat do to you?"

He looked up but didn't comment before he went back to poking it around his plate.

"Hey, Riley," Sienna said, leaning across me to batt her eyelashes at him. Her date was sitting right next to her, but she seemed to have forgotten that. And he didn't seem to mind at all.

If he even noticed. He'd spent half the night following around a producer, trying to talk his way into a job on the show. "What exactly does a carpenter do? You build stuff, right?"

I fought the urge to roll my eyes, but Riley just nodded at her. "Yeah, that's pretty much the job description."

When he didn't encourage the conversation any further, Sienna lost interest and went back to Instagramming every aspect of the evening.

I flipped over my phone and checked the time. "It's only a few more hours. Then we can leave. I know you're hating this."

"I'm not hating it, B. I just..." He sighed. Then he shoved his chair back and grabbed my wrist.

He pulled me up from my chair, and I followed him towards the edge of the darkened room, weaving between people and tables. I was almost running to keep up with him.

"Riley! Where are we going?"

He didn't answer.

When we hit the wall, he looked in both directions before tugging me towards his left with a new determination. We reached a door, and when he tugged it open, he led me through, light spilling into the darkened auditorium. We were now in a quiet, well-lit hallway to the side of the stage. As the door closed behind us, I extracted my hand from his grasp.

"Riley, stop. Talk to me. What's going on?"

He spun around and had his lips on mine before I could even comprehend what he was doing. He pushed me up against the door we'd just come out of, his mouth possessing mine. Branding me, owning me. His kiss was hard and desperate, and after a moment of surprise, I kissed him back with everything I had. Kissing him was all I'd wanted to do all night. When he pulled away, my gaze was unfocussed.

Holy hell.

The man had always been able to curl my toes, but there was something in that kiss that did me in. He could have undone his fly and taken me right then and there and I wouldn't have batted an eyelid. In fact, I would have welcomed it. I knew exactly what hot, fast sex with him felt like, and it was never a bad thing.

His gaze was sharp and burned through me as he hovered inches from my mouth. I moved in to kiss him again, but he stopped me.

"Is that how you kiss all your friends?" he demanded.

"What?" I was lost in the haze of his tongue in my mouth and his hard body pressed into mine.

"I'm not your fucking friend, Bianca. A friend wouldn't kiss you like that."

My eyes widened. What was he even talking about?

"You told the reporter out there that we were just friends."

Oh. That. "Is that why you've been such a grump tonight?" I asked, putting my hands on my hips and trying to look mad at him. He was hot when he was cranky. It was partly why I'd picked so many fights with him over the years. His eyes always darkened and laser-beamed in on me, and his eyebrows got the cutest wrinkle between them. I always wanted to kiss him and touch him until the scowl went away.

He folded his arms over his chest. "I haven't been a grump."

I laughed. "Yeah, Riley, you have."

"Why are you laughing?"

"Because you're being ridiculous. You were the one who said we should at least try to be friends! Isn't that what we've been doing here? Trying to build a relationship? A relationship usually involves being friends, you know."

He dropped his arms. "So, you do want a relationship?"

I took a step closer but didn't touch him. "Yes. You idiot. I do."

"Then why didn't you tell that reporter I was your boyfriend?"

I threw up my hands in exasperation. "Because you're not! We went on one date. Two if you include this one. We haven't had any talks about exclusivity. I didn't want to assume. Plus, you looked so uncomfortable out there on the red carpet, I wasn't sure you'd even want to be with me after all of that. If I'd announced us as a couple you would have had a media circus out the front of your house by tomorrow morning. I wanted to at least talk to you about it before I just lumped all that on you." There was so much more to being in the public eye than he even knew. Dangers, too, that he needed to know about before he signed himself—and Sadie—up for that sort of life. My family bore the scars of those dangers. My mother, and the loss of my sister, a constant reminder that not everything was golden in Tinsel Town.

"Oh," he said.

I stepped into his space, and his arms wrapped around me. And for the first time all evening, Riley relaxed. His posture softened, and he dragged me in, burying his face in my neck.

"Sorry," he whispered, and I rolled my eyes.

"You're forgiven. I knew we couldn't last too long without an argument. Truly, I was surprised we'd managed this long."

"But, hey, I apologised, and you forgave me. That never used to happen. So high fives for progress."

I laughed as I slapped his hand and he pulled me back in. He leaned down and brushed a kiss over my lips.

"Mmm," I murmured. "Let's just stay out here for the rest of the night."

"Fine by me," he whispered.

No sooner than the words had left his lips, the speakers in the wall announced that the Gold Logie would be up next. Riley leant back, making me pout.

He grinned. "We better get back, Miss Gold Logie nominee."

I ran my hands up his arms and over his muscled chest to his tie. He let me loosen it enough that I could undo the top button and lean in to kiss his neck. He groaned.

"I'm not going to win anyway." I let my teeth graze the sensitive skin while the announcer named the nominees.

"BB James, for her portrayal of Elaina on *Ocean Bay*."

There was smattering of applause, but Riley's hand made its way under the split in my skirt, and I'd found his lips. So I almost didn't hear the announcer say, "And the award goes to... BB JAMES!"

Riley jerked back, and my eyes widened before I burst into laughter. "Well, shit!"

I thanked the cosmetic gods for smudge-proof lipstick while Riley helped me tug my dress back into place. Then he opened the door and let us out.

"BB? Is she here tonight?"

The announcer squinted through the stage lights as I skirted the edge of the room, heading as quickly as possible for the stage. But right before I hit the steps, I glanced back over my shoulder.

Riley leant on the wall with his arms crossed, watching me. When our gazes met, he gave me a grin and brought his hands together to clap me.

God, he was cute.

Unable to wipe the smile from my face, I took the stairs one at a time, careful not to faceplant, and accepted my award. I leaned into the microphone, looking out at the sea of faces, none of which were anything more than a blur with the lights blinding me, and thanked my parents, manager, the crew, the writers, directors, and my cast mates.

"And I'd like to thank some people who have always been

there for me. To Elodie, Jamison, Low, Reese, and to Riley." I turned in the direction of where I'd left him, standing by the wall. "To the best *friends* a girl could ever hope for." I threw him a wink and hoped he was smiling.

21

RILEY

"I'm so proud of you," I whispered in Bianca's ear as we strolled hand in hand toward the exit.

I squeezed her fingers, and she looked up at me with a coy smile that took my breath away.

"Thank you. That means a lot."

Damn, she was beautiful tonight. That dress was a complete knockout, and despite the misunderstanding over where we stood, the night had ended on a high. Being here with her, at one of these events, instead of watching from home while jealousy consumed me every time her date touched her, was a pleasant change.

Her winning the gold was just the cherry on the top. She'd spent the rest of the night being congratulated by her peers, and she was inspiring when she was in her element. She was made for this life. If I hadn't been the one working with her all those years ago at a racetrack bar, I would never have believed it had even happened. She was so far from that girl I'd once dated that I barely recognised her.

We pushed through the lobby doors and stepped out onto the street, only to be blinded by flashing cameras.

I tightened my grip on Bianca's hand and surveyed the scene. There was less security out here now than there had been earlier, and the crowd barricades had been taken down. The fans had all left, but the paparazzi were hanging around, probably hoping to find someone drunk and disorderly, or leaving with a fellow cast mate. Something scandalous they could sink their teeth into. Something they could deliver to their editors that would get them the headline in tomorrow's newspaper.

"BB! Congratulations! How do you feel?"

"Amazing. I'm so thrilled, honestly," Bianca said graciously.

I kept us moving towards the limo across the street. Stopping would mean being swarmed; I'd learned that lesson at the hospital.

"We hear you're up for a Ridge Leone project! Tell us all about it."

I tucked my arm around her, pulling her close to me. Ten more steps and we'd be at the car, and she'd be safe. I really hated these vultures. They made me so uneasy. They were ruthless with their need to get the story or the exclusive photo.

"Oh, I don't know about that. I'm very happy where I am with my *Ocean Bay* family."

I got the door open and turned to face the paps. "Sorry, fellas, Miss James has to go." I pushed her inside the car and put one foot in to follow her.

"Are you her bodyguard? What's your name?"

I stared down at her gorgeous face, now hidden from view from the photographers, and safe within the limo. She had that come-get-me smile she'd always saved for me back when we were dating. And in that moment, she was the girl I knew. The girl I'd once loved and the one I'd pined over for years.

I turned back to the photographers as I leaned on the door. "I'm not her bodyguard. But here's an exclusive for you. We aren't just friends."

I threw them a wink before I sat on the seat, lifting in my other leg and shutting the door. Outside, the paps exploded with questions. I laughed at the way they pounded on the windows, but when Harrison drove away, I watched in shocked amazement as some tried to run after us. My heart pounded.

Bianca chuckled beside me, and when her warm hand landed on my thigh, I turned in her direction.

"Playing with the media already, Riley? That's a seasoned pro hobby."

I shrugged. "I wanted them to know you were my girl." Then I paused, running my finger down the side of her face. "I want *you* to know you're my girl."

Her lips spread into a smile so blinding I was sure my heart would stop.

"I like the sound of that." She brushed her lips over mine, her tongue flicking out just briefly, but then she pulled back.

I frowned. Now that we'd made it official, all I wanted to do was take her home and kiss her until she saw stars.

"Do you want to go to an afterparty? We'll have to surrender our phones, but they're always a lot of fun."

"Whatever you want. It's your night. We should celebrate your win."

She nodded happily and gave Harrison directions. But when we stopped in front of the swanky Bondi mansion, a crowd of paparazzi swarmed the car. Two security guards tried to hold them back, but they were woefully outnumbered.

"Whoa," Bianca said quietly, her eyes big as she took in the crowd. "I've never seen this sort of media turnout at an after-party. This is insane."

A troubling thought occurred to me. "Do you think this has anything to do with me announcing us as a couple?" I asked and clenched my fingers by my sides. It had been a stupid, egotistical move. I'd hated her calling me her friend, and I'd wanted everyone to know we were more than that. I'd wanted every man who'd ever looked at her to know she was mine and she was off the market. But now, staring out at this swarm of photographers, I worried I'd majorly fucked this whole thing up.

But Bianca's laugh, like windchimes in the breeze, floated through the car. "Don't be ridiculous. They aren't here for me. I'm too old to be of any interest to them at an afterparty. They know I'm not going to get drunk and dance on a table. Trust me, there's much more exciting things happening for them to try to get a glimpse of than you and me announcing we're a couple."

But I couldn't ignore the rising sense of unease. "I don't want to let you out of this car, B. I don't want you getting hurt."

She seemed as if she was going to laugh off my concerns again, but then a pap banged on the window behind her. She jumped. Several more people knocked at the windows.

"Are the doors locked, Harrison?

"They are, Miss James."

She was a little pale when she took my face between her palms and stared me in the eyes. Then nodded. "Okay. Let's get out of here then."

22

BIANCA

*E*ven though night had long fallen, the sand beneath my feet held the last traces of the day's warmth. I held my heels in one hand, my other hand wrapped around Riley's fingers.

"Better?" I asked, running my thumb over his palm. The waves lapped at the edge of the shore, the sounds of the ocean soothing after a long evening of too much conversation.

"Yeah. This was a good idea."

A breeze blew over my bare shoulders, but it wasn't cold. A sure sign summer wasn't far away.

"I love this beach. We do a lot of filming here, and those days are always my favourites." There was something about the beach that soothed my soul. The moon was barely a sliver in the sky, so the darkness that surrounded us was deep as we walked along. It was as if we were the only two people on Earth.

"You're ruining your dress," Riley said.

I shrugged, and to prove my point, I pulled him down in the sand to sit next to me.

"Wait." Riley tugged off his jacket and laid it down on the sand for me to sit on.

I truly couldn't have cared less about the dress. I knew I'd never wear it again anyway, so it didn't matter if the sand ruined it. But it was nice of him to be a gentleman. We sat side by side, and for a long time, we just stared out at the dark ocean, breathing in the salt air. I laid my head on Riley's shoulder, and that was how we stayed until I eventually looked up at him.

"Thank you. For tonight. I know it isn't your thing. But it meant a lot to me that you came anyway."

He nodded, then dropped his lips to my upturned face. His lips brushed over my mouth, soft and slow at first, teasing, before they pressed more firmly. His hand smoothed along the side of my face, his fingertips burying beneath my hair, finding the nape of my neck, and pulled me closer.

My lips parted, allowing him to deepen the kiss, and it felt as old and familiar as every other time we'd kissed over the past ten years. But it somehow still felt new and exciting as well. It was a strange mix of promises clashing with old feelings, and when he guided me to lie back on the sand, I went willingly.

His big body covered mine as he braced himself on his forearms and kissed me until tiny moans escaped my mouth. My core throbbed at the feel of him against my breasts, his erection pushing into my leg.

I shifted beneath him. I didn't care that we were on a beach. It was so dark and one a.m. in the morning. There was nobody here. And I wanted him. I'd wanted him from the minute I'd seen him in that tux. I'd wanted him for a whole lot longer than that. And judging from the way he was kissing me, he wanted me, too. His lips trailed off the edge of my mouth and down my neck, moving across my chest. My back arched as he moved aside the material covering my breasts, his mouth taking my nipple. I writhed beneath him, my legs opening as if they had a mind of their own, and the breeze blew over my bare mound.

Excitement spiralled through me. This was so bad. So

public, but with no one around, and in the safety of the darkness, all that did was spur me on. We'd had outdoor sex before. We'd had sex so many times and in so many places it was hard to keep track of them all. Ten years' worth of sexual exploits all saved up in my memory, for nights I was alone and wishing we could get this thing right.

And now here we were. It finally felt right.

I palmed his erection through his pants, fumbled for the zip on his fly, then flicked it open and shoved his pants down over his ass. I wanted him inside me.

But he pulled back and out of my grasp. I tried to reach after him, but he grabbed my wrist and pinned it to my side.

"Stop. I don't just want to fuck. Not yet. Want to taste you first," he mumbled against my skin before sliding down my body to the split in my dress.

He pushed the silky black material high, so I was completely exposed to the cooling night air. And then he covered my core with his warm mouth.

My hips jerked, and though he still had one of my hands pinned, he couldn't do anything about my other hand which flew to the back of his head. I ran my fingers through his short, dark hair as his tongue licked through my folds in long, slow strokes. Over and over again, his tongue caressed me until I ached to be filled.

"Riley," I moaned, and knowing what I needed, he slipped two fingers up inside me.

With the practiced ease of a man who knew my body as well as I did, if not better, he found that spot inside me that made me see stars. And within moments, my walls clenched down on his fingers, and I cried out, holding him to me while I convulsed in pleasure.

As I came down from my orgasm high, I realised I had his hair clenched in my fingers, but he didn't seem to mind. When he kissed me, I tasted myself on his lips, but then the head of his cock was probing at my entrance, and the feel of him inside me was all I wanted. Normally, the sex between us was quick, hot, and fast, but tonight Riley seemed content to take his time. He nudged inside me, inch by inch, until I was stretched and full. And then he moved. His hips rolled slowly, his cock slipping in and out so leisurely I thought I'd die from the drawn-out torture. But with each stroke, my pleasure heightened. He was toying with me, building me up by stopping to kiss me, and to suck or squeeze my nipples. My clit throbbed.

"Fuck you looked so hot in that dress tonight. I've been desperate to do this from the moment I saw you."

I moaned, tightening around him. I'd wanted it, too.

He gradually increased his pace until I was panting, and then he reached between us, finding my clit with his fingers and rubbing over the already sensitive bud. And I was done for. I shattered around him for the second time.

"Fuck, Bianca." His cock pulsed, his groan in my ear only increasing my pleasure when he found his own release.

He stroked in and out a few more times, his pace slowing as we both trembled and fought to catch our breath, and then he collapsed down on top of me.

I buried my face in his neck and closed my eyes, memorising this moment. It was the same moment I'd lived for all those years. The same moment that had gotten me by when we were so damn angry with each other we couldn't even see straight. But this time, instead of trying to cling to it, to hold on and wrap myself in it because I didn't know if or when I'd get it again, I relaxed. He was mine now, and I was his. I wouldn't have to wait months until the next event that our friends held. I wouldn't have to go through a screaming match in order to have this moment I so desperately craved. This moment of tenderness that always seemed to break down the walls between us—it was something I could have as much as I wanted now. Now that we were a couple.

I smiled up into the inky-black sky.

Riley lifted his head and kissed the corner of my mouth. "What are you smiling at?" he asked.

"This. Us. You. It feels good. It feels right."

A smile tugged at his lips. "I couldn't agree more."

23

BIANCA

*T*he minute I cracked one eye open, I wished I hadn't. Blinding light speared in, stabbing through my brain, making me wince.

I rolled away and tried to bury my face in the pillow, but rolling was a bad move. My stomach lurched, and suddenly, I knew with certainty that I was going to be sick. Both eyes flew open, and I raced for the bathroom, barely making it before my stomach emptied. Sweat broke out on my brow, and my stomach clenched painfully. I retched again.

Oh my God. I was dying.

Riley appeared in the doorway, and even through bloodshot eyes, I noticed how damn adorable he looked, all sleep-tousled, his hair sticking up at odd angles and his boxer shorts low on his hips. My gaze traced the V of muscle that led below his waistband before another round of nausea overtook me and I hurled up the last of whatever we'd drunk when we'd gotten home last night.

Riley knelt by my side, pulling back my hair while I tried to wave him off. "Go. Nobody wants to see this," I moaned.

"Stop. You're sick. Let me help you."

I shook my head, but then his big hand was rubbing warm, slow circles on my back, and it felt so nice I stopped protesting. When my stomach seemed to have settled, I sat back on the cool bathroom tiles and slumped against the basin. Riley left but then came back with a glass of water and some ibuprofen. He smiled sympathetically while brushing limp strands of hair from my eyes.

My eyes watered, but I tried to smile. "Thank you. Sorry."

"No, I'm sorry. I didn't even realise how much we drank last night. I hate that you're sick."

He frowned, and I fought through the fuzzy memories. Winning the gold. Riley and I going all the way on the beach, in what had to be one of the most romantic experiences of my life. Going back to his place, where we'd cracked open a bottle of wine and toasted my win. We'd sat up until the sun rose, talking like we hadn't talked in years. We'd finished that bottle, and another, in between talking and kissing and touching. We'd gone to bed in the early hours of the morning, and I'd fallen asleep, curled into his body. His home was so quiet. It was warm and comfortable and lived-in in a way my place, with its sleek lines and cold metal, wasn't. It had been a night where everything felt right and easy.

I hadn't even noticed how drunk I was. But I was feeling it now.

"Come on, let's put you back to bed. In a few hours, you'll be feeling a whole lot better."

He put one arm around my back, the other beneath my knees, and lifted me off the bathroom floor as if I weighed nothing. I rested my head on his shoulder, loving the way his arms felt around me.

He padded down the hallway to his room, but the open door of the bedroom next to his caught my eye. It was painted a bright purple, and the walls were covered with photos of teenage girls smiling at the camera, and posters of actors and singers. I spotted a few of one of the young guys on my show. A single bed sat in the middle of the space, neatly made with a white bedspread with tiny purple flowers on it.

My eyes widened. "You weren't supposed to have Sadie today, were you?" I tried to scramble out of his arms. "I can go." Jesus, I hadn't even considered his daughter. That would be just my luck, to be standing here with my hair a mess, mascara smudged everywhere, and wearing nothing but one of Riley's t-shirts when his daughter came home for the weekend.

But Riley's arm tightened around me. "Relax. She's at her mum's this weekend."

I stopped squirming. Because I didn't even know how I'd manage to make it home in this state.

Riley walked us back to his bedroom and deposited me gently on the bed, pulling up the clean white sheets and climbing in beside me. I rolled to face him. The space between his eyebrows wrinkled, and I reached out to smooth it with my thumb.

"What's the matter?"

He sighed. "There's something I need to tell you."

"Okay," I said slowly, a hint of worry creeping through me. I didn't like the look on his face, and I had a feeling I wasn't going to like what he said next.

"It's about Sadie." He propped an elbow underneath his head. "She's moving in with me. Full time."

"Oh," I said, my eyebrows raising. "That's...nice. Right?"

Riley's frown deepened. "It's more than nice, B. It's some-thing I've wanted from the minute I found out she existed."

"Of course." I nodded, trying to sort his words through my foggy brain. "Why didn't you tell me she was moving in?"

What did that mean for him and me? I hadn't seen Sadie in years, not since she was a little girl. I knew Riley only saw her every second weekend, so she hadn't really been on my radar. Which I realised now, was incredibly self-centred of me. But I was used to being alone. I hadn't had to consider a partner in a very long time.

Riley pushed off the bed and pulled on a t-shirt. I wanted to pout as his abs disappeared beneath the material. Though the opportunity to look at his ass was a nice consolation prize. But when he turned around, his face was tight.

"Hey," I said, reaching out a hand to him, careful not to move too fast in fear of setting off my stomach again. "What's wrong?"

He shook his head and went to leave the room, but then he stopped. "She's not a baby, you know, Bianca. It's not like you'd have to change her nappies or give her bottles. She's fifteen."

"I know?" I wasn't sure where he was going with all this.

"I didn't tell you because every time we talk about her, you get *that* look on your face."

"What look?" I asked, confused, and a little annoyed myself. I didn't like his accusatory tone.

"That look that says you'd rather be talking about anything in the world apart from my daughter."

My prickle of irritation grew. He was being unfair. "That's not true."

He sighed and came back to sit on the bed. "I don't want to fight about this. Not after last night."

My mind flashed back to making love with him on the beach. Something we hadn't done in years. We fucked a lot, but we hadn't made love since we were twenty. I softened. I didn't want to fight either.

"I do want to hear about your daughter. The two of you are a package deal, I know that."

He nodded. "Even more so now. Her mum is moving, and she wants to live with me. This is huge, Bianca. I've tried so hard to form a relationship with her. I want her here with me more than I want anything in the world."

I nodded.

"But I want you, too. I don't want Sadie being around more to be a dealbreaker for you. And I'm scared it is. I know you don't like kids."

I ran my fingers along the edges of the sheet. "That's not true. I like them. I just don't have any experience with them."

I didn't say it out loud, but the real problem was that Sadie made me nervous. I knew how much Riley adored her. If I was going to be with him, she would become a big part of my life, too. And that meant I'd be bringing a child into my world. A world that was full of people trying to take advantage of you. Paparazzi taking your photo without your permission. Reporters chasing you while you drove. People watching your every move. My sister had been a casualty of this life, and it scared me to bring another child into it.

But I wanted Riley so much. It was selfish.

I so desperately wanted to be selfish.

Riley reached out and took my hand. "Look, this is all a bit premature anyway. We've been a couple less than twenty-four hours. We have time to deal with all this. Sadie is moving in next weekend, but that doesn't mean you need to meet her right away. We can hang out at your place until you're more comfortable with the idea of her."

I shook my head, not happy that he was babying me. He completely had the wrong idea. I wasn't worried about her hating me. I was an actress on a pretty popular TV show. And she was a fifteen-year-old girl. She'd love me. I needed to tell him about what had happened to my sister, but when I opened my mouth to try, a new worry occurred to me. Riley seemed to be protesting an awful lot.

"Are you saying that because you don't want me meeting her?"

"No! Of course not."

I nodded. We were both overreacting. Sadie wasn't my daughter. The media probably wouldn't even care if Riley had a kid. Not unless we got married, but lord, that wasn't even on the horizon. Definitely not something I needed to consider now. I couldn't date Riley without meeting his daughter. Especially not if she was going to live here. So I pushed all my worries aside and smiled at him reassuringly. "Good. Because I want to meet her. I really do."

I pulled his hand to my mouth and kissed his palm, deciding to keep my family secrets quiet for a little longer.

24

RILEY

*C*loud nine felt pretty damn good. Bianca and I were together. We were official, and even though I still sensed some hesitation on her part, she was adamant that she wanted to meet Sadie tonight. I'd tried to talk her out of it, considering she was hungover enough to be vomiting, but she'd waved my concern away, curled up in my bed, and gone back to sleep. I tucked a blanket around her still form before picking up my phone and scrolling through to Sadie's number.

The photo I'd added to her contact information made me smile. She was sitting in front of a cake covered in chocolate frosting. The two of us had baked it together, for no reason other than we both felt like chocolate, and a packet mix was all I had in the cupboard. Moments after the photo had been taken, I'd shoved her face right in the cake, making her squeal. But she was such a good-natured kid. After the initial shock, she'd picked up the remains of the smushed chocolate mess and hurled them straight at me, starting an epic food fight. It had taken us hours to clean the kitchen afterwards, but it had been worth it. The memory of that day was more important than any amount of cleaning.

I shot off a text message, suggesting that we go to La Mer for dinner. It was one of the swankiest restaurants in the city, and I knew Sadie would love it. I was already imagining the ten minutes we'd have to wait while she Instagrammed each course. Bianca's phone rang in shrill tones from the lounge room, and I winced, the noise cutting through my head. Bianca wasn't the only one sporting a hangover this morning. Though at least I wasn't vomiting. Bianca didn't stir, even when the phone rang again. I pushed off the bed and tiptoed out to where she'd left the offending device, just wanting to be sure it wasn't her parents. I didn't want to wake her. She'd looked practically green in the few minutes she'd been conscious earlier. But if her parents were calling with an emergency, that would be different altogether. I squinted at the screen. Tangie. Her manager. I put it back down. Nope. She could wait until Bianca had at least slept for a few hours.

I crawled back across the bed to where Bianca lay on her side, the gentle rise and fall of her chest assuring me she was still asleep. Good. She needed it. I fitted my chest to her back, tucked my knees in behind hers, and buried my nose into her hair, feeling completely content. My daughter was happy and excited and only days away from moving in with me full time. And I had the woman I'd wanted ever since I'd lost her. I relaxed into the mattress and let Bianca's soft, warm body lull me to sleep.

When I woke up, it was to Bianca tugging off my sleep shorts. The sun outside the window seemed low, dark shadows stretching out across the ceiling. We had to have slept most of the day away. My arm was still locked around Bianca's waist, forcing her to reach behind to touch me. She stilled, realising I was awake, then glanced over her shoulder.

"I was going to wake you up in the best way possible. But your shorts won't budge."

"Drawstring," I whispered before nibbling at her ear. "How are you feeling?"

She turned away from me again, wiggling her ass against my erection. "Much better. You?"

Even if I'd felt sick enough to curl up and die, I wouldn't have told her that when her fingertips were slipping beneath the waistband of my shorts. She twisted so she was facing me, then pushed me flat to my back, her eyes hooded as she straddled me, shifting down my body, taking my clothes with her. My balls clenched as the air hit them, and my cock stood tall, a drop of liquid shining at the tip, just waiting for her.

"Take your shirt off," I commanded. I was pretty sure she was naked beneath that thin material and I wanted to see.

Her fingers clenched in the hem of the oversized shirt I'd given her from my drawer last night. She dragged it up her thighs and then higher, across her belly, revealing that she was indeed, completely bare beneath. I reached out a hand to touch her, but she stopped me.

"This is just about you. You can look, but right now, I just want to touch you."

I frowned and began to shake my head, but then she pulled the shirt off the rest of the way, and my brain short-circuited. She leant over me, her hardened nipples brushing my chest, and made her way down my body, kissing, licking, and nipping as she went. My cock throbbed at the sight of her naked body, and her warm, wet, mouth dipping closer to where I really wanted it.

She'd said no touching, but when her tongue shot out and licked the drop of liquid from my tip, I couldn't stop myself. I ran my fingers through her hair. She lifted her gaze to meet mine and gave me a sly smile. Then, without breaking eye contact for a moment, she closed her mouth over my cock and sucked me deep.

By sheer force of will, I kept my hips chained to the mattress beneath me. What I really wanted to do was jerk so my cock would plunge even farther into her warmth. But I fought that urge and watched while she controlled the show. She ran her tongue along the underside, flicking it over the head, each time taking me a little deeper into her mouth. Her pretty pink lips ran up and down my length, shining in the late afternoon light and completely capturing my imagination. My breathing increased as the feel of her wrapped around me stole my oxygen. She cupped my balls and tugged at them gently until the head of my cock hit the back of her throat. I groaned. God, she felt good, her practiced tongue swirling around me in the way she knew I loved. She increased her pace, and I dared to let my hips move a little, thrusting into her mouth, testing how much she could take. But the gleam in her eye and the small moans of pleasure she let out told me she was more than just okay.

"Let go," she murmured between sucks.

I closed my eyes, letting the sensation building in the base of my spine and my balls take over. I gripped her hair harder and thrust into her wet, soft mouth, until I couldn't hold on another moment. My release ripped through me, emptying into her throat. She moaned her satisfaction but didn't let up with her sucking and licking. When I couldn't take any more, I moved her away from my cock and up to my lips. I cupped her face between my hands, then kissed her hard on the mouth. She was smiling coyly when she pulled away, and I dropped my head back on the pillow, completely boneless and spent.

I flung an arm over my face but grinned when she started laughing. My breath caught again with how stunning she was. Her hair was tousled, last night's mascara still smudged around her eyes, but she'd never looked more beautiful. I found her lips, kissing her, slow and soft this time.

We kissed until words I wasn't ready to say, and she wasn't ready to hear, fought to break free.

"My turn now," I whispered. Better to steer the conversation back to sex. Something safe and familiar for us. I'd scare her off if I voiced any of the feelings coursing through me.

But she pushed off the bed and moved around the room towards the door.

I scrunched my face up in disgust.

She threw a pillow at me. "It's late. If we're going out for dinner, we need to have a shower."

Right. Dinner. I supposed we had to leave this bed. I consoled myself with the fact I could bring her back in here in just a few hours. I nodded, grabbed my phone, and checked for a text message from Sadie, but the battery had died.

"It needs to charge, but go get ready, and we'll just swing by her house. If she's not up for it, the two of us can at least go get some food. I'm starving."

"Me, too," Bianca said as she walked backwards towards my bathroom door. She paused in the doorway. "Riley. I said *we* need a shower..."

I was up, across the room and kissing her before she could change her mind.

25

BIANCA

*M*y fingers shook as I attempted to swipe on my mascara, and after three unsuccessful attempts, I admitted defeat and put the wand down. I stared into my reflection in Riley's bathroom mirror.

"You've got this. She's going to love you."

I nodded firmly and picked up the mascara again, ignoring the fact my hand hadn't stopped shaking. Why the hell was I so nervous? This was ridiculous. I had a nation full of teenage girls who loved me. Why would this one be any different?

Because she *was* different. I knew exactly how important she was to Riley. Which meant that tonight had to go well.

"You ready?" Riley asked, leaning on the bathroom doorframe. I capped my mascara wand and closed the gap between us, finding his hand with my own.

"Absolutely," I said with a confidence I had to fake. I didn't want to give him any sign of how nervous I was. But of course, he saw right through me.

He grasped my face between his palms and stared deep into my eyes. "Stop stressing. It's going to be fine. I promise."

A handful of the butterflies swirling around my stomach

flew off. "Do you think she'd accept bribes in the form of Tate Jennings signed posters? Maybe an introduction?"

Riley's lips quirked up at the side. "Isn't Tate Jennings at least twenty-one?"

"Something like that."

He shrugged. "I suppose he's better than Chris Hemsworth."

I laughed and kissed his cheek. "Babe, no one is better than Chris Hemsworth."

Riley rolled his eyes so hard I was surprised they didn't fall right out of his head.

"Come on, Hemsworth hater. Let's do this." I linked my fingers through his, and he let me lead him down the hall to the front door. I was still laughing when I stepped aside so he could open it wide. We stepped out onto his porch, the door swinging shut behind us with a crack.

A wall of noise hit us like a punch to the face.

Swarms of people who had been waiting out on the footpath rushed across Riley's lawn, circling around us. Within seconds we were completely surrounded. My fingers tightened around Riley's. I was used to the paparazzi, but this was like nothing I'd ever seen before. At worst, I had one or two guys with cameras outside my place each day. They were generally respectful, and from time to time I even used them to my advantage, letting them take shots of me when I had a movie coming up or I had a new brand promotion going on. But this was next level. I was too shocked to even move. How had they even found out where I was? Or where Riley lived?

"BB! How do you feel?"

Forcing myself out of my Bianca mindset, I shifted into the fake persona I'd diligently crafted for BB over the years. I smiled and let out a tinkling laugh that sounded nothing like my own. "About the award? I feel great. It was an honour to even be nominated. But, guys, we have somewhere to be, and you're on private property. So if you'll excuse us..."

I tried to skirt around the woman thrusting a microphone in my face, but she stepped in my way. My hackles rose.

"Not about the award. About the sex tape." She turned to Riley. "What about you? Did you know you were being filmed?"

The blood drained from my face. All traces of BB and her fake confidence dissolved. Leaving me with nothing but Bianca and the cold, hard, fear that I hadn't misunderstood the woman's words.

More microphones were shoved in front of me, and cameras flashed while I groped for words.

"Excuse me?" I asked lamely.

"Wait. You don't know?" The woman's face took on a snake-like quality, her glee over being the one to inform us written all over it.

I shook my head. Beside me, Riley's large frame vibrated. I glanced up at him, and his face was like thunder.

The reporter didn't even seem to notice that Riley was moments away from exploding. She gave us a smug grin and thrust a phone at me. Horror clamped down on my throat as the images on the phone became clear. A couple, on the beach, having sex. The woman's breasts on full display, her black formal dress hiked up and pushed aside to reveal her sex. The man in a discarded tuxedo, moving to go down on her.

My eyes filled with tears, blurring the images. Not just any woman. Not just any man. Riley and me. The video was dark, but it had to have been taken with professional equipment, as it was clear enough for the two of us to be identified. My gaze whipped from reporter to photographer, each one trying to get a reaction from me. I knew I shouldn't. I knew I had to hold it together. Say no comment and walk off until my manager could deal with the epic mess Riley and I had created. But I couldn't.

"How could you," I said quietly. "Which one of you was it? This isn't some game, you know. It's my life!"

My knees buckled, and with crippling certainty, I knew I was going to faint. My stomach rolled, and dizziness blurred my vision as I fell. Distantly, I braced for the impact of the ground, but then strong arms caught me around the waist, and I found the strength to fight through the fog. I buried my face in his shirt, breathing in his fresh clean smell and the scent of his cologne, until I felt a car seat beneath my thighs. He slammed the door, and I shielded my face from the onslaught of camera flashes and fists banging on the windows while Riley pushed his way to the driver's side. Then he was in and backing his jeep out of the driveway, with seemingly no care given to anyone who might be standing behind the vehicle.

I pulled out my phone and Google-searched my name. "Oh God," I moaned when the video filled the first page of search results. I hit play, unable to look away, and stared in disbelief at the screen.

"Don't watch it," Riley said, manoeuvring the car through the suburban streets.

He took turn after turn, but I was oblivious to where we were. All I could do was watch the twenty-minute-long video. The moment that had been so special, so romantic, was now tarnished and dirty. And if the video wasn't bad enough, the comments people were making were horrifying. Some made jokes. Some commented on my body. Some expressed how disgusted they were and how they'd never watch *Ocean Bay* again. Not one person spoke out about how wrong this was. We shouldn't have had sex there, on the beach. That was a stupid, rookie mistake, but I'd been so caught up in the night, in winning, and in Riley that it had felt like the most natural thing in the world. We were in the wrong. But whoever had posted this all over social media had no soul.

"Shit," Riley muttered, peering into the rearview mirror. "They're following us."

I couldn't bring myself to look. All I could do was stare at the images on the screen. That moment had felt so private. So special. We'd been making love for the first time. And now it felt cheap and nasty. Ruined by some jackass who only cared about the money a video like that would make.

"God, I'm so fucking stupid. What the hell were we thinking?"

I glanced over at Riley in dismay. His mouth was set in a firm line as he increased his speed to lose our tail. He had the advantage of knowing this area well, though, since it was home. And after he'd turned down several side streets and headed back the way we'd come, he sat back in his seat, relaxing just a fraction. And I envied him. I envied him and that tiny bit of relief he'd found. Because I was desperately wondering if I'd ever feel that again. He reached across the console and found my fingers. I gripped his like he was the only thing saving me from falling. Because maybe he was. Panic, embarrassment, and anger swirled around my heart and my head, making it impossible to think clearly.

"We weren't thinking. We were just in the moment."

I closed my eyes. It sounded so simple. "What are we going to do?" I whispered. "We can't go home. There'll be another media circus at my place."

"Shit."

Shit indeed. We were royally screwed.

26

RILEY

*M*y skin was too tight. Every muscle in my body burned, wanting to explode free, but of course, that didn't happen. All I was left with was the aching sensation of a hole opening up in my chest.

Shit. I drove aimlessly, rubbing Bianca's thigh while she stared blankly at her phone, playing that damn tape over and over again. I cringed, hearing our laboured breathing, her moans, me calling her name as I came. Fire burned through me at the complete and utter invasion of privacy. We'd screwed up by having sex in public. But that didn't give whoever the fuck had taken that video the right to film it and broadcast it to the world. I wanted to kill each and every one of those filthy photographers and reporters. Or better yet, go to their homes. Take photos of their children. Touch their belongings. Taint every damn thing they'd ever loved with the same feeling of disgust and loathing I had now. Make them see how it felt to have the woman you loved fall to pieces in the seat beside you and have no power to do anything to stop it.

I didn't need to watch the tape, because my brain kept playing the scene over and over again anyway. Where had the pap been? Hiding in the bushes? Behind a sand dune? Had he been farther away with a telescopic lens? I hadn't noticed a thing when we'd been on the beach. It had been so dark and quiet. I'd thought we were completely alone.

And because I'd assumed, I'd let Bianca down. A growl formed in my throat at the thought of every Tom, Dick, and Harry watching that video, all around the world, seeing my woman at her most vulnerable. Seeing every private part of her body—parts only her man should see.

That thought hit me like a fucking sledge hammer. I lifted my arm and slammed my fist down on the steering wheel. Once, twice, three times.

"Fuck!" I yelled.

I pulled over to the side of the road, sure now that we had no one following us, and shoved my way out of the car. I punched the bonnet, leaving a dent, but I couldn't bring myself to care. Pain radiated through my knuckles and up my arm, but I barely felt it. Yanking open Bianca's door, I reached in, pulling her sobbing form from the vehicle once more. She clung to me like a koala, and I strode up the path. I hadn't given any thought to where I was going, I just knew I needed to get her somewhere safe.

I knocked loudly on the door until the sound of footsteps came from behind the solid wood. It swung open noiselessly.

Eliza stood in the doorway. Shock filled her face first, then anger.

"You idiot," she hissed at me. "You're all over the news! What the hell were you thinking?"

Her gaze landed on Bianca, and for the first time, Eliza seemed to realise I wasn't alone. Bianca's sobbing form shook in my arms, and the look on Eliza's face softened just a smidge before she turned back to me.

"What are you doing here?"

"I'm sorry," I said. "I lost the paparazzi then all I could think of was getting to Sadie. I just needed to know she was safe. I needed to keep them both safe," I pleaded desperately, begging her with my eyes to understand.

"She is, but you should know. She's seen the tape. She was the one who showed it to me."

Something inside me shrivelled and died. As I'd driven, in between fuming over the tape and trying to comfort Bianca, my other overriding thought was getting to Sadie. Making sure she was safe was priority number one. And making sure she didn't see that fucking tape was a close second. I should have known she'd have already seen it. She was all over social media, and by the sounds of it, so were Bianca and I.

I gave Eliza a helpless stare and clutched Bianca a little tighter. "Please, Liza. Can we come in? We've got nowhere else to go. There's paps everywhere. And I need to talk to Sadie."

Eliza hesitated for another moment, then sighed, opening the door wider. "Fine. But Jesus Christ, Riley, you've really fucked this up. I don't know what the hell you're going to say to your daughter. That's not the sort of thing any fifteen-year-old should see."

Didn't I know it.

Eliza stepped aside, and I mouthed 'thank you' at her as I passed. She gave a curt nod and pointed to the living room, following behind me. Thick grey carpet lined the floor of the large area, and my boots sank into it when I crossed the space and deposited Bianca gently on the lounge. She pulled back from me with red-rimmed eyes, my shirt soaked from her tears. She looked over my shoulder at where Eliza stood with her arms folded across her chest, then back to me.

"I'm so sorry," she whispered.

And my heart fucking broke. Pure devastation tormented her features. Her shoulders slumped, and tears stained her cheeks. Eliza sighed from the doorway before turning away, her soft footsteps padding down the hall.

"Hey," I said quietly, kneeling in front of her and taking her chin in my fingers. I forced her watery blue eyes to meet mine and let her see the determination and fire I knew burned there. "This is not your fault."

"Everybody is going to see that tape, Riley." Her words were slow and choked and full of self-loathing. "Everyone. It's already all over social media." She buried her face in her hands. "This will end my career. Elaina is the sweetheart of the show! She's practically a nun! They're going to fire me. And no credible studio will ever look at me again."

Her shoulders shook with fresh sobs, and I pulled her into my arms, wishing with everything I had that that wasn't true. I knew her career meant everything to her. It couldn't be over.

"It's not your fault," I said again, kissing her tears. God, my heart was breaking, watching her in so much pain.

"Actually, it is." A voice came from behind me. I whipped my head around to where Sadie now occupied the space that Eliza had stood in just moments earlier.

"Sadie," I said, getting to my feet to go to her, but she held her hand out in a stop motion. I stopped. Her eyes were blood-shot, and damn if that didn't just add another knife to my heart. I was right when I'd said this wasn't Bianca's fault. It was mine.

"Sadie, please." I begged, but she shook her head.

"Everyone knows it's you on that video, Dad! You telling the reporters that you two weren't just friends, then the tape. Everyone knows, even if they can't see your face. They're all tagging me in it and asking when my dad became a porn star."

Shame burned in my chest, and the knowledge that my actions had hurt my daughter was a pain like nothing else. I closed my eyes, wishing I could rewind time and not be so damn stupid.

"It was a private moment, Sade. Someone violated that."

She shook her head, her body trembling. Then she hissed, "A private moment? How was that a private moment? You were on a beach for the whole world to see!" Her stare burned through me. "I hate you. You've ruined my life."

She may as well have ripped my heart straight out of my chest. Nothing could have hurt me more. She was a good kid, not the type to throw those words around without meaning. And the worst thing was, I couldn't even blame her. I hated myself more than she ever could.

27

BIANCA

I closed my eyes as Riley's daughter's words cut through me like a knife. The pain and devastation on her young face, and the pure anguish on Riley's, was like a blinding light. It took away every ounce of the self-pity I'd been wallowing in since we'd been surrounded on Riley's front lawn, and in its place left nothing but worry for Riley and Sadie. I'd been a teenage girl once. I knew how they worked. This was going to damage the relationship Riley had worked so hard to build. There was no way it couldn't. We'd ruined that in one stupid, thoughtless moment.

I stood stiffly and pulled my phone from my pocket. "I should leave. I'll call an Uber and wait out the front."

But Riley shook his head. "I'll drive you to a hotel. I don't want you going out there alone."

I so badly wanted him to come with me, but I knew Sadie needed him more than I did. "You should stay. Try to talk to her."

"I think she needs some space. I'll come back first thing in the morning."

I wrapped my arms around his waist, marvelling at how much he cared for me, even when his own world was falling apart. He was a good man. A man I didn't deserve.

"I'll be fine."

"Yes, you will. But I'm still coming with you. I know my daughter, B. It's better to give her some space."

I nodded, although it was selfish, because the truth was, I didn't want to be alone.

I waited in the car while he said goodbye to Eliza and told her he'd be back in the morning. Then he drove us to the nearest hotel. I kept my head down and sunglasses on while he booked us a room, then ushered me to the elevator. I prayed no one would recognise us and tip off the media.

We walked in silence to the room, but as soon as we got inside, he pulled me against him, and I went willingly, desperately needing the comfort of his arms. He held me close to his chest, and I trailed my fingers over the muscled planes of his back. I breathed in his scent, memorising it, letting it calm my aching heart. And then I tilted my head back, looked into his impossibly beautiful face, and decided to be selfish one last time.

"Kiss me," I whispered.

His brown eyed gaze searched my face then he gently laid his lips to mine. His touch was soft, full of unspoken words, and my heart both swelled and sank simultaneously. Our lips parted, our tongues meeting and moving in unison, like we'd done so many times before. His kisses made me stronger. But I knew it wouldn't be enough. No amount of kisses was going to undo this mess. His arm tightened around my waist, tugging me closer, walking us backwards to the bed that sat in the centre of the room.

He perched on the edge, while I stood in the gap of his legs and just stared at him. This man—so good and sweet and kind. We'd spent years trying to get our lives together, trying to find a way for the two of us to work, and finally we had. Finally, we'd both been in the right place at the right time, only to have it all ruined mere days later.

What had made me think I'd get the fairy tale ending? What had made me think that, this time, maybe fate would smile on the two of us and just let us be? But there had always been something. We'd never worked.

Maybe that was just the way it was supposed to be.

I bit my lip as tears filled my eyes. I didn't want these thoughts. But I couldn't stop them. The look on Sadie's face. The pure, utter disgust she'd aimed at me, and the heartbreaking tone in her voice when she'd told Riley she hated him. I couldn't forget it. I never would. That scene would be burned into my memory for life. There was nothing more important than the two of them repairing their relationship. I knew what it was like to grow up without a parent. I might not have lost mine completely, but my mother was barely a shell of the woman she'd once been, so often lapsing into herself for weeks or months at a time. She was barely present, unable to live fully in a world that didn't include my sister.

His fingers linked between mine, and I stared at them, trying to blink back my tears. A sense of déjà vu washed over me— memories from the day Eliza had turned up at Riley's house with five-year-old Sadie at her side. I'd gazed down into that little girl's brown eyes and known instantly she was Riley's. There was no mistaking it. The eyes I loved on him were mirrored back at me from Sadie's rounded face. I'd known then, the same thing I knew now.

I'd lose him.

"B. Look at me. It'll be okay. A sex tape isn't the end of the world. It worked out pretty well for Kim Kardashian."

I nodded, wishing my career potentially being over was the only problem here. My phone had been ringing nonstop, my manager calling more than anyone else. But I'd ignored them all. They could wait. They could wait until morning, because tonight I didn't care about my career. All I cared about was the man I knew I had to let go.

28

RILEY

*B*ianca's nimble fingers made short work of the buttons on my shirt. Each one slipped from its place as she moved her way down my chest, exposing my skin to the air. She lingered at the bottom, looking down at where her hands were clenched in the material before she pushed it back off my shoulders. The dress she'd worn for what was supposed to be a special dinner out, disappeared over her head. I waited, watching her carefully until she straddled my legs, climbing onto my lap.

The sadness in her gaze hollowed my insides. I just wanted to go back. Turn back the time, twenty-four hours, and make better decisions, just so I wouldn't have to see her this way. I grasped her bare thighs, sliding my hands higher, skimming the sides of her body. The strapless bra found its way to the floor, leaving her with only a scrap of lace covering her mound. Her bare breasts bobbed in my face, and I caught one nipple with my mouth. It beaded beneath my tongue, and I sucked greedily, desperate to make her feel good. To feel something other than the shame and embarrassment I knew she was trying to bury. Her creamy skin beneath my mouth and hands was enough to make me forget my own name, and I wanted to have the same effect on her.

When her fingers threaded into my hair, her head dropped back, and tits pushed forward, I knew what she wanted. What she needed.

I would have been content to hold her all night. I hadn't expected sex, but the agony in her voice as she'd asked me to kiss her was too much. She needed me. My hands. My mouth. My cock. Not my heart. She didn't need me telling her I loved her, complicating matters further, and changing things when her world was already upside down. She needed what was safe and familiar. I could take away her pain and problems, at least for a little while. And then, I'd hold her. I'd hold her and support her, and we'd get through this thing together. I had the rest of our lives to tell her I loved her. I could wait for the right moment. Make it special.

I dug my fingers into the flesh of her hips, lifting and turning her so she was lying on the bed, spread in front of me like a goddess. All those blonde curls fanned out around her head, big blue eyes full of pain and hurt staring up at me. Something primal in me rose, the need to protect her roaring through my veins and pounding in my ears. I hooked my fingers in the lace, sliding it off her legs then returning to the junction of her thighs. Spreading them wide, I placed kisses down her stomach and over her bare skin until I reached her core. I left an open-mouth kiss there. Her hips rolled. Good.

Her folds were glistening pink, and I slicked my tongue through her, finding her clit, circling, then rasping over it. Her hips rolled again, her fingers tugging through my hair while she moaned, "More."

I licked my fingers and pushed two of them up inside her tight opening, searching for that spot within, stroking it over and over as she made tiny noises in the back of her throat. She rocked back and forth, working her flesh against my lips and tongue, urging me on. Her body trembled and as much as I wanted to see her fall over the edge right then and there, I also knew that would just bring her back down to earth before she was ready. And the selfish part of me wanted to go with her. I wanted her beneath me when she came. I wanted her crying out into my mouth and begging me not to stop.

So, I moved my hand away, sitting up to unbutton my jeans and yank them off. She watched me with hooded eyes, her gaze focusing on my cock as I set it free. She sat up, grasping the hard length, and I hissed when her mouth closed over the head. Fuck. So warm. I let her mouth run my length a few times, unable to pull away, until an overwhelming need to get inside her overcame me. I wanted her clamping around my cock, my seed spilling inside her. I wanted to brand her, mark her as my own. I wanted her to know that no matter what the hell had happened or would happen in the future—she was mine.

I lifted her head and covered her mouth with my own, pressing her back into the mattress. Her legs wrapped around my hips, and my dick found home, sinking deep inside her without resistance. We both stilled, her pussy so tight and warm around me I saw stars. For a long moment, I just held her, tight and safe within my arms. Where she should have always been. And then she moved, rolling her hips beneath me, and I matched her speed, taking things slow, kissing her lips, her cheeks, her eyelids until I couldn't stand it anymore. Our pace increased, building in intensity, my balls aching to release.

I reached between us, finding her clit while I fought to hold myself in check. Her fingernails scraped down my back and ass, pressing into the flesh, urging me on with her cries of more. With a loud moan that filled me with pride, she clamped down on me, and I groaned, her release setting off my own, deep inside her body.

We rode out the wave together, our movements gradually slowing. Our heated skin pressed together, and I rolled us so she lay on my chest. She laid her head down over my heart, and I wondered if she could hear the way it beat for her. Always for her. I picked up a piece of her hair and ran it absently through my fingers, marvelling at the silky smoothness between my fingertips. I was so damn content, so blissed out on the post-orgasm high and the feel of my woman on top of me that it took me a moment to notice the moisture on my chest.

"Hey," I said quietly, shifting so I could see more than the top of Bianca's head. "Are you crying?"

She tried to pull away, to bury her face back in my chest, but I grasped her chin, tilting her face up so I could see the tear streaks that ran down her cheeks.

"You are. Shh," I soothed. "It'll be okay."

She shook her head and sat up. She took the white hotel sheets with her, covering her bare breasts.

I frowned.

"It's not, though, Riley," she said sadly.

I pushed myself up so I was sitting, too, and reached for her, but she shifted away. My heart thumped.

"What's going on here?"

"We've been an official couple for what? Two days? And look what's happened. We're all over the news. Neither of us can go home. Your daughter and your ex hate you. And I've probably tanked my career."

Listed out like that, I could hardly deny that it had been a shitstorm. "It'll blow over, B. People will forget about this and move on."

She shook her head. "Some people will. But the people who count, like your family, they won't. I saw the look on Eliza's and Sadie's faces. They hate me."

"They don't even know you." I tried to take her hand, but she edged farther away.

She got off the bed and rummaged around on the floor for her clothes. My breath hitched. "Where are you going?"

Her bare skin shone in the low light cast from a lamp. She turned away to put her underwear on and then slipped her dress over her head before turning back to me. She walked slowly around the bed and came to perch on my side, the mattress dipping slightly under her weight. Her gaze met mine. My heart pounded at her expression. Gone were the soft smiles and coy looks she'd given me last night. Gone even were the sadness and pain that had plagued her since we'd found out about the tape. In its place was a strange blankness, and with ice running through my veins, I realised I'd seen that look on her face once before. Ten years ago, when she'd walked out my door and hadn't come back.

"I'm going to go to stay with my manager until this all blows over." She took a deep breath, and for an instant, her mask slipped. I saw the pain and hurt behind it. But so quickly, she switched that off. "We can't do this. We aren't good for each other. I won't stay here with you and watch your relationship with Sadie break down because of me. She's too important."

No. I shook my head, trying to understand what she was saying. "Are you breaking up with me right now?"

She bit her lip, and I saw my chance. If she was hesitating, this was a knee-jerk reaction. Not what she really wanted.

"Sadie and I will be fine, B. She's not your concern."

She dropped her gaze to the rumpled bedspread. "It's not just that. You hate my lifestyle. I saw how uncomfortable the paparazzi and the award ceremonies make you. You think that's going to get any easier now? Once the paps get a hold of who you are, do you think you'll have any sort of privacy as long as you're with me? Your quiet life will be over. You won't just be

Riley anymore. You'll be BB and Riley. They'll follow you around, analysing your every move. They'll send photographers to wait outside Sadie's school and ask her if she's seen our sex tape. They'll ask what she thinks of her father going down on BB James in the middle of a public beach. Is that what you want?"

I recoiled at the thought. "Of course that isn't what I want! But if that's the only way to have you, then that's what I'll do."

Bianca shook her head. "I can't do that to you. I know we haven't exactly been friends all these years but I've always cared about you. I watched you fight for your relationship with Sadie every step of the way. You got a proper job, bought your house, sacrificed so much so you could do this all for her. And now she's moving in with you. Do you think Eliza will let her do that if you have paps making your life a living hell? You'll lose her, Riley. I can't let you lose her for a hook-up."

Her words were a slap to the face. As physically painful as if she'd just punched me. "A hook-up," I said dully.

But then my blood began to simmer as her words sank in. This was exactly like last time. "A fucking hook-up? That's what this was to you? Here I was, thinking we had it together this time. That it was something more than just fucking." And suddenly, I was fuming. Despite all the dramas her lifestyle brought with it, I wanted it. I wanted everything to do with her, but she'd never been able to accept me as I was. Or to accept that I had a daughter.

I shifted to the other side of the bed, found my jeans, and yanked them on. "I'm an idiot. I should have known."

Bianca stood, and we faced each other across the wide king-sized bed. The bed I'd held her on just minutes earlier and contemplated how full I felt. The woman standing across from me now suddenly looked like a stranger. The gap between us as wide as a canyon.

"Should have known what? That someone would film us on the beach having sex?"

I snorted. "Should have known it would end like this. It always does."

Her eyebrows pulled together. "What does that mean?"

It meant I was stupid for thinking things could change. That people could change. "Doesn't this all sound familiar to you? This is exactly what you did ten years ago when we broke up the first time. You found out about Sadie and you bailed."

Her mouth dropped open. But I wasn't done. "We were happy. No, we were more than happy. I was fucking in love with you. Did you know I had a ring? Jamison and Low told me I was crazy, but I just laughed and told them that there was no doubt in my mind that you were it for me. That when you know, you know. I wanted to make you my wife, Bianca! But you bailed as soon as things got rough. Sadie and Eliza came back into my life, and you couldn't deal. My whole world had been turned upside down, and you didn't even bother to stick around. You just left."

Her gaze went dark. "That isn't fair, and you know it."

No, I didn't. That was exactly what had happened, and it had been the reason we'd barely been able to be in the same room for the last ten years. That sexual chemistry between us had never diminished, but she'd broken my heart when she'd walked away without a second thought. No, that wasn't true. She came back when she was horny. And I guess nothing had changed.

"Isn't it? Can you honestly look me in the eye and tell me you didn't leave me all those years ago because a boyfriend with a child and an ex in tow wasn't a part of your Hollywood dreams?"

Her eyes narrowed.

Fuck me. I hated this. How had we gotten back here so quickly? Back to arguing about old hurts instead of just focusing on the future. This was what we always did, and it killed me every time.

A little of my hurt and anger dissipated. "B," I said reaching toward her, but she yanked her hand away, fury shaking her shoulders.

"You're an asshole," she spat, picking up her bag and shoving the strap over her shoulder. "I never had Hollywood dreams. My dreams were never that big. I've stayed in Australia all these years just so I could be near you, and now you throw that back in my face. Fuck you. I broke up with you all those years ago so you could go back to your ex and your daughter. The three of you never got a shot at being a family, and I know how important family is to you. I loved you enough to let you go."

I blinked. What? She'd never told me any of this. But through my surprise, anger coursed. "You broke my goddamn heart, Bianca! I never wanted Eliza! I wanted you!"

But she shook her head. "If it weren't true, why were you back with her just weeks after we'd broken up? You think I missed that? We broke up, and I spent weeks hoping you'd come back to me. Hoping you'd turn up on my doorstep and tell me that I was wrong. That we were meant to be together. When I found out the two of you were together, I knew I'd been right. The three of you are a family. I don't fit in it. I never did."

I paced the room, so frustrated I could scream. "You broke up with me, Bianca. You. Dumped. Me. And yes, Eliza and I tried to have a relationship after. But you and I were broken up. And it wasn't weeks later. It was months later. What did you expect me to do? Never date again? You dumped me and didn't look back. By the time Eliza and I started something up, you were already walking red carpets on the arms of A-listers. No room in your life for ex boyfriends. We never even had sex, B. That's how pathetic Eliza and I were together. We tried, for

Sadie, but there was nothing between us. No spark. No lust. Certainly no love."

She threw up her hands and let out a groan. "Dammit, Riley, what does it matter now? We always end up back here, don't we? Every damn time. Everything in the past is all water under the bridge, isn't it?"

I stopped pacing. The room went still and deathly quiet. We stared each other down.

"We don't work." She whispered. "There's something fundamentally wrong with the two of us. We just always end up hurting each other, and I can't do it anymore. I won't."

My heart hurt. "So you're giving up. That's it? We're over?"

She lifted one shoulder in a shrug. "Better that we end it now, before there are real feelings involved."

Her words were a slap to my face. "Don't lie. You know this is more than sex."

She just stared at me.

A lump formed in my throat, so large I thought it would choke me. Because for all the horrible things we'd said to each other over the years, none had ever hurt as much as hearing her say there was no feelings between us. Because for me, there always had been. I'd been in love with her for ten fucking years. I couldn't get over her. I knew with certainty, that a million years could pass, and she'd still be the only woman I wanted. Eliza was great, but she wasn't Bianca. No one was. And that was why there had been no one since. I hadn't even gone looking for a one-night stand. Because she was it for me. She always had been.

But she didn't feel the same way. And nothing I said was ever going to convince her otherwise.

When she turned and walked to the hotel room door, I let her go.

29

BIANCA

*T*he hotel room door closed behind me, and my heart splintered into a million pieces. A sob rose up in my throat, and I fled down the hall, barely making it around the corner before I slumped against the wall. My misery escaped in an agonised cry, a sound I'd only made once in my life. The night my sister had died. Even through my pain, that noise shocked me to my core. I gulped in air, trying to stop the tears from rolling down my face, trying to stop my body from trembling, but it was no use. There was no coming back from the things Riley and I had said. That tiny shred of hope I'd carried all these years, that voice in my head that whispered we belonged together, and when the time was right, it would happen...in a few short minutes, we'd blown all hope to smithereens.

He'd left me with a gaping hole inside, one I knew would never mend itself. There would be no one else who held me the way he did. There would be no other man who lit my soul on fire. I knew walking away was the best thing for him, and for Sadie, but God, it hurt.

My shoulders shook as I cried, until the *bing* of the elevator startled me. A middle-aged couple got off, giving me a curious glance, but I ducked my head and rushed into the elevator, stabbing at the close-door button. The elevator descended, and despite being the middle of the night, I rummaged through my handbag and pulled out my sunglasses to cover my watery eyes.

I practically ran through the hotel lobby and straight into one of the waiting taxis, giving the driver Tangie's address. And then I huddled on the backseat, wrapping my arms around my middle in an attempt to hold myself together.

"About time!" Tangie yelled when she opened her front door to find me standing there.

I burst into a fresh round of tears, but Tangie didn't even seem to notice. She just bustled me inside her modern, city apartment that overlooked the beach, and waved her manicured hand in the air. "I've been trying to call you for hours! Where have you been?"

I couldn't even answer I was crying so hard, tears streaming down my face. I'd done more crying in the past twelve hours than I had in years.

Tangie frowned at me. "BB, I don't know why you're crying. This is not a bad thing! So a few million people saw your snatch."

My mouth dropped open in shock and I stared up at her from where I'd perched on her lounge. Oh my god. She had not just said that.

"What?" she asked, as if that were a completely normal statement. "At least you were well-groomed. Now if you'd been rocking a full bush, *that* would have been a PR nightmare."

"Oh my god. Please stop," I begged, holding up a hand. "Please don't say snatch or full bush ever again."

She laughed, the sound tinkling across the room as she came and sat beside me, putting her arm across my shoulders. "It's really not so bad."

I shook my head. "It's not just that. It's Riley..."

She nodded her head knowingly. "Ah yes. Riley. The bane of my existence."

I quirked an eyebrow at her, but she'd already stood to move to the kitchen, and I followed her, curious as to what she meant by that.

"How?" I asked, watching while she pulled two white mugs from an overhead cabinet.

She sighed. "You think I don't know he's the reason you've always made me turn down any overseas projects?"

I shrugged. "I never had Hollywood dreams, Tangie. You knew that when you took me on as a client. *Ocean Bay* has always been enough for me."

"You can't bullshit a bullshitter, B. You've been in love with that man for your whole adult life. You didn't want to leave him."

I threw my hands up in the air. "It doesn't really matter, does it?"

I couldn't deny what she was saying. I *had* stayed for him. I'd stayed for my mother. But I'd also stayed for myself. I wasn't lying when I said *Ocean Bay* had always been enough for me. That was true. I just wanted to act for the pure joy of throwing myself into a role and becoming someone else for those few minutes. I'd never wanted the fame that came along with it. Though I guessed any chance of obscurity was gone now, after the world saw my sex tape.

"Riley and I are done. For good this time. I need to move on."

Tangie spun around, a teaspoon still clutched in her fingers. "Really?"

I rolled my eyes. "Could you try sounding a little less delighted?"

She pointed the spoon at me. "Then you can go to LA." It was a statement, not a question.

"Why would I want to do that?"

"Because I haven't turned down that job offer on the Ridge Leone project."

Unbelievable. She was truly the worst manager ever. I opened my mouth to yell, but she cut me off with a wave of her hand.

"Stop. I already know what you're going to say. I'm the worst manager ever. I don't listen. I'm fired. Yadda yadda. Let's just skip that and get to the bit where you agree to taking the part and I start making phone calls."

"No."

"Yes."

"Tangie!"

"BB!" she mocked. "Look. You are going to get hounded in this country for that tape. You think that's going to die down anytime soon? Hell no. This is the biggest scandal to hit the Australian TV in the history of forever. Go to LA where you're a relative unknown and sex tapes are a dime a dozen. I can have you on a plane tomorrow. Do the movie. It's four months, tops. Then come back and pick up your role on *Ocean Bay*."

"If I even have a role left to go back to. A sex scandal hardly fits with their dinner time slot," I said wryly.

She pinned me with a look. "Have I ever let you down?"

I shook my head. She was a pain in my ass but she was an A-plus manager. I wouldn't have had half the opportunities I'd had without her.

"Then trust me."

I tilted my head. I couldn't deny, the thought of running away and leaving this whole mess behind me was appealing. "Four months."

She nodded, shifting her weight from foot to foot, practically dancing on the spot with her building excitement.

"And then I'm back. And you won't give me a hard time about doing more movies. Because despite there possibly being some truth in what you said about Riley, movies aren't where I want to be."

She saluted me. "Scout's honour."

I let out a long sigh, but my lips lifted at the corners. "Fine. I'll do the movie. I'll go to LA."

30

BIANCA

*T*he LA skyline was undoubtedly beautiful, with the sun sinking behind the city buildings, but I could barely bring myself to care. I closed the glass doors and turned away from the view and back to Tangie. She bustled around the extravagant hotel room the production company had put me in while we shot *Back Blade*. The schedule had blown out, and we'd been here five months instead of the four I'd been promised, but Tangie had gotten me extended leave from *Ocean Bay*. She'd assured me the producers were all fine with it. They were excited for the publicity my starring in a big-budget movie would bring their little Australian TV show.

And I definitely owed them some good press. The show had copped abuse left, right, and centre after the whole sex-on-the-beach scandal. Mobs of people had called for me to be fired, claiming I set a bad example for the teens and young families who watched the show. But the show had steadfastly stood by me and refused to cave. And for that, I owed them everything.

Tangie pushed a rolling hanger across the white floor tiles to where Bree sat on a stool, her makeup brushes all spread out on the bench behind her. I'd been a complete brat and demanded that the company fly my friend and old makeup artist out here to do my makeup for the awards ceremony tonight. We'd met years ago when she'd briefly dated Jamison in his pre-Elodie days. Then she'd come back into my life as my makeup artist in the early days of *Ocean Bay*. On my first day, I'd found myself in her makeup chair, and we'd been friends ever since. The movie producers hadn't even blinked an eye when I'd told them nobody could do my makeup like Bree could. They'd just booked the ticket. I would have liked to have flown Reese and Elodie over, too, but that would have been pushing my luck.

Truth was, I'd pretty much been a complete brat the entire time I'd been in LA. I'd been a pro on set, because that was my job and I wasn't going to let anyone down, but I'd spent the rest of my time hiding in my trailer. The other cast members had invited me for drinks on numerous occasions, but I'd turned them down so many times that they'd stopped asking. The film company had offered to rent me an apartment, but I'd refused that, too, insisting that I was fine in the hotel. Deep down, I knew I was scared of putting down any sort of permanent roots.

I was homesick. I missed Sydney beaches and my job on *Ocean Bay*. I missed my friends, my parents, my coworkers. Most of all, though, I missed Riley.

I felt his absence like a gaping wound. Even when we hadn't been together, I'd never gone five months without seeing him. There was always some event within our mutual friends' lives that meant we saw each other at least once a month. To go five whole months without speaking to him had only widened the black hole that had opened up in me the day I'd left.

Bree eyed me curiously, then motioned to come sit in front of her so she could do my makeup. She'd only gotten off the plane a few hours ago and looked tired. Dark circles rimmed her eyes. Shit. I was the worst friend ever. So selfish.

I let out a long sigh. "I'm so sorry I dragged you all the way here," I said to her. "I just...God. I don't know. You don't even do makeup anymore, but here I am, acting like a total diva and flying you all the way out here."

Bree chuckled. "Are you kidding? I'm a bit jetlagged, but a free trip to Hollywood, just to do your makeup? You should be a diva more often."

"But Damien and the girls, and your job..."

She shook her head. "The girls have Damien wrapped around their little fingers. And he's a terrific dad. He has the fort well and truly held while I'm gone."

I could believe that. Bree had done well for herself and come so far from the angry young woman she'd once been. Meeting Damien had mellowed her, and motherhood suited her well. Her twin daughters were blonde-haired rays of sunshine.

"You want to talk about whatever's bothering you?" Bree asked, startling me from my thoughts.

I shook my head. "Later. Let's just get ready. I haven't even chosen a dress yet. Want to help me pick? Then you can do my makeup to match."

Bree agreed, and I jumped off my chair, heading for the rack of dresses Tangie had abandoned to take a phone call on the balcony. I ran my hand over a sparkling gold number then stripped down to my underwear. I shimmied into the dress and turned around, waiting for Bree to do me up. Then I stood in front of the full-length mirror Tangie had placed in the middle of the room for this exact purpose. Whoa. The dress was something else. My cleavage spilled over the top, and the material clung to my hips, showing off my curves. I turned to the side, smoothing the material over my belly and frowning at the way it pulled taut. I shook my head.

"Nope. I look pregnant. Definitely not this one."

I tugged the dress off and tried on all the others on the rack before flopping down on the lounge, still in just my underwear.

"Arggghhh!" I yelled as Tangie finally came back in from outside. "Tangie! None of these fit! What am I supposed to wear?"

Tangie frowned without looking at me. "What do you mean, they don't fit? You're like a tiny doll. Everything fits you."

I stood, padding over to where the two women stood and gestured at the rack in frustration. "Well, they don't!"

Dammit. There I was acting like a brat again. I knew whose fault it was that none of my clothes fit. I'd been stress eating the entire time I'd been here. It was hardly a wonder that I'd put on some weight.

I glanced from woman to woman, but both stared at me with their mouths hanging open.

"What?" And then I realised they weren't just staring at me. They were both staring at my belly. I covered my stomach self-consciously.

"Can you two stop that? Yes, I've put on a bit of weight."

Bree and Tangie exchanged a glance then stared back at me.

"Bianca," Bree said gently. "Are you pregnant?"

I rolled my eyes. "Great. If you guys are asking me that, the reporters probably will, too. Especially if I rock up wearing one of those dresses. Tangie, can we get some other choices in time?"

Tangie shook her head, quiet for the first time in the entire ten years I'd known her. "B. Are you sure you aren't? You don't just look like you've put on weight. That looks like a baby bump."

I turned and studied myself in the mirror. I'd been avoiding them lately, because I had noticed I was putting on weight. But that was only because of the copious amounts of chocolate I was eating every time something made me think of Riley.

I shook my head. "I can't be. I haven't had sex with anyone in months. And I'm on the pill."

"Have you had your period lately?"

I nodded. "Yep." Though when I thought about it... "They've been quite light and irregular, though. Which doesn't normally happen. I was going to go to the doctor once I got back home to Sydney, but then the schedule got extended... It's probably just because I've been so stressed."

Bree crossed the space between us and squeezed my fingers. "Some women still have bleeding throughout their pregnancies...it can be completely normal. Maybe you mistook that for your period?" She gazed down at my rounded belly. "Because that's a baby bump, Bianca."

I dropped my hands, running them over the slight swell, the tight skin. No. It couldn't be a baby bump. The last time I'd had sex with anybody was with Riley after the awards ceremony...

"Oh my god." I gasped. I pushed off the lounge and ran to my bathroom, slamming the door. With a sudden rush, I remembered making love with Riley on the beach. In the hotel. Unprotected. Like we always did because we trusted each other to stay on top of STD tests, and I always took my pill religiously. But then I remembered vomiting the morning after the night on the beach...

No. I'd done a pregnancy test the first week I'd been here in LA. I'd remembered throwing up my pill and I knew that might have meant my contraception hadn't worked. I'd taken a test, just to be sure. It had been negative.

But the way Bree and Tangie had looked at me with such certainty... Tangie didn't have kids, but Bree did. She'd know, wouldn't she?

With my heart in my mouth, I crouched to riffle through the cupboard underneath the bathroom sink and found the two-pack pregnancy test, one already gone. I pulled out the remaining one and held it in trembling fingers before taking it over to the toilet.

When I was done, I placed the test on the bathroom sink,

washed my hands, and sank heavily to the cold floor to wait. Bree and Tangie knocked at the door, Bree asking if I was okay, Tangie calling out that Jerome was here, and we were going to be late. But I couldn't bring myself to care. Jerome would be pissed. He'd been accompanying me to all my publicity events, just like he always had, pre-Riley. He loved the attention, and I was happy to let him have it. He wouldn't want to miss the red carpet.

I focused anywhere but at the test. I forced my gaze over the ceiling, the tiles, the towels I'd hung neatly after my shower...but inevitably, it eventually landed on my belly. I traced the small swell with my fingers.

I knew before I even picked up the test and saw the two blue lines that it was positive.

31

RILEY

*E*lodie and Jamison's living room was chaos. Sophie, their toddler, ran around squealing her excitement over having a houseful of new people to play with. Reese and Low sat on the lounge in front of the TV, encouraging her. Elodie kissed the gurgling baby on the cheek and held him up for Jamison to take.

It was a happy scene. But it did nothing to improve my mood. I leaned on the wall and took a swig from the beer bottle I'd grabbed from the fridge. Shit. I shouldn't have come to this thing. I should have just sat at home, by myself. Here, I'd have to watch Bianca walk the red carpet with that over-tanned, over-buffed loser she was dating. At least at home I could have nurtured my misery alone. Now I'd have to hide it or be the asshole who brought the whole party down.

"Riley, come sit!" Reese called, patting the space on the lounge beside her. She'd had a few drinks, and her cheeks were flushed.

I tilted a beer bottle towards her. "Nah, I'm good. I'll go start the barbecue."

She frowned, but then Elodie squealed over some A-lister

who had just appeared on screen, and I took the opportunity to make my exit. Elodie and Jamison's barbecue sat right by the open door. Plenty close enough that I could still hear the TV and the running commentary from my friends. I clicked on the gas, watching as the flame ignited.

"You all right, bro?"

I looked up to see Jamison and Low following me outside. I turned back and fiddled with the dial so I wouldn't have to face them. I'd known the two of them for so long, they'd know just from the expression on my face that I wasn't okay. I hadn't been for months. Not since she'd left.

I shrugged and tried to force a smile. "Yeah. I'm fine."

"We're happy to hide out here with you and drink beer all night," Jamison offered.

"I'm not hiding."

"Yeah, you are. But we get it."

I picked up a sausage from the plate beside the barbecue and tossed it onto the grill. It let out a satisfying hiss. "I can't stand that guy she's dating. He's a fucking tool."

Low nodded in agreement. "Reese says they're not dating, though. That he's just her arm candy."

I gave him a withering look. "Does it matter? He's still going to be all over her." I shook my head, dumping the whole plate of meat onto the grill, then stabbed at it with a pair of tongs. I couldn't do it. I just couldn't watch his hands on the small of her back, or the way she'd lean into him when the reporters asked them to pose for photos. And he'd pose effortlessly, like some runway model, of course. Nothing like the awkward posing I'd done. He undoubtedly fit into her world better than I did. With his shining white teeth and ease in front of the cameras. The two of them were everywhere. The next IT couple, according to the gossip magazines.

Our sex scandal long-buried by her moving on with someone else.

"She's next!" Elodie yelled from the living room.

"You guys go," I mumbled. "I'd rather be alone anyway."

Jamison and Low exchanged a look, then Low clapped me on the shoulder. "We'll be back in five. Remember. The meat is already dead. No need to murder it again."

I flipped him the bird, and he laughed as they returned to the living room. Bianca had said much the same thing the night of the award show. I took another swig of beer and tried to stop the flood of memories. That night in the limo. Kissing her. Touching her. She'd been mine for such a brief moment, but it was all I'd thought of for the entire time she'd been gone. How could it be over? How could she have just walked away?

"There she is!" Reese squealed from the living room.

I closed my eyes and tried to breathe. I didn't need to watch. I didn't need another reminder of everything I'd lost. She was on the other side of the world, with another man. Why would I subject myself to watching that?

Fuck me.

I yanked open the door and strode across the room. Reese lifted her head when I entered and gave me a small, knowing smile. I ignored her, my gaze focussing in on the flat-screen TV mounted to the wall. And there she was. The woman who owned my heart and soul, taking the hand of that douchebag Jeremy or whatever his stupid name was, and sliding out of a limo. She stood, straightening her dress...

Elodie gasped. "Is that a..."

But Elodie's words drifted away as Bianca's long blonde hair fell down over her bare shoulders, cleavage spilling from a gold dress. She stared right into a camera, and for half a second, it felt as though she was looking for me.

"A baby bump!" Reese yelped, snapping me out of my trance.

What?

"Holy shit," Low muttered, then threw a glance at me.

My brain struggled to keep up.

"Riley...." Jamison said quietly. His face was full of sympathy.

"It couldn't be, could it?" Reese asked, seemingly unaware of my confusion. "She couldn't be pregnant. She would have told me..."

Realisation shot me through the heart. Her boobs were definitely bigger. Her hips flared where they hadn't a few months ago, and when my gaze landed on her belly, my stomach rolled. I knew her body. She was the only woman I'd been with for so damn long, I knew it like the back of my hand. I knew she had a freckle on the underside of her left breast. I knew she had a scar from a childhood accident on her thigh. And I knew that her belly was toned and flat. I knew because I'd run my hands and tongue all over it so many times that the feel of her skin beneath mine was burned into my memory.

She tried to cover herself with a large purse, but I saw it. And evidently, so did everyone else.

The first reporter on the red carpet didn't even bother with pleasantries. "BB, wow! That dress! We were all stunned when you stepped out of the car. Are you pregnant?"

A hush fell over the room, and I stopped breathing, waiting for her answer.

Her eyes went wide, her mouth falling open. "What? No..." She shook her head, and for a split second my heart beat again. She wasn't pregnant. I'd been wrong. We'd all been wrong.

But then her date, Jerry or whatever, stepped towards the microphone with a laugh. He put his arm around Bianca and pulled her close. Then he rested a hand on her belly.

I wanted to reach through the TV, rip off his arm, and club him over the head with his own severed limb.

"Might as well tell them, babe. There's no hiding it in that dress."

My heart stopped.

"I can't believe she didn't tell me," Reese cried.

"Congratulations, you two! Do you know if it's a boy or a girl?" the reporter asked Jerome.

He smiled into the camera, his white teeth flashing. "No, we decided a surprise was better."

Bianca's expression was frozen, her eyes wide and her lips slightly parted, but Jerome had told me all I needed to know. When I looked over at Low, his face filled with pity.

"Not such a fake relationship after all then, huh?" I bit out before going back to the barbecue to rescue the meat that was turning black. Just like my heart.

I couldn't sleep. I was so tired my eyes ached, and I'd gotten into bed, but I couldn't put my phone down. After a strained dinner at Jamison and Elodie's place, where nobody talked about the elephant in the room, I made an excuse to leave. No one objected. The party had become subdued, with Reese trying to call Bianca over and over, and everyone studying me awkwardly. But home was no better. Being alone in my room just gave me too much time to think. And too much time to obsessively stalk Instagram and Facebook for any scrap of detail. And there was plenty of it. Jerome had plastered his Instagram with photos of him and Bianca. Bianca's account was silent, but Jerome was announcing to the world that he had a new baby mama, and her fans were all over it. I scowled at all the congratulations messages. Fuck. Would she move to LA permanently now? Or would they move back here? Would I have to see them at every function our friends put on?

I couldn't do that.

It had been one thing to see her at events when we'd both been single. But I couldn't go and watch her with another man. I tossed and turned until sometime around dawn I finally slept.

"Dad!" Sadie said, shoving me.

I sat up blearily, blinking in the harsh light flooding into my bedroom.

"Are you awake?"

I scrubbed my hands over my face, fumbling around my bed for my phone. "What time is it?"

"Late. You slept all day."

"What? I did?"

She nodded. "Mum is here to pick me up. I just came to say bye. See you in a week?"

I blinked away the haze. "Right. Yep. I'll pick you up from your mum's next weekend." I ruffled her hair and pulled her close. "I'll miss you, kiddo. I like this house a whole lot more when you're here."

She laughed and shoved me away. "Yeah, yeah, I know. You tell me all the time."

She was right. I did. But the past few months of her living here had been the only bright spot in my life. She was a great kid. She'd copped some shit when my sex tape scandal had been all over the place, but she'd made me so proud with the way she'd handled it. Completely owning it and never letting anyone get to her. She'd laughed her way through the whole thing, and eventually life had gone back to normal.

She'd been angry with me, understandably, but after much grovelling and a shopping spree, she'd come round. Eliza and her husband had moved, and Sadie had stayed. Just like we'd planned.

"Say hi to your mum for me, okay?"

She nodded. She kissed my cheek then got off the bed. In the doorway, though, she turned back.

"Dad?"

"Mmm?"

"Have you checked your social media in the last hour or two?"

"No, you just woke me up, remember?"

"Your, ah... Your friend. BB? She's all over the tabloids."

I sighed. "Yeah, I know. She announced last night she was pregnant. Or rather, her boyfriend did."

Sadie shook her head. "You dodged a bullet there, Dad. What a train wreck. That Jerome guy was caught kissing some brunette at the afterparty. The photos are everywhere. I know you liked her, but she's always in the media for something. And it's never anything good."

"What?"

She shrugged.

"He was kissing someone else?"

She pointed at my phone sitting on my bedside table. "It's trending on Twitter. You can't miss it. See you next week."

She waved, then a few seconds later the front door closed.

I snatched my phone up and stabbed at the Twitter icon. My heart sank as I scrolled through the feed. Sadie was right. Candid photos of Jerome all over some brunette in the corner of a club were everywhere, with hashtags like #wheresBB and #babydaddydrama along with photos of Bianca and Jerome on the red carpet.

My blood boiled. That stupid prick. I wanted to fly across the world and punch him in his cheating, too handsome face. Didn't he know what he had? Obviously not, if he couldn't even keep it in his pants on the day they'd announced they were having a child together. I got up and paced around my bedroom, anger coiling my muscles too tight. Fuck! She didn't deserve this. She'd already had to get through one scandal in the last year. She'd only just had time to put that behind her, and now this? I shook my head and tried to relieve some of the tension in my shoulders, but no amount of pacing was calming my fists balling at my sides.

I grabbed my phone again and brought up her number. My finger hovered over the call button, but what the hell was I going to say? Congrats on your pregnancy, sorry your baby daddy can't keep it in his pants?

"Argh!" I yelled, throwing my phone onto my bed. I couldn't call her. It wasn't my place. She'd made her position perfectly clear when she'd up and left the country to get away from me.

I sucked in deep lungfuls of air and groaned. Who was I kidding? Even if it made me the dumbest, lovestruck fool in history, I couldn't just sit back and do nothing. Not when she was on the other side of the world, hurting.

I picked up the phone again, and this time, there was no hesitation. I knew what I needed to do.

32

BIANCA

*T*angie and Marco, Jerome's manager, screamed at each other across my hotel room, while I sank deep into the plush lounge, wishing I was anywhere but here.

"This is a PR disaster," Tangie screeched, her face red as she stood toe to toe with Marco. "Jerome has royally fucked this up for everyone. How the hell are we going to spin this?"

Marco was just as angry, his entire body so tense he was practically vibrating. "Well, maybe if you'd told me your client was knocked up and going to wear a skin-tight dress so the whole bloody world knew it, we could have gone in with a game plan!"

Jerome sat beside me on the lounge, the two of us watching the back and forth between our managers like it was a tennis match.

He leaned over. "I really am sorry, Bianca," he said to me quietly.

I wanted to be angry with him. He'd outed my pregnancy, falsely claimed to be the father, and then gone and made out with some woman he'd been seeing, naïvely unaware of how much attention would be on him after the shitshow he'd created. I wanted to be angry, but the whole situation was just ridiculous. And in the scheme of things, so unimportant.

I had a tiny baby growing inside me.

And compared to that, everything seemed insignificant. Just the thought of a baby was both overwhelming and terrifying. Tangie had made me stay in LA for the weekend to attend this crisis meeting, but then I was on the next plane back to Sydney. I had no reason to be in LA. And every reason in the world to go back home.

Back home and straight to Riley's door to tell him he was going to be a father again.

I was done with LA. For good.

I rested my hand on my little baby bump, still shocked over the fact it wasn't just bloating from overeating. Tangie and Marco droned on and on, but I tuned out. A band of panic tightened around my chest at the thought of being a mother. I'd never even really considered having kids of my own. After what had happened with my sister, and with my job, I'd always been adamant that I didn't want to bring an innocent child into the storm. A child was something the press could use to hurt me. Just like they'd hurt my mother. They'd destroyed her life the night they'd taken things too far.

But when I thought back to those moments on the beach, being in Riley's arms and making love, rather than just fucking...this baby was the product of that. Maybe we hadn't said the words, but I'd loved Riley for most of my adult life. I'd been willing to walk away when walking away only affected me. But now I had someone else to consider. Maybe he wouldn't take me back. I'd somehow become the story of the year, what with a sex tape, then a baby daddy scandal. I knew my coming back into his life would just be one more drama in a long list of them. But he had to know. He had to have the choice. I would never deny him the chance to be involved with this baby, the way Eliza had denied him with Sadie all those years ago.

I'd picked up the phone to call him a hundred times over the last two days. But every time, I'd cancelled the call before it had connected. It wasn't something I could do on the phone, from across the other side of the world. It had to be in person. I had to see his face when I told him this baby was his. The way he reacted would tell me exactly how he felt. And from there, I'd be able to make some sort of decision on what the rest of my life would be.

Tangie and Marco were still screaming at each other, but I was done listening.

"Enough!" I yelled over the top of them.

They both stopped and stared at me.

"Jerome and I aren't together. He did nothing wrong." I glanced over at him. "Nothing wrong by hooking up with someone else anyway. Telling everyone the baby is his even though we've never even slept together is another story altogether."

He held his hands up in mock surrender. "I told you, I'm sorry about that. I just got caught up in the moment and thought it would be good publicity. I didn't think it through."

I rolled my eyes. He was young and green and obviously self-centred. I just couldn't bring myself to care. Let the whole world think Jerome was this baby's father and that I was the poor pathetic sap being cheated on. Riley would know the truth. And so would the people we cared about. Sadie. Our friends. Our families. It didn't matter what the rest of the world thought they knew.

I pushed to my feet. "I'm done with this. My flight leaves in five hours, and I need to finish packing. So if you don't mind..." I glanced in the direction of the door.

"But—"

Tangie started up again but I held up a hand in a stop motion. "No, Tangie. Spin this however the hell you want. I don't care. I'm going home."

She gave me a disappointed look, then threw a murderous one at Jerome and Marco before snatching her purse from the kitchen bench. "Fine. I'll see you back in Sydney then."

I nodded as the three of them filed out of my room, leaving me blissfully alone. I padded to my bedroom where an open suitcase lay on the bed, my clothes and shoes strewn about. I picked up a shirt from the bed and folded it neatly, placing it inside the suitcase when knocking on the door started up. I groaned.

The knocking turned into banging, and my blood pressure rose. "All right, Tangie! I'm coming!" I yelled, crossing the room and pulling open the door.

"Not Tangie," Riley said gruffly on the other side.

My mouth dropped open and I stared at the man I hadn't been able to get out of my mind since the minute I'd walked away from him. I fought to speak, to voice the confusion slamming through me, but nothing happened. The whole world slowed down, and I suddenly felt like I was moving through a fog.

Riley's gaze dropped to my belly then lifted to meet mine. Determination shone bright and strong in his eyes. "Can I come in?"

I nodded dumbly and stepped aside. He shouldered a backpack and walked by me.

"Is that all you brought with you?" I asked, snapping out of my trance.

"Yes. I don't plan on staying long."

"Oh." I couldn't help the way my chest deflated. My fingers itched to reach out and touch him. To run over his two-day stubble and into his plane-tousled hair. To press my lips against his and to feel his arms come around me. To hear him say everything would be okay. That he still wanted me, even after I'd run away. Even though I was pregnant and about to turn his life upside down.

He dumped his backpack on the living room floor and turned back to face me.

"I saw what happened the other night. With Jerome and the baby and that other woman. And I just...shit." He ran his hands through his hair but didn't make a move to say anything else.

"You just what?" I prompted. My brain raced a million miles an hour, but I couldn't come up with a single reason as to why or how he was standing in my LA hotel room. None of this made any sense, and I was wholly unprepared to see him so soon. I'd thought I would have the entire plane ride back to Sydney to think about what I'd say when I saw him.

There was so much to explain, and I needed a moment to recover.

"Riley, why are you here?"

He lifted his head, and his eyes blazed with an intensity I'd never seen from him before.

"Because that guy isn't good enough for you. If he's cheating on you now, the day you announce your pregnancy, then he's always going to cheat. You deserve better." He turned away and paced the room. "I couldn't stand the thought of you dealing with all this alone. Again. And before I knew what I was doing, I was booking a flight and driving to the airport."

My heart thumped hard. "You flew across the world just to check on me?"

He stopped pacing and stared at me as if I'd just said the stupidest thing he'd ever heard. Then he strode across the room, stopping just centimetres in front of me so I had to look up to meet his gaze.

"No," he said fiercely. "I came to tell you I love you. And that

I don't care if you're having someone else's baby. I love you and I want you to come home with me."

Then he dropped to one knee.

"Marry me."

If I hadn't felt the thick carpet beneath my feet, or the breeze from the air-conditioning vent, I would have thought I was dreaming. Because only in a fantasy land could this wonderful, amazing man be telling me he loved me after everything I'd put him through. It was impossible that he'd want to take on a baby that wasn't his. Except that it was his. He just didn't know it yet. I couldn't even process the proposal. That was entirely too much to comprehend. I knelt to the floor in front of him, my legs unwilling to hold me any longer.

He ran the backs of his fingers down the side of my face, then to the base of my neck. I closed my eyes as I leaned into him, too shocked and amazed to say a word, and he dipped his head, his lips hovering just over mine.

"Please, B. Give me another chance. Come home with me. Marry me. He can be involved with the baby. As much as he wants, but I want you. *You* belong with me. You always have."

Something inside me broke. Five months of thinking about him, missing him, regretting every lost moment over the last ten years. The walls I'd built that held all of those things together snapped, and I reached up to cup his face, pulling back just enough that I could look into his eyes, finally finding my words. "I love you, too. I always have. I'm not with Jerome. And I—"

He blinked, surprise flooding his features, as if he'd expected to have to beg. But then his grip on the back of my neck tightened, and his mouth crashed down on mine, swallowing the words I still needed to say.

All thought disintegrated as his mouth moved with mine, desperate and wanting, his lips opening and his tongue seeking entrance. I clutched him to me, afraid I'd heard wrong, afraid none of this was real. His muscled shoulders bunched and tensed under my hands. The warmth of his chest pressed against mine. Very real feelings stirred low in my belly.

"Are you really here?" I whispered when his lips trailed off my mouth.

He chuckled before he kissed his way down my neck, swirling his tongue over my skin. I moaned at the sensation.

"Do you think I'm a mirage? Pretty sure a mirage couldn't kiss you like this."

His mouth found mine again, and he kissed me so deeply my head spun. His kisses sent sparks of pleasure straight from my lips to my core, and I wrapped myself around him, unable to get enough. My brain was foggy with lust, and the overwhelming need to be with him consumed me. But he had to know first. I couldn't process any of this, especially not the proposal, until he knew. I pushed to my feet, pulling him up with me, but then took a step back, putting some space between us. I knew it was the only way I'd get the words out without succumbing to the need pulsing through me.

For two days now, I'd thought of this moment. Thought of nothing else really, except telling him he was the father. I'd spent the whole time nervously worrying about what he'd say. Things weren't good between us, and it had been five months since we'd been together. What if he'd moved on? What if he thought I'd done it on purpose? But now, all those fears evaporated. He was here. Straight off a twenty-plus-hour flight, telling me in the flesh that he loved me and wanted me. Nothing could have made this moment more special. And now I felt nothing but excitement.

"I need to tell you something," I said coyly, watching his face.

"You do. You still haven't told me whether you'll marry me or not. But tell me quick, because after five months of not seeing you, talking is not what I want to be doing."

I laughed, loving his playful tone. The pain I'd been harbouring since we'd been apart fading away. A bright future full of happiness taking its place. I took his hand and moved it to my little belly. "I wasn't talking about the proposal. I meant this. You're the father, Riley. Not Jerome."

Riley stilled.

"What?" He spat the word out like it tasted bad.

And with that one word, my overfull heart deflated and then broke as he snatched his hand away, his expression going blank.

33

RILEY

My baby.

That was *my baby* she was carrying. Which could only mean that it had been conceived five months ago. Five whole months. A bitter taste rose in my mouth, and I took a step back.

"Riley?" she asked, a tremble in her voice. She stepped towards me, but I held up a hand to stop her coming any closer.

"I don't understand. I thought you'd be happy? You just said you loved me..."

A devastated laugh tumbled from my lips. A choked noise even I didn't recognise. It sounded wrong. So full of hurt and pain it should have been a sob. Bianca flinched.

"And you said you loved me." I choked on the words, because suddenly everything she'd said meant nothing. She was a liar.

She shook her head, her beautiful blue eyes filling with tears, a sight that tried to undo me. My body wanted to reach out and touch her, soothe her, but my brain yelled accusations of betrayal, reminding me she was just like Eliza. Someone willing to keep my child away from me. Would she have even told me at all if I wasn't here, standing in front of her? Would she have just stayed in LA forever? My blood boiled.

"I do love you," she cried.

Ha. More lies. "You don't. If you did, you would have never waited five months to tell me you were having our baby, Bianca. Five months! You know how much what Eliza did broke me, and yet here you are, just repeating the same thing." I shook my head and turned away from her, unable to look at her now I knew she'd never really cared for me. Never really known me at all. How could she keep something like that from me?

"I'm an idiot." I picked up my backpack from the floor and slung it over my shoulder. But I couldn't make my feet move. Despite everything, despite my brain yelling to get the hell out of that room, I didn't want to leave her. That was my baby she was carrying, and like a fool, I knew with certainty that none of this could stop me loving her. But how could I stay? When she thought nothing of keeping something so huge from me?

Bianca let out a huge sigh. Then she closed the gap between us, moving with determination, and pulled the bag from my shoulder. I fought with her half-heartedly until she gave me a look and yanked it from my grasp. I let her.

"Riley. Look at me."

I didn't want to. The flash of anger had subsided into plain old hurt. I was trying desperately to get the anger back, but I couldn't do that if I looked at her. I'd get lost in her eyes and I'd forgive her instantly. And that would make me an even bigger fool than I already was. I shook my head stubbornly.

She grabbed my face between her hands. "Riley Clarke. Listen to me and listen to me good. I love you, but you are stubbornly stupid sometimes." There was laughter in her eyes. For the life of me I couldn't understand why. Did she care so little that she thought laughing was an appropriate response to my heartache? Jesus. That was cold.

"I didn't call you because I didn't know. I found out on Friday, Riley. Friday. As in three days ago. If you go into my bedroom, you'll see that everything I own is packed into a suitcase. And on the bedside table, you'll see a plane ticket to Sydney. It leaves in five hours."

Hope rushed in despite my attempts to tamp it down. "You were coming back?"

She nodded. "And I was planning to take the first Uber straight to your house. I wasn't keeping the baby from you. I wouldn't do that. I just couldn't tell you over the phone."

Relief filled me. Then guilt. I'd just yelled at the mother of my child. My stomach rolled at the thought. I knelt on the thick hotel room carpet, circling my arms around her waist, resting my head against her belly. "I'm so sorry, I just thought..."

A surge of protectiveness rose. Her fingertips ran through my hair as I tried to process the myriad of emotions without breaking down and crying.

"It's okay. I know you. I knew exactly how big this would be for you, which is why I was coming back. You can be as involved with this baby as you want."

"Marry me," I mumbled into her belly. "Does that tell you how involved I want to be? I meant what I said. You belong with me. You and our baby."

She sighed, and when I glanced up at her, my heart sank at the sad look on her face.

"I can't. It's too soon, and this is all too crazy. We haven't even dated! We've just been one whirlwind of disaster after another. I need to know we can get our shit together before I can commit to marrying you. Because when I do marry you, I want to know it's forever. Don't you?"

That was true. And at that point, I didn't even care. I'd give her whatever she wanted. I'd do whatever she needed. If she needed time, I could give her that. But there was no doubt in my mind. She was the one for me. And someday, she would be the one wearing a white gown, who met me at the altar.

I stood and ran my hands through her hair, tilting her head up to me. "I already know, Bianca. I'll keep asking, and one day, you'll say yes."

"You're awfully cocky for someone who just got turned down."

I grinned, then clutched my heart dramatically like she'd shot an arrow through it.

She placed one of her delicate hands over the top of mine and leant in. "You know what I will say yes to right now?" she whispered in my ear.

I quirked an eyebrow.

"Getting naked with my man and showing him exactly how much I've missed him."

I scooped her up into my arms, her squeal of delight in my ear, and stormed towards the bedroom. "Funnily enough, I'll say yes to that, too."

34

BIANCA

*R*iley insisted on taking a shower before getting down to it, and I'd pouted at him as he'd disappeared into the bathroom, leaving me alone in the bedroom. With one sweep of my arm, all the clothes and the suitcases on my bed fell to the floor in an untidy heap, and I stripped out of my workout clothes. I stared down at my sports bra and cotton underwear and decided that...nope. That was not what I was going to be wearing when I hadn't seen Riley in five full months. I stripped out of the daggy underwear set and riffled through the pile on the floor, searching for something sexier, but then the water in the bathroom stopped. I whipped my head up and stared at the en suite door, but it didn't open. Abandoning my search for lingerie, I laid out on the bed, completely naked, figuring that was the end goal anyway.

Riley rattled around in the bathroom, but the door still didn't open, and eventually my gaze wandered to my belly. It seemed like a small bump for five months. But it was noticeable. And now that I knew, I felt stupid for not realising sooner. My breasts were fuller, my nipples darker. I'd put on a little weight around my hips and thighs. That was probably courtesy of the late-night binge-eating more than the baby. But suddenly, I realised that Riley was going to see me naked. I didn't dislike the way my body had changed. I'd starved myself for years to get the sort of figure I 'needed' to be an actress, and now I had a few curves. But what if Riley wasn't attracted to this version of me? Even as I thought the words, I knew how ridiculous they were. I was having the man's baby. And he'd just told me he loved me. I knew that had nothing to do with what I looked like naked. But still.

I suddenly felt too bold, too on display, lying on the bed like some wanton sex goddess. So I pulled back the covers and slipped beneath them just as Riley walked out of the shower with a white towel wrapped low on his waist. Those delicious lines ran either side of his hips and down beneath the towel. My mouth watered.

I sat up, forgetting my momentary lack of body confidence, and prowled across the bed on all fours. I couldn't help it. I'd always been so damn turned on by him, that even when we were screaming at each other, all I wanted to do was rip his clothes off.

I sat on the edge, and he came to stand in front of me. I spread my legs so he could stand between them and he sucked in a sharp breath as he no doubt got a glimpse of my bare pussy. But before he could do anything, I untucked the edge of his towel and let it fall to the floor. His thick cock was already gloriously hard beneath it, and I ran my hand over the head and down his length. I took my time, refamiliarizing myself with everything I'd missed over the last five months.

Wetness pooled between my legs, and like a magnet, my gaze was drawn to his face. He had his eyes closed, his chin resting on his chest, his abs contracting as he fought with himself. I wanted him to let go. I wanted to see him unravel.

I reached between his legs and cupped his balls, squeezing

them lightly and stroking over them. Then I lowered my head and added my mouth to the assault. Riley's head rolled back, and he groaned long and loud. I sucked one ball into my mouth, now using my hands to work his cock, making him clench. Then he sharply pulled away.

"Jesus, B, stop. I'm going to come if you keep that up. And I'm not coming before you do. Lie down."

I bit my lip. There was that rush of self-consciousness again. It was one thing to be sitting in front of him, but if I laid back on the bed, he was going to see every inch of me. Damn it. Why had he not turned up late at night when it was dark?

I shuffled back on the bed, drawing my knees to my chest.

He frowned.

"What's wrong?"

"Nothing. My head is just full of voices that don't deserve any credit." For so many years, I'd had people telling me what my body should look like. Slim but not skinny. Fit but not muscly. And for ten years, I'd listened. It was part of my job.

He kneeled on the bed, his expression soft as if he knew exactly what I was thinking. I reached for his cock again. I wanted to go back to concentrating on him so I didn't have to think about myself. But he moved out of reach, and I pouted at him. He tucked a strand of loose hair behind my ear and smiled gently at me.

"I can make the voices go away." He kissed one of my knees that I still had pulled to my chest, then my fingers which were locked tightly around them. He tugged at my wrists, and I let my hands drop to the mattress.

His big hands rested on my knees, then he whispered. "Now lie back."

I did as I was told, reminding myself over and over that this was a man who loved me. Who had spent years worshipping my body and knew it better than I did. The man whose baby grew in my belly.

My back hit the soft blankets, and Riley gazed down at me. I watched his gaze wander over my face, then lower to my breasts then the swell of my belly. It lingered there a long time before he lifted his head again. And the look in his eyes took my breath away. Pride, protectiveness, love—everything was there in his eyes while he stared down at me. He swallowed hard. His broad shoulders pushed my knees wide. And this time, I let them fall open easily, welcoming the sight of his big body looming over me. He held himself on his arms, supporting his weight and lowered his mouth to mine. His lips were soft, and the kisses he gave me were gentle. My heart swelled. His lips parted, his tongue slipping inside to meet mine. I pushed up, wanting more, wriggling so his cock brushed against my entrance. I moaned when the tip of him touched my clit.

His kisses trailed off my mouth, to my neck and lower to my breasts. He cupped them both, his fingers flicking over my nipples, pleasure shooting through me. Until that moment, I hadn't noticed how sensitive they were. But now I revelled in it. When Riley sucked one nipple into his mouth, I arched my back, urging him on. I wanted to watch him as he discovered my new body. I wanted to watch and make sure he liked what he saw, but the feelings unfurling within me wouldn't allow me to. My eyes fluttered closed, and sensation roared through me.

Still palming one breast, he used his other hand to travel lower, and I thanked the lord, because my core was throbbing for his touch. But he stopped at my belly. And then he sat back, in the gap made by my wide-spread thighs. His fingers trailed over my bump. So softly, he traced every inch of skin, then cupped our growing baby with both hands before lowering his head to kiss me just to the side of my navel. My heart doubled in size. I hadn't planned on having a baby. I didn't know how to be a mum. But if I was doing this with anyone, I was glad I was doing it with him. No one else would ever look at me the way Riley did.

He didn't say anything, just continued his path south, kissing and licking his way over my mound to my folds. He didn't hesitate for a moment. He ran his tongue straight through the centre of me, making me cry out. If I'd thought my nipples were sensitive...

"Still thinking?" he asked.

His tongue ran over my clit, and I shook my head violently. No. I wasn't thinking. Not about whether my body would still turn him on anyway. I'd seen the evidence of that in every look and every touch since he'd laid me down. Now, all I was thinking about was the orgasm I knew was coming.

His tongue dipped low, and he licked in long, slow strokes, occasionally pushing his tongue inside me, just enough to make me beg for more. He made tiny noises of satisfaction when my hips rolled, trying to get more friction against his mouth. Then he slid two fingers inside me, immediately searching for that spot that we both knew would be my undoing. Five months apart hadn't changed anything. He still knew all my sensitive places. Still knew exactly how to get me off. His fingers moved in and out of me while he sucked on my clit. Over and over again he hit the parts where I wanted him most, until my internal muscles clamped down on his fingers and blinding pleasure soared through me.

I cried out, jerking and clutching his head, his shoulders, anything I could to ground myself as I rode out the wave of pleasure. When it subsided, his cock replaced his fingers, and he was sliding in and out of me with ease. He kissed me, and I tasted myself on his lips, but I tasted him, too. He was warm and familiar, and we moved together, my hips rising to meet his, his gaze holding me in place as he thrust into me in.

"I love you," he whispered in my ear.

Tears welled in my eyes. I pressed my fingernails into the skin of his back and held him tight.

"I love you, too."

He stilled and looked down at me. "We can't fuck it up this time, B. I'm done with all that. If you push me away again, I'm not going. Anytime you want to run, I'll follow. I need you to know that."

I nodded and pulled him back to my chest as he picked up the pace again. He pumped in and out of me until he groaned my name, his wet heat spilling inside me.

I stroked my fingers over his skin, over the planes of his body. I knew. But he wasn't going to have to chase me. I was done running. I was done pushing him away. I was home.

35

BIANCA

*A*fter fifteen hours, the plane drone had finally lulled me into a restless sleep. Before that, our trip home to Sydney had been quiet. Riley and I sat together, holding hands, both of us lost in our own thoughts. So often I found myself subconsciously rubbing my belly. Every time I ran my fingers over the swell, a little spear of panic shot through me.

Unwilling to be separated from Riley again, I'd cancelled my original flight, and we'd spent the last few days in a bubble. But now we were heading back to reality, and coming home meant facing our future. There were so many hurdles to jump. Sadie, and the fact she hated my guts, was a big one. My job on *Ocean Bay*, another. Tangie had assured me my role was safe, but the producers didn't officially know about the baby yet. Though, I could guess they'd seen the tabloids. I couldn't imagine they'd be too pleased to be writing an unplanned pregnancy into the storyline of the twenty-something pure and innocent I portrayed on the show.

But the one overriding thought was the baby. And the pure terror that wrapped itself around my throat every time I thought about bringing a baby into my life.

I traced the bump. So tiny. How was I supposed to keep something so small and precious safe? The world I lived in was brutal. Ready to cut you down at the first sign of cellulite or a pimple. Your every move under a microscope. Things might have died down a little while I was overseas, but as long as I was acting, my indiscretions were out there for the whole world to see. Was I really going to bring an innocent baby into this mess?

After too many hours to count, the plane bumped and skidded along the runway, and we shuffled to the exits. Keeping my frustration with the slow-moving line in check was difficult. I just wanted some fresh air and to be away from crowds for a while. My neck ached, and I had knots in my back from sitting in the cramped space for so long. Fatigue made me slow as we waited for our bags and eventually made our way out of the airport.

"You have no idea how grateful I am to see your beat-up old junk bucket," I said, sinking into the ripped fabric seat of Riley's jeep. He'd left it in the long-term parking area, and I was glad we didn't have to wait for a taxi or an Uber. I just wanted to get home. I put my hand on his thigh and squeezed it gently, loving that I was allowed to do that now. "You sure you're not too tired to drive?"

He shook his head. "I've had that much coffee and Red Bull, I'm surprised I'm not having heart palpitations."

"Let's get out of here then. I'm ready for my own bed."

He leant across the centre console and kissed me below my ear, making me shiver.

"You got it. Sleep, then we'll get an appointment with your doctor, okay?"

I nodded. While we'd been in LA we'd realised that I'd had no prenatal care. That was a scary thought, but there'd been no point seeing a doctor in LA when we'd be leaving in a few days.

So I'd put it out of my mind and promised Riley we'd see someone as soon as we got back.

Riley navigated his way out of the parking garage and onto the city streets. I watched through the window while trees, buildings, and people blurred by, my eyes not focussing well with the overwhelming exhaustion that was threatening to consume me.

I was verging on sleep when I recognised where we were. "Wait! Riley, stop."

"Huh?" he asked but pulled over on the side of the road anyway. "What's wrong? Is it the baby?"

"No, no." I pointed to the graveyard we were about to pass. "There's an entrance gate up there. Can we stop for a moment? I..." I sighed. "I just need to stop. Please."

I hadn't been to my sister's grave in almost half a year. No matter how tired I was, I couldn't drive past.

Riley must have seen something in my eyes, because he nodded, put his indicator on, and navigated back onto the road. He took the turn off into the cemetery, then I guided him through the maze of streets to the memorial area. He didn't question me as we got out of the car. He just jogged around from his side, linked his fingers through mine, and followed me to my sister's garden.

It hadn't changed in the months I'd been gone. Fresh flowers still sat in the vase by her name plaque, telling me Dad had made his weekly visit in the last day or two. It was neatly kept, no weeds growing around the edges. I knelt in front of the rocks that lined the edges and put my hand on the soil. My other hand came to my belly instinctively.

This baby would have made my sister an aunt. Would that have made her happy? Would she have had children of her own by now? Cousins for my child? I still remembered the way she'd always babied me. Even when I'd been six and she'd been ten, she'd been quite the little mother. Mostly bossing me around, but she'd been my confidante, too. When Mum had gotten too wrapped up in our careers, yelling at me when I couldn't remember my lines and storming off in frustration, it had been Brittany who had hugged me and told me to ignore her. It had been Brittany who had made a game of remembering my lines.

Yes, I decided with certainty. She would have been so excited about this baby. And she would have been an amazing aunt.

A tear dripped down my face, and I brushed it away, but another followed straight after. Despite my best efforts, I couldn't hold them back. It was so unfair. She should have been here. And now I was having a baby. I was bringing a child into the world that had killed my sister. I clutched my belly tighter. This baby would be photographed and stalked and tormented from the day he or she was born. It wasn't right. I'd never intended for this to happen.

The tears fell fast and hard, and when a sob escaped, Riley gathered me up in his arms and held me. He didn't say a word. He just held me and let me cry. I knew I was overly emotional from the long plane ride and probably from baby hormones. My sister had been gone for so long, I shouldn't suddenly be feeling the loss so keenly. But exhaustion mixed with fear for my unborn child gripped me like a vice, and it was a long time before I could get myself together.

I wiped my face, sniffing back the last of my tears, and looked up at Riley through watery eyes. "I had a sister."

He nodded, and then he led me to a nearby park bench and pulled me down on his lap. I rested my head on his shoulder and breathed in his scent until I didn't feel like crying anymore.

"She was killed in a car accident. A bad one. When she was ten."

"How old were you?"

"Six. I was in the car, too."

His arms around me tightened.

"Did you know I was a child actress?"

He shook his head, and I smiled.

"I guess you never Googled me then, huh?"

He shrugged, then a hint of red stained his cheeks. "I did, but I was really only looking for photos of you."

"For your spank bank," I said knowingly, and we both laughed. It felt good. Laughing made it easier to tell him the rest of the story without breaking down again. I got off his lap and sat beside him, twisting so we faced each other.

"My sister and I were cast as siblings on a popular American TV show for kids. Kind of like the early *Hannah Montana*, I guess. I was only four when we got the roles. My role wasn't very big. I was really just a recurring extra who had the occasional line. But my sister was the lead. And she was amazing. She made that show. She was cute as hell and could deliver a one-liner like a seasoned pro."

I sucked in a deep breath of fresh air and let it settle in my lungs before I continued. "Mum managed us. She'd been an actress in her time but never had more than a few small roles. Nothing that ever set her apart from the dozens of other starlets looking for work in LA. But Brittany had something she didn't. Maybe I did, too. I don't know."

He kissed the top of my head. "You do have something, B. I'd bet my life you had it back then, too."

I shrugged. "Maybe. But Mum became obsessed with our careers. Especially Brittany. She was the ultimate stage mum. Pushing us into every media opportunity possible."

I bit my lip, thinking of the woman holed up in her little house, unable to leave because of the damage the outside world had done to her. Guilt filled me. "Don't get me wrong," I added quickly, not wanting Riley to get a skewed idea of who my mother was. "She was a good mum. She loved us. She tucked us in at night and sang silly songs in the car. She often chose the manager hat over the mum hat, but it came from a place of love. I truly believe that.

"The night Brittany died, we'd been doing a press thing for the show. There were people everywhere. Too many. Someone had tipped off the tabloids, and they'd spilled it to the public. The event was already over capacity, but people were climbing over railings, and there wasn't enough security to keep up. I don't remember it all. I just remember being pushed and shoved by a crowd, and holding my sister's hand tight, scared I'd get lost, until someone picked me up and shoved me into a car. Mum got in the driver's seat and took off, yelling at us to put our seat belts on."

Glimpses of dark roads and headlights flashed through my head, and I had to blink the images away, because the unease they stirred in my gut still made me feel sick.

"Dad later told me that Mum had been desperate to get my sister and me away. She was afraid we'd be hurt, so she'd pulled the plug on the event. But the tabloids had been relentless. They'd been pissed they'd been denied access to the story and they'd chased our car. Mum took a corner too fast in an attempt to get away. The car rolled."

"Jesus," Riley said softly.

"We landed upside down at the bottom of a short embankment. I had my seat belt on. So when I came to, I was upside down, but basically unhurt. But all I remember after that is the screams. My mother's screams. And then screams from the ambulance and police."

I twisted my hands in my lap. Still, even after all these years, it was difficult to say the words. "Brittany didn't have her seat belt on. She was thrown from the car. Pronounced dead on arrival."

Bile rose in my throat. "I don't want that for our baby, Riley. I never thought I'd have kids. I love my job. If I could have stayed away from acting, I would have. But it's always called me. I'm not happy doing anything else. But I never planned on bringing a baby into this!"

My voice cracked again, and Riley ran his hand up and down my back in long, slow strokes while I fought to control the rising panic.

He grasped my chin between his fingers and tilted it up, so I was forced to look at him. "That's not going to happen to our baby. I promise you that."

He said the words so fiercely and with such promise that every inch of me desperately wanted to believe him. But none of us could predict the future.

"You can't know that, though."

"Maybe not. But what I do know is we don't have to make the same mistakes your mother did."

"I have to give up acting," I said.

He shook his head. "And do what? You love acting, Bianca. It's part of you. You can't give it up."

"Then what?"

He ran his fingers through his hair. "I don't know yet. I didn't lose my sister, but I still have all the same fears you do. I fear for you every day that you aren't with me. But that's also no way to live a life, so I've learned to keep it in check. And now that's what you're going to have to do. What *we'll* do. Together."

"You really feel that way about me?" How had I missed that? I knew he hated the paparazzi but I'd always assumed it was because he didn't want his face in the magazines. I'd never even considered it was because he was worried for my safety.

He nodded. "I'd kill any one of those bastards if they hurt you, B. And I'll do the same thing for our baby. We'll take all the precautions. Get alarms, a bodyguard. I'll stay home with him so we can keep his life as private as possible. I don't know, but we won't make the same mistakes your parents did."

The fear and panic lessened a little as I realised I wasn't in this alone. My fears were shared, and that made the burden a little easier to carry.

His gaze burned into mine. "Do you trust me?"

Without hesitation, I answered, "Yes." And I meant it with every inch of my soul. I'd never trusted anyone more.

36

BIANCA

*S*adie was on one of her week-long trips to her mother's place, and when Riley insisted I stay with him, I didn't protest. There was nowhere else I wanted to be than in his bed. We barely left it. We'd slept, our limbs entwined, only to wake up, fumbling for each other in the dim light and making up for all the time we'd lost. We'd ordered food in between marathon rounds of sex and spent hours soaking together in Riley's old clawfoot tub. We didn't talk anymore about our worries over the baby. We just enjoyed each other, and this precious window we had where time seemed to stand still. But the clock had ticked on, and the honeymoon period we'd been blissing out on had to come to an end.

Sadie was due back any minute now, and I was still here.

"Are you sure this is the way you want to tell her, Riley?" I scrubbed a hand over my face for the umpteenth time that day, my stomach sinking at the thought of Sadie walking into her home and finding me here with her dad.

But Riley just kissed my cheek. "I told you, we don't have to say anything about the baby just yet. But she has to know we're together. You're important to me, and I'm not going to hide you like you're some mistress I'm sneaking around with on the side. I love you."

I gave him a weak smile, still convinced this was going to go horribly wrong, but I wasn't the girl's parent. It wasn't my place to decide what was best for her. If this was how Riley wanted to officially introduce me to his daughter, then this was how it would go down. But my gut churned with warning anyway.

Outside, a horn honked twice, and I stiffened, anticipating the moment Sadie would throw the door open and find me standing here like a chump. A freaked out, nervous-about-meeting-a-teenager, pregnant chump.

"Dad! You here?" Sadie called, waltzing in and dumping her backpack by the door.

Riley squeezed my hand. "Yes."

Sadie looked up, a grin on her face when she saw her dad. Then she noticed me, and I watched as her eyes travelled along our bodies, to where our hands were joined. The smile fell from her face.

"What is she doing here?"

Sadie's ice-laced voice froze my heart. I hadn't expected her to run up and hug me, of course. But the outright hostility in her voice was painful. I hadn't even officially met the girl, and she already hated my guts. I had no grand illusions of her loving her father's new girlfriend, but I wanted to at least be friends. Though I knew the odds of that ever happening were slim, especially after all she'd been through with our sex-tape scandal.

Riley ignored her tone and instead smiled brightly. "She's here because we're together. For good this time." He put his arm around me, tugging me closer.

I went, but it felt forced.

Sadie's eyes narrowed. She was roughly the same height and a similar build to me, but the look in her eyes was withering.

"What do you mean you're together? Dad! How dumb are

you?"

Riley stiffened at my side. "Sadie..." he warned.

But Sadie was far from done. She whirled on me. "You need to leave. You dragged him into a sex scandal that's only just died down, then you ran off to hide on a movie set while he was left here to pick up the pieces with a broken heart. Though why he even cared you left, I can't understand." She shook her head like she was completely disgusted.

And the worst part was, I knew where she was coming from. I was disgusted about the way I'd run off as well. My stomach ached at the thought Riley had been nursing a broken heart all these months.

Sadie turned back to her father, seemingly determined to tell us exactly what she thought of the entire situation. "Don't you care what everyone is going to say? She's been sleeping around Hollywood, getting herself knocked up by some jerk half her age, and now you're just going to take her back?"

Her gaze shot to my belly, and I fought the urge to cover it. Riley was so stiff beside me, I was surprised he hadn't snapped.

"You're just going to have some other man's sloppy seconds?" Sadie threw out the barb, and I felt it as keenly as if it had actually sliced my skin. Even though she was fifteen and angry and I knew she was just lashing out, it hurt.

Riley exploded. "Enough!" he roared.

Sadie's gaze snapped back to him in shock. Even I looked up at him in surprise. Riley and I had had some epic arguments over the years, but I'd never heard him raise his voice like that, and evidently, neither had Sadie.

"Riley," I said in a low voice, putting a calming hand on his shoulder as if he were a skittish horse. "It's okay."

"It absolutely is not okay," he said in a lower voice but one that still shook with anger. He took two steps towards Sadie, who was now silent. "You listen to me and listen to me good. You and I are a team and we always will be. But you won't speak to me, or anyone for that matter, like that. We brought you up better. I love her, and you're going to have to accept that."

Sadie's jaw clenched. "You love a woman who is having a baby with another man? You're an idiot. You think she loves you back?"

Riley practically vibrated with anger. "You're grounded," he spat out.

Sadie's mouth dropped open. I cringed. This wasn't going to help anything.

"Riley—"

"And for your information, Sadie, the baby is mine."

The silence that fell over the room was deafening.

"What!" Sadie choked out, her eyes filling with angry tears as she stared at Riley and me in horror.

I groaned. So much for easing Sadie into all this and not dumping it on her.

"You heard me. The baby is mine. And you're going to have a baby brother or sister."

Sadie shook her head. "I'm not."

"Oh yes you are." Riley retorted. "In fact, we're going for an ultrasound this afternoon. And you're coming."

Both Sadie and I gaped at him. Having a snarling teenager with us the first time we saw the baby was not exactly how I'd envisioned our appointment going. But when Sadie looked to me, I just bit my lip. I couldn't protest. I did want her to be involved...just not when she was being completely hostile.

"Argh! I hate you!" Sadie screamed and stormed up the stairs, slamming her bedroom door at the top.

I jumped as the sound echoed through the house.

Riley sank down into a chair and ran his fingers through his hair. "Well, that didn't go well."

I almost laughed. That was the understatement of the year.

37

RILEY

I hate you.

Logically, ever since I'd found out I was a dad, I'd known that at some point, Sadie would tell me she hated me. But after getting to fifteen and it not happening, I'd kind of stopped bracing myself for it. As the 'part time' parent, I'd fallen into the 'fun' parent role. Eliza had always had to deal with the discipline and the hard stuff, while I'd spent my weekends with Sadie taking her to amusement parks and the beach. And Sadie was a great kid. She'd always been so mature for her age, she'd never really given either of us much to discipline her over. She got good marks at school, because she enjoyed it. She seemed to like boys, if I went by the posters adorning her walls, but she wasn't one for sneaking off to parties. She was a good, *nice* kid. So hearing her say she hated me wasn't something I could just brush off. And I'd heard it twice in the last six months. It wasn't any easier the second time around. If anything, it was worse.

"Hey," Bianca said quietly from beside me on the lounge. "You okay?"

Her small hand ran over my biceps and up over my shoulder to squeeze the back of my neck gently. I leant into her touch, because it felt so damn good, and then, feeling hollow, I laid down, placing my head on her lap and kissing her bump. I closed my eyes as her fingers trailed through my hair.

"She didn't mean it."

"I know. But it still sucks. That wasn't how I imagined telling her would go."

To her credit, Bianca didn't say 'I told you so'. I knew she'd had reservations about her being here when I told Sadie, but I was so sick of everything being a mess. I'd just wanted it all out in the open and for everyone to be happy and getting along. I hadn't meant to tell Sadie about the baby. I certainly hadn't meant to ground her, then force her to come to the ultrasound with us.

I sighed. "I'm sorry, B. I can't go back on what I said about her coming to the ultrasound. She won't respect me if I just go back on my word."

Bianca made a small sound of affirmation, then said, "It's fine. Maybe it will help her feel like a part of this whole thing. I want her to be there. I'd rather she be there willingly, of course, but this baby will be a big part of her life, too. Maybe this will help her focus on the good that has come from this disaster."

I wasn't so sure but nodded anyway. Silence drew out between Bianca and I, and the lure of sleep pulled me down. Jetlag was a bitch. But I didn't want to sleep. Bianca would have to go home now that Sadie was back, and I wasn't at all prepared for it. I wanted her with me, night and day, but I knew that couldn't happen. I needed to soak in every moment now.

"Riley?" Bianca asked quietly.

"Mmmm?" I answered sleepily.

"What if there's something wrong with the baby?"

I cracked one eye open. "Ay?"

"I've had no prenatal care. I haven't taken any vitamins or

rubbed any cream on my belly, and that book I started reading on the plane? It said I should be able to feel it moving by now."

"You haven't felt it move yet?"

She shook her head, looking worried. "What if I've hurt it?"

I sat up and pulled her against my chest. "Stop. You haven't done anything wrong. You didn't even know."

"I should have known, though. What kind of woman doesn't realise they're pregnant for months? I was just so caught up in my own dramas... God. I'm an awful mother already. This poor kid is doomed."

I chuckled at her melodramatics. Once an actor... "You are going to be a terrific mother. You know how I know that?" She shook her head, and although she was trying to laugh, I could see real fear in her eyes. Which dried my laughter in my throat. She wasn't acting at all. She really was terrified she was going to be a terrible mother. "I know because you're scared. Which means you already love our tiny baby and you want what's best for it."

"What if I'm not what's best for it, though? I have a crazy job that takes up a lot of my time. I'm selfish. I've barely even held a baby and I've no idea what you do with one twenty-four hours a day. I've no maternal instincts, Riley. I've never had that 'oooh, a baby' gene that other women seem to have. I've never felt some biological clock ticking." She listed off all the reasons she'd be no good for this baby on her fingers, then she flopped back on the lounge looking defeated. "I suppose when this baby hates me, at least he or she will have something in common with her big sister."

I frowned. "Sadie doesn't hate you, and neither will this baby."

She let out a long sigh, then she pushed to her feet, holding out her hand to me. "I really hope you're right. Because I'm entirely out of my depth right now. But it's time to put my big-girl panties on, because we need to leave for the hospital or we aren't going to make our appointment on time."

Bianca went to wait in the car while I knocked on Sadie's door and told her it was time to leave. Muffled grumbling came from the other side, but then she opened the door and stormed past me. I followed her down the stairs and out of the house and winced as she yanked open the back door on my jeep, climbed in, then slammed it behind her. The whole car rocked, and I took a deep breath and reminded myself that this was difficult for her and that I needed to be patient. But damn, she wasn't making it easy.

The car ride to the hospital was tense and quiet, and I kept glancing over at the two women who my whole life revolved around. Bianca stared off into space, her hands resting on the swell of her stomach. Sadie bored holes through the window with laser precision focus, refusing to make eye contact with me for the entire drive. One woman terrified, the other angry. Awesome.

Bianca's manager had organised for us to go right in to see the doctor, bypassing the public waiting room for fear of causing a scene, and we were only there for a few moments before we were sent farther down the hall for the ultrasound technician to do her thing. Sadie found a chair in the corner and slumped in it with her arms crossed over her chest. While Bianca climbed up on the table and laid back, lifting her shirt to reveal her smooth skin.

"Okay," the ultrasound tech announced. "I'm Bernice." She sifted through a file then pulled a stool over to Bianca's side. "I just need to lower your pants a little and tuck this cloth in to protect your clothes. Is that okay?"

Bianca nodded, and I moved to her other side. Her hand immediately found mine, and I squeezed it reassuringly.

"First time seeing your baby, huh?" Bernice said kindly.

Bianca looked so nervous, and I was worried by how pale she'd suddenly gone, so I answered for her. "Yes. First time. We've only just found out."

On the edge of my vision, I saw Sadie roll her eyes but I ignored her. Too distracted by Sadie's snarkiness and Bianca's nerves, I realised I hadn't even given myself a moment to feel anything. But shit. I was about to see my unborn baby for the first time. And then I suddenly realised why Bianca was so pale.

Bernice squirted some gel onto Bianca's belly, and B closed her eyes as a wand was pressed on top. Immediately, a steady thumping sound filled the room, and there, on a fuzzy black screen, appeared the outline of a tiny baby. The blood drained from my face. Holy shit. It was real. It was really real. You didn't need to be a professional to make out anything. There was a fully formed baby in Bianca's belly. And it was mine. It was ours.

My gaze met Bianca's and held it, the sound of our baby's heart beat echoing between us.

"Everything looks perfect for how far along you are," Bernice said cheerfully. She moved the wand around and peered at the screen, stopping only to tap some numbers into the keyboard.

A grin split my face, and I leant forward to kiss Bianca on the top of her head. "See?" I whispered in her ear. "He's perfect. Just like his mother."

Bianca blinked back the moisture in her eyes and tilted her chin up to kiss me. And all I could think was how much I loved her, and how much I loved the baby we'd created together already. It couldn't have been a more perfect moment.

"It's not even cute," Sadie said brattily from the corner. "It looks like an alien. Its head is huge. Good luck pushing that out."

I sighed. Well, it was almost a perfect moment. Now that we knew the baby was healthy, the next step was getting his big sister on board.

38

BIANCA
3 MONTHS LATER

I had never realised how slow a single week could be until I was pregnant. Unemployed, and pregnant anyway. I couldn't go back to *Ocean Bay*, not with a noticeable baby bump that couldn't be written into my character on the show. Tangie had arranged extended leave for me, and I was due to go back to work when the baby was three months. But right now, still five weeks away from my due date, going back to work seemed a lifetime away. I was stuck in some sort of limbo. I didn't like to leave my apartment much. The press followed me every time I did, yelling questions about where Jerome was and why I was hanging out with my ex. In the past, I'd had a somewhat friendly relationship with the paparazzi, but now they scared me. I was terrified they'd all crush me for the chance at a photo of my bump. This baby's life seemed infinitely more precious than my own. Risks I'd taken when it was just me seemed reckless and unimaginable now that I had someone else to think about

I picked up my phone, dialling Jerome's number, and waited impatiently for him to answer. I'd taken to doing that at least once a week.

"Hey," he said sleepily.

I looked at the clock, realising that with the time difference, it was likely the middle of the night there and I'd woken him up. Tough luck. He still owed me.

"Just checking to make sure you haven't started any new rumours."

"I haven't said a word beyond *no comment*. I swear. You don't have to keep reminding me."

The press still all thought Jerome was the father, and since he was in LA and I was here, they were constantly sniffing around for some sort of story. They'd been relentless. Jerome and I had both agreed to not comment at all on the status of our relationship and the fact the world thought he was my baby daddy. Neither of us would give the press anything. Me protecting Riley and Sadie. Him protecting the newfound fame he'd found, even if it was for all the wrong reasons. But at least he'd kept his big mouth shut. And beyond that, I didn't care what he did.

"Good."

He mumbled something about trust, which was laughable, but I ignored him and hung up.

I wandered aimlessly around my living room, straightening photo frames that were already straight and then flipping through a parenting magazine I'd read cover to cover. I threw it down on the coffee table, frustrated, and rubbed my lower back. It had been aching all day and just made me even more irritated than normal.

Things were still frosty between Sadie and me. To the point that I'd stopped going over there. Most days, Riley dropped in at my place on his way home from work, but he could never stay long. He didn't like to leave Sadie alone at night. Tangie was still cranky at me for screwing up the whole gig in LA, and though my friends all dropped by from time to time, it was lonely being at home by myself so much, with nothing but a baby bump for company.

At least I could feel him moving now. We didn't actually know it was a boy, we'd chosen not to find out, but Riley seemed certain, so I went along with it. It was easier than saying "he or she" every time. The ultrasound had showed the baby's placenta was on the front of my uterus, which was why I hadn't been able to feel him move, but now that he was so big, it was impossible not to. I smiled, thinking about the first time he'd kicked Riley. The look of pure delight on his face had filled my heart with so much joy, and I longed for the day I'd see our baby in his arms.

But then I realised that seeing him in Riley's arms meant I'd actually be a mother. And I still wasn't sure how I was going to deal with that. Every time I thought about it, I immediately pushed the idea from my head.

A knock at the door startled me, and I waddled over to open it and let Riley in. He kissed me, smelling of sunshine and sweat and wood, having come straight from work. He bent to kiss my bump, just the same as he always did. But then he pulled back and frowned.

"Are you okay?"

I opened my mouth to insist I was fine but then I closed it. Was I okay? Honestly?

"No." I shook my head slowly, realising I really wasn't fine at all. "I mean, I am. The baby is good and everything. I think he's been turning somersaults today. I just..." I threw up my hands. "Riley, we have five weeks to go, and this baby hasn't even got a bedroom. I've got no bassinet!"

I paced the length of the living room before something dawned on me and horror turned my blood to ice. "Riley, he's going to have to sleep in a cardboard box! Or a drawer like it's the nineteen-twenties. And then the paps will get a shot of him asleep in a washing basket or something. The magazines will pay a fortune for that, and then Department of Child Services will be on my doorstep, taking him away from me!"

I rubbed my belly protectively as Riley laughed.

"Why are you laughing?" I wailed.

Riley sobered immediately. "Oh, shit. You were being serious?"

"Yes!"

He was still chuckling when he held his arms out to me, and I stepped into his embrace grudgingly. My annoyance softened as his arms circled me, and I rested my head on his chest.

"You've been cooped up in this apartment too long."

"I know."

"I'm going to ask you something. Again. And this time I'd really like you to say yes."

I buried my face in his chest. I knew what he was going to ask. Because he'd asked me twice in the past few months since we'd gotten back together.

"I love you, B. Marry me. This baby is coming so soon. Marry me and move in with me. I don't like you over here, by yourself, stressing out over the paparazzi while I'm wandering around my big house, wishing you were there. I'm not going to stop asking until you agree. So you may as well just agree now."

He smiled down at me, and it was so boyishly charming that I almost said yes. Almost. But just like the other times he'd asked, I hesitated. And he sighed.

"Okay, okay. It's another no. You're lucky my self-esteem is pretty high, because all these knock backs would seriously wound a lesser man."

I giggled and pulled his mouth down to meet mine. "I love you. I'm just not ready to get married...but..."

Riley raised one, hopeful eyebrow. "But? There's never been a but before."

I considered what I was about to ask. I'd been holding out on moving in with him, even though I knew it was the logical next step. I wanted to. So badly. Sleeping apart from him was torture. I wanted to do all that pregnant, couple stuff. I wanted to wake him at three a.m. and tell him to go get me ice cream with hot sauce and pickles. Not that I actually craved those things. Gross. I just wanted the opportunity.

But I'd been trying to give Sadie as much time as possible to come around. I'd hoped we would have been able to form some sort of friendship, or at least a tolerance for each other by now, but it really hadn't happened. If ever I was over there, Sadie disappeared to a friend's house or into the depths of her bedroom. She'd iced me out at every opportunity. But whether Sadie was on board or not, I was running out of time. I didn't want to be here alone anymore. I didn't want to be bringing this baby home to a house that wasn't a family home, the way Riley's home was. I wanted this baby to have full-time access to his father. And Riley deserved that, too. The chance to the be the parent of a newborn. The chance Eliza had robbed him of. I didn't want to do the same. "I would like to move in with you. If you'll have me, of course."

Riley looked stunned for a moment, then let out a whoop that the paps on the street outside probably heard. He picked me up and hugged me so tight I let out a gasp as the baby pressed down on my bladder and I fought not to pee myself.

"Too tight!" I yelped.

He immediately let me go. "Oh shit, sorry, sorry! I just got over excited. You're serious? You're going to move in?" His eyes were as wide as a kid on Christmas morning, and I realised for the hundredth time how lucky I was that this man had waited ten whole years for me. He could have gone off and married someone else, but he hadn't. And here he was, patiently waiting on me again. I loved him with every inch of my being.

"You know what?" Riley asked, scanning the room for god

only knew what. "Don't answer that. You're moving in. No taking it back." He stormed into my bedroom. I followed slowly, because I really did need to pee now. There was so much pressure in my lower belly I felt like I was going to explode.

When I reached the bedroom, Riley had my suitcase open and was throwing clothes into it haphazardly. He yanked open a drawer and dumped out my entire underwear collection.

"Riley!"

He waved his hand. "Nope, not listening. You're coming home with me. And you're coming home with me tonight."

He went back to emptying out my wardrobe, and I grinned as he worked. I was going home with him. Home, to be a family.

I had most of Bianca's clothes packed when she sat on the edge of the bed.

"I want this Riley, I really do. But before we move me into your house, what are we going to do about Sadie?"

For a brief moment, I cherished the way she said 'we'. Not, what are *you* going to do about your daughter. She was thinking of us as a team, and I loved that. But she had a point. I sat beside her and sighed. "I don't know. We could ship her off to military school?"

Bianca rolled her eyes. "You don't mean that."

I nodded. She was right. I'd never even for a minute consider sending Sadie away. Not after fighting for access for her entire life. I loved that girl more than life itself, even if her behaviour lately had been less than admirable. "She'll get used to it," I said eventually, not really all that sure if my words were true. Sadie was fighting back against all things Bianca and baby pretty loudly.

"What if she threatens to move back in with her mother?"

"It won't come to that. But even if it does, that has to be her decision. You're the woman I love, and you're carrying my child.

Living over here, alone... It's not good for you or the baby. You need to move in. I *want* you to move in."

She fingered the edge of the bedspread. "I know. We need to not royally fuck it up this time, though. Not like when we told her about the baby."

"Agreed. You keep packing. I'll go home, talk to Sadie, and come back and pick you up in a few hours."

She squeezed my hand. "Come back soon, okay?" She ran her soft lips against mine. "I can't wait to sleep in *our* bed tonight. And to be your live-in girlfriend."

I wrinkled my nose. Live-in girlfriend. It wasn't even close to a good enough title for the way I felt about Bianca. I wanted her to be my wife. I hadn't looked at anyone else for almost my entire adulthood. She was it for me. I didn't know why she was holding back, when I knew I was it for her, too. But I'd give her the time she needed, I'd keep asking, until that one day where she'd say yes.

I leant in and kissed her neck. "I'm going to make my live-in girlfriend come so hard tonight she sees stars," I promised.

"Is that some sort of signing bonus?" she asked with a sexy smile.

"It's an everyday bonus. Get used to it." I stood and gave her a mock salute, loving the way her gaze had suddenly turned hot.

"One hour. I'll be back. Be ready, or I may have to throw you down on the back seat of the car for old times' sake."

She laughed and shooed me out the door. I went. Grudgingly. I was dreading this talk with Sadie, but at least there was a reward waiting on the other side. And Sadie had had plenty of time to get used to the idea. She was a mature, young woman. She'd see sense, and everyone would be happy.

Especially me. I'd be surrounded by the two women I loved and the little bundle about to make his entrance into the world.

40

RILEY

"Sadie?" I called the minute I walked in the door. The stairs squeaked as I thundered up them, making a beeline for her bedroom. The white painted door opened when I reached it, and I stopped short.

A broad-shouldered teenager, already a few inches taller than me, filled the doorway.

"Nathan?" I asked, immediately recognising Elodie and Jamison's eldest son, but having no conceivable idea why on earth he'd be coming out of my daughter's bedroom at eight p.m. at night. Then I remembered Eliza's warning about our daughter's crush on the boy.

My protective dad gene turned up to one hundred, and agitation tightened my skin. The urge to demand what the hell was going on here was on the tip of my tongue, but I'd just told Bianca I was going to try to talk to Sadie calmly, and opening the conversations with accusations about what she was doing with a teenage boy in her bedroom was not the way to do it. My gaze darted past him to where Sadie sat on the bed. Fully clothed, at least.

"You, go," I said to Nathan sharply.

With a quick glance back at Sadie, he darted down the stairs.

I stiffly sat beside her on the bed. She didn't say anything. No yelling about kicking her boyfriend out of the house, which told me she knew she was in the wrong. Jesus, was he her boyfriend? I pushed the idea away. One drama at a time.

"We're going to talk about that later," I said as sternly as I could muster.

She shrugged.

"But right now, there's something important I need to talk to you about."

I shifted on the bed so I was facing her, but Sadie still sat with her feet hanging down, kicking at the carpet with the tip of her Converse sneakers.

"Sadie..."

She turned, mirroring my pose, and lifted her head to look at me. "Dad..." she mimicked.

I couldn't help but smile. She was a little smart-ass sometimes. "We need to talk about Bianca."

Sadie rolled her eyes and went to stand, but I grabbed her wrist and tugged her back down.

"No. Sit. I've given you months to get used to the idea of Bianca and me. But you haven't come around by yourself like I hoped you would. You don't even give her the time of day, even though she's been trying to get to know you. And I realise now, that that's my fault. Because I haven't been honest with you. I've been treating you like a little girl, and I know you aren't one anymore."

That seemed to get her attention.

She sat back down. "You've been lying to me?"

Her voice sounded small and hurt, and I understood why.

"More like I just haven't told you the full story. Bianca and I used to date, a long time ago. Back when we were in our early twenties, we worked at a bar together. Did you know that?"

She shook her head. She seemed interested, so I continued.

"We were friends for a while, and then we started seeing each other. I fell for her, Sadie. Hard. I was head over heels in love with her."

"What happened, then? She didn't love you back?"

I shook my head sadly, remembering so clearly those early days with Bianca. All the mornings I'd woken up with my arms around her naked body, all the whispered words of love, all the plans we were making for the future. "No. She loved me back." I mulled over my words carefully. "But then you came into my life. And she immediately fell in love with you, too. Just like I did. You were all blonde curls and big eyes and, baby, you made me so damn happy. Maybe too happy."

"I don't understand," she said looking confused.

"I didn't either, at the time. Bianca began distancing herself. And I admit, I thought it was because she didn't want to be burdened with a guy who suddenly had a five-year-old in tow. I spent a lot of years being hurt and angry about that. But that wasn't it at all. She loved me enough, and *you* enough, that she stepped aside. I've only just found out myself, but Bianca's had a lot of loss in her life. Bianca didn't want that for you. She wanted you and me to have a shot at being a family. With your mum. She wanted you to have a normal, happy childhood."

"What? But you and Mum sucked at being together. All you did was fight."

I grimaced. "You remember that?"

She shrugged. "Bits of it. I mostly just remember being happy when you moved out and we got to do fun things together on the weekends instead." She was pensive for a moment, then tilted her head to the side. "Did you love Bianca the whole time you were with Mum?"

I let out a long breath. "Yes," I admitted. "After Bianca broke up with me, I was hurt, and your mum was there for me. She's a good friend like that." I gave her a wry grin. "But as you might have noticed, your mum and I are better as friends. I love her, but..."

"But not the way you love Bianca."

I smoothed back her hair, then pulled her head to me and kissed the top of it. "You're pretty perceptive for a fifteen-year-old, you know?"

She laid her head on my shoulder like she had when she was five years old, and I stilled as the flood of memories washed over me. Then I put my arm around her and squeezed her.

"I want you to be happy," she said quietly. "I do. I know I've been acting like a brat, but the whole sex tape thing..."

"I know. We screwed up, and you got hurt in the process. I never apologised for that, and I should have. I'm really sorry, Sadie. We won't ever do anything like that ever again."

"Good. Because that's disgusting. Nobody needed to see that, Dad."

I snorted. That was the truth. But then I sobered because there was more to be discussed. "Bianca's moving in."

She pulled back sharply. "What! No!"

"I need her to be here, Sadie. I love her, and she's having my baby. I missed out on your first five years. Please don't make me miss out on your little brother's as well."

She looked up at me with big brown eyes. "It's a boy? I'm getting a brother?"

"I think so."

She mulled that over for a time, and I stayed silent, praying the next words out of her mouth wouldn't be 'I'm going to live at Mum's.' Because if she did decide to leave, I knew it would break me. I was so damn close to everything I wanted, I just needed Sadie's nod of approval.

"If Bianca moves in, I get to name the baby," she declared.

I choked on a laugh. "And what would you name it?"

She didn't even hesitate. "Draco."

I pulled a face. "As in the evil kid in *Harry Potter*?"

She shrugged. "Slytherin for life."

"Not a chance in hell, kid."

She pouted, but then she kissed my cheek and stood. "Maybe Bianca will like it and the two of us will outvote you."

Relief crashed down on me. She might not have said the words *Bianca can move in*, but I felt her blessing in them anyway. And in that moment, I really hoped she and Bianca would join forces and gang up on me. My heart swelled at the thought of them working as a team and laughing together, even if it was at my expense.

I just hoped I didn't end up with a kid named Draco.

I turned the radio up as high as my ears would allow and cruised through the city streets on the way to pick up Bianca. An excited buzz thrummed through my veins, as heady as any drug. I was picking up the woman I loved and bringing her home. Our house. And I couldn't wait another minute. I pushed my foot down impatiently on the accelerator only to be on the brakes again when the light at the intersection turned red.

"Come on, come on," I muttered impatiently. The streets outside were lit up, despite the late hour. It was Friday night, I realised. Early for most then. People moved from club to club, running to avoid the light rain that had just begun to fall. I'd been one of them, once upon a time. But now the thought of spending my night in a smoky bar, surrounded by sticky floors and strangers didn't seem very appealing. Not even close to as appealing as staying at home with my little family.

The song switched to *Living on a Prayer* by Bon Jovi, and I grinned and sang along, even though I wasn't normally one to sing. But I couldn't help it. I was so jazzed up, I needed an outlet, and since I was stuck in the car, singing was all I had. The light went green, and I inched forward with the traffic before the road opened up and I hit the accelerator for real. My thoughts were full of family board game nights, and bringing Bianca breakfast in bed, a tiny baby swaddled in a bassinet next to her. Damn. The thought nearly took my breath away. I knew she was worried about being a mother, but I wished she saw what I saw. I wished she could see what I already knew. That she was going to be amazing.

A screech of tyres cut through the song, and I whipped my head to the right to see headlights barrelling down on me. Blinded, I didn't have time to do anything before the car slammed into me with a sickening crunch of metal against metal. And everything went dark.

41

BIANCA

*W*hen the clock hit ten p.m., I'd call him. Not a minute before. That was the promise I'd made with myself. Riley had gone to talk to Sadie over two hours ago, and I hadn't heard a peep from him since. I wanted to give them time to discuss everything but I was going insane. She'd see reason, wouldn't she? Losing her now would kill Riley, and that would kill me. I was so nervous my leg had developed a twitch.

The time on my phone finally changed to ten p.m., and I hit the call icon next to Riley's name. My stomach swirled as I waited for him to answer. But it just kept ringing. Was he taking so long because the talk had gone badly? Was he right now driving her to her mum's place? The thought made me feel ill.

"Pick up, pick up, pick up," I muttered, but the phone went to voicemail. Shit.

I dropped it on the coffee table and paced the living room again. I was worried and tired and uncomfortable. The ache in my back had gotten worse. I just wanted to go soak in Riley's bathtub, put on some comfy PJs, and crawl into bed.

"Screw it." I grabbed my car keys from their spot on the white kitchen bench, pulled out the handle on the suitcase Riley had shoved half my clothes into earlier, and locked the front door behind me. His house was only fifteen minutes from mine, and there was no reason for him to come pick me up. I was still perfectly capable of driving myself, even if my belly did almost touch the steering wheel.

The dull ache in my back intensified as I drove, and halfway there, I noticed pain low in my abdomen as well. I wanted to cry. Pregnancy sucked. I was so huge, something was always hurting. It was still too early for labour, and I knew a good back rub would help the pain. I'd make Riley give me a long massage before he even thought about giving me those orgasms he'd promised. The idea of his hands soothing the ache in my back was more appealing than an orgasm right now anyway.

I pulled up at Riley's house, frowning when his jeep wasn't in the driveway. There was a light on upstairs in Sadie's room though. I got out my phone and called Riley again. Still no answer. Well, now what? Pain stabbing through my belly made my decision for me. "Ow," I muttered, rubbing at the sore spot. "All right, all right, baby. I'm getting out of the car." The door of my convertible swung open effortlessly, and I used the frame to haul myself up into a standing position. My belly was so tight and heavy, though, that it drained what was left of my waning energy. I had to stand there for ages, leaning over the car, trying to catch my breath.

A sharp pain stabbed through my back and abdomen, and something gushed within me. My heart slammed against my chest in shock as liquid ran down my legs. It wasn't a trickle. And there was no mistaking it for something else.

My waters had just broken.

"No," I whispered, staring at the amniotic fluid puddling around my feet. It was too early. I was only thirty-five weeks. I still had at least two weeks to prepare. To paint the nursery. I had no baby clothes! No car seat. Nothing.

"Riley," I yelled in panic before remembering his car wasn't here, which meant he wasn't either. I looked around the dark street helplessly. My breaths came in short, shallow gasps until the pain stabbed through me again.

A head appeared in the upstairs window. "Bianca?" Sadie's voice yelled.

I had to wait a beat before the contraction passed and I could talk again. "Yeah, it's me," I called back weakly. "Where's your dad?"

"He went to get you. At least, I thought he did?"

Another pain gripped my belly, and I doubled over with a cry. Oh my god. I fought to control my emotions as the pain ebbed away. These contractions had gone from uncomfortable to painful in the space of minutes. Was that normal? My heart thumped. I didn't know what to do. I was scared. I wanted Riley.

Sadie appeared out of the darkness, making me jump. Her light-coloured PJs, and long, blonde hair was ghostly, streaming out behind her as she ran around my car. "Bianca?" She asked in a small voice when she reached my side. "What's wrong?"

I smiled at her, trying to be reassuring, but another pain gripped me, stealing my words. When it subsided, I looked up into the girl's frightened face and realised I didn't get to be the one to fall apart right now. "I think I'm in labour. How long ago did your dad leave? He's not answering his phone."

She bit her lip. "Ages ago. I've been wondering where he is."

I nodded, not letting her see how worried that information made me. Where the hell was he? It wasn't like he'd stop off for a drink at the bar. He'd said he'd be right back to pick me up.

Another contraction hit and I tried to stifle a groan, but the noise seemed to startle Sadie into action. "Shit, Bianca, you need to go to the hospital. Can you drive?"

I shook my head, because no way was I getting back in that

car and trying to drive myself somewhere with pains like this. "I think we need to call an ambulance."

Sadie's eyes went wide, her fingers trembling, but she nodded, and I watched her stab out 000 for emergency.

"Yes, hello. I need an ambulance, please," she said in a steady voice.

In the darkness, her hand found mine and squeezed it. I looked down at her fingers clasped around my own, and even through my worry about being in labour and my missing partner, the sight filled me with happiness.

"They're on their way," she said, finishing the call.

"Thank you," I whispered. "I'm really glad you're here."

She nodded, suddenly seeming older than her fifteen years. "I'll stay with you until we find Dad. Where the hell is he?"

My eyes misted over, emotion overwhelming me. "I don't know."

And then we stood in the darkness until sirens pierced through the night.

42

RILEY

*S*omething was dripping. The constant *drip, drip, drip* was all my foggy brain could comprehend. *Drip. Drip. Drip.*

I cracked open one eye but quickly shut it as a bright light pierced through and splintered my brain. Nope. Wasn't doing that again anytime soon. Audio only seemed the safer bet. *Drip. Drip. Drip.*

With my eyes closed, I slowly became aware of other noises, but they just confused me more. They were all mixing together until it became one big blur of noise. I couldn't hear the dripping anymore. And I missed it. The drip was better than the chaos that swirled around me now. I forced myself to concentrate and identify the individual noises. Sirens, horns, people yelling, someone screaming. Where was I? There was no two ways about it. I was going to have to open my eyes again.

But even when I did, I couldn't make sense of what I saw. Everything looked wrong. Lights flashed, people peered in at me through cracked glass, and they were all upside down.

"Hey, mate," a voice called. "What's your name?"

I turned my head stiffly, wincing at the pain in my neck. I

squinted through the darkness, trying to find the voice that had spoken to me. If someone could just explain where I was and what had happened...

With a sudden rush of clarity, the fog in my brain cleared, and I realised I was still in my car. It wasn't the people who were upside down.

It was me.

Adrenaline coursed through my system, and I panicked, thrashing from side to side trying to free myself from what was left of my car. Something cut into my neck, choking me. I couldn't breathe. I couldn't breathe!

I opened my mouth to yell for help, but nothing came out. Jesus Christ. What was going on? I looked to where the man who'd asked me my name was and realised he was still there, speaking to me in a slow, calming voice.

"Whoa, whoa, mate. Eyes on me."

I did as he said because the thrashing wasn't getting me anywhere.

"You need to stay still. You've been in a car accident. You're upside down, and we're working to get you out. We're almost there, but you just gotta chill till we can get you, okay?"

"Okay," I managed to get out. God, it was loud. *So* loud. What was that noise?

"What's your name?"

"Riley." At least I remembered that much. Good start.

"Riley, I'm Ethan. I'm a paramedic."

I frowned. He had long, dark hair and a leather jacket. A chunky, masculine-looking ring of black and silver adorned the hand he was gesturing at me with. And tattoos crept up the side of his dark skinned neck.

"Riley, you with me?"

"Huh? What?"

"I asked where you have the most pain?"

"You don't look like a paramedic."

Ethan grinned. "Off duty. I was out on my bike."

That explained some things. I did a quick sweep of my body. "My head. Hurts."

Ethan nodded. "Yeah, you've got a pretty nasty gash on it. I'm going to hand you some gauze. Do you think you can hold it to the wound?"

I nodded, then thought better of it and replied with words instead. "Yes."

He winked, then yelled to someone. "Hold up for a second. He's awake, and I'm going in."

The metallic grinding noise stopped, and Ethan crawled through the smashed-out window, pressed something soft and white into my hand, then helped me hold it to my head.

"They won't let me stay in here while they're cutting you out, but you need to hold that there, okay? I can't see how deep it is, but since you're awake, it may not be as bad as it looks. Head wounds bleed a lot. Try to stay conscious, okay?"

"Got it."

A phone rang, and Ethan peered around the mangled wreck of my jeep. "Your phone has been going off ever since we got on scene."

"Glove box."

Ethan popped the button on it, but nothing happened, so he tried again with a closed fist. It sprang open, and he fished through the mess of papers until he came up with my phone. It was a lot less damaged than my jeep was.

Ethan eyed the screen. "Sadie?"

"My daughter. She's only fifteen. She's alone."

"I'll talk to her," he said, shuffling the rest of the way out of the car.

The grinding noise started up again, and I groaned. I still had no real recollection of what had happened. All I remembered was lights and noise and then nothing. Eventually, the grinding noise stopped, and the driver's-side door pulled away.

Ethan's face appeared in front of me again. "Hey, mate. Just gotta get this collar round your neck, then we'll get you out."

"I'm fine," I insisted but let him put the collar on anyway.

Then Ethan stepped away, and two other guys cut me out of my seat belt, lowering me carefully onto a stretcher.

"I'm fine, really, this is unnecessary," I complained, trying to sit up.

I had a headache like nothing I'd ever felt before, but other than that I had nothing more than minor aches and pains. I'd live. I was pretty sure of that. But I let him push me back down and load me into the ambulance. Where else was I going to go? My jeep was a write-off. And my head probably did need stitches.

Ethan shone a light in my eyes, took my pulse and my blood pressure and few other things as sirens blared and we raced through the streets to the hospital. He sat back and met my gaze. His face was grave.

"Shit. Why are you looking at me like that?" I asked. "Am I dying and I just don't know it?"

He shook his head. "Nah, you should be right. All your stats are good, considering the state your car was in. You're bloody lucky."

"Then what?"

"Your daughter..."

Fear gripped my throat like a vice. "Did you talk to her? Is she okay?"

"She's fine. But she's been calling you because your missus is in labour."

"What?" I roared, struggling to sit up again, but I was strapped to the damn backboard. I winced at the pain in my head. "Let me up!"

Ethan got in my face again. "Riley. Chill. They were in an ambulance on their way to the same place you're going right now. You're not going to get there any faster by moving."

"It's too early, though. She's not due for five more weeks." I struggled against my restraints some more. She couldn't be in labour yet. I had all these plans about how that would go. Bianca would wake me in the middle of the night and whisper that the baby was coming. I'd drive us to the hospital, and I'd be there to see my son enter this world. I'd missed Sadie's birth. I didn't want to miss another one of my children making their entrance. Fuck.

Ethan sighed. "Mate, you're going to need some scans and tests to make sure you don't have bleeding on the brain once we get there. Sounds like your wife was pretty far along. I think you should prepare yourself for meeting your kid a little later." He placed what was supposed to be a calming hand on my shoulder, but it was anything but.

I eyed him with a steely gaze that told him exactly what I thought of his tests.

"Not a chance in hell. Give me something to sign if you need to, but do it quick, because as soon as this ambulance stops, I'm going to find my family."

Ethan sighed. "Fine. If I let you up, will you at least let me put some butterfly strips on that cut?"

I nodded, and he undid the clips, letting me sit up and pull off the cervical collar. As we rolled into the hospital emergency bay, Ethan stuck one last plaster to my head and eyed his work.

"It'll hold, but you have to get looked at properly as soon as that baby is here, okay?"

I didn't answer. I'd had worse injuries playing football. I'd do the tests, but not until I knew that Bianca and the baby were okay. The vehicle stopped, and I was out the door and running for the entrance, Ethan yelling directions to delivery behind me.

My legs were wobbly, but nothing was going to stop me from getting to my family. I took the stairs to labour and delivery ward two at a time, my head pounding and my vision blurring. But with every step I prayed I'd make it in time. And that this baby would be okay.

I skidded into the delivery ward waiting room, quickly noting Sadie wasn't there, then rammed the buzzer by the locked door repeatedly. After what felt like a lifetime, a static voice came over the small speaker in the wall, then buzzed me in once I'd identified myself.

The nurse sitting at the desk on the other side of the door held a chart in her hand and glanced up as I entered. She blinked.

"What on earth?" the woman asked, standing and taking a step back.

I could only imagine what I looked like. Head all held together with tape. Hair messed up and full of blood. Eyes wild, chest heaving. Shit.

"Bianca James," I urged. "Where is she?" I whipped my head around the space but I was at a cross intersection. There were four different directions Bianca could be, and I was wasting time.

"Sir, you can't go in there if you're under the influence of drugs or alcohol. And your head is bleeding," the woman said.

"What? I'm not!" I yelled.

She edged towards the phone. That stopped me in my tracks. Was she...scared of me?

I held my hands up and tried a lower, calmer voice. "Please. I'm not on anything. My partner is here somewhere in labour, and I need to get to her." I took a step forward, but the woman held up her hand.

"Stop right there. I'm calling security."

Well, fuck. That was just great.

43

RILEY

I couldn't believe after everything else that had happened tonight, I was about to be kicked out of the delivery ward for being a suspected junkie.

"Please," I begged the nurse, trying to appear as non-threatening as possible.

But the old bitty had already made her mind up about me and wasn't letting me past. I could storm by her, of course, I was twice the woman's size, but where would that get me? No closer to finding my family. I clamped my fingers into fists and fought down the urge to scream. Where was Bianca?

Behind me, the door buzzed open again, and I spun around, expecting to see security guards. But Ethan, my paramedic, waltzed in in his heavy boots and jeans and clapped me on the shoulder. "You find her yet, mate?"

"No, not yet. I'm having a few problems being...admitted."

Ethan and I both turned back to the nurse, and in stunned disbelief, I watched as the old dragon lady's expression turned from wary to...something I couldn't even name. Did she just bat her eyelashes at Ethan?

He sauntered over and put his arm around her shoulders, his

dark skin contrasting sharply with the pale white of the woman. "Irene, this is Riley, and he really needs to see his girl. He was one of my patients and he won't go get treated until he sees her. And as you can probably imagine, just by looking at his head, I really want him to get treated so he doesn't die of a brain bleed and lose me my job. I cleaned him up in the ambulance, but it's temporary."

The woman, Irene, gazed up Ethan's muscular frame, and I almost rolled my eyes.

"Room twenty-two," she said without even glancing back at me. "But clean up first. Wash those hands!"

"Thank you," I called, more to Ethan than the nurse, and took off down the hall.

"I'll be in the waiting room to take you for those scans the minute you're done, Riley. No excuses!"

I threw him a thumbs-up, found the nearest bathroom to scrub the dried blood from my hands and face, before sprinting again through the corridor. My heart thumped as I scanned the numbered doors, rapidly approaching the one that had a twenty-two stencilled on the front. I skidded to a stop in front of it and pushed it open with a gentleness that was at complete odds with the way I felt inside. Inside, I was a complete mess, my emotions pinging around my body like fireworks. But on the other side of the door, the room was quiet and smelt fresh and clean. The lights had been dimmed. And there in the middle, were the two most beautiful women I'd ever seen in my life. I searched the room, but there was no one else here. No tiny baby, and Bianca still appeared very pregnant. Relief swept through me, and I breathed a full breath for the first time since Ethan had told me she was in labour.

"Dad!" Sadie yelled. She ran from her position at Bianca's side and threw her arms around me.

I winced when pain shot through my side but kissed the top of her head.

"Oh my god, you're here. Bianca's water broke, and we had to get an ambulance, and I didn't know what to do and—" Her eyes went wide as she took in the makeshift gauze bandage keeping the cut above my eye closed.

"Shh," I soothed. I grasped the sides of Sadie's face, tilting it up. And saw how very scared she was, but also the strength and determination of the young woman she was becoming. "You did everything exactly right, Sadie."

She nodded, her shoulders sagging a little. "Are you okay?"

"I'll be fine."

She took a step towards the door. "Can I go then? I don't want to be here for the bloody bits."

I grinned. "There's a waiting room just outside. I'll come check on you soon."

I was over at Bianca's side before the door even closed. She was standing, leaning heavily on a raised bed. She breathed slow and even, and when she looked up at me, she seemed to take a moment to register who it was.

"Where have you been?" she panted. Then her mouth dropped open, and her fingers reached up, hovering over my banged-up head. "What happened?"

"Sadie didn't tell you?"

She shook her head. "No, she—" She fell silent, dropping her head down on folded arms and rocked her hips side to side as a contraction racked her body.

My heart clenched at the low moan she let out. I couldn't help but touch her. She had a long, thin black shirt on, and I ran my hands down her spine while she swayed. After some time, she lifted her head and smiled weakly at me.

"Where's the nurse?" I asked, ignoring her earlier question

about my head. I could explain all that later. All she needed to concentrate on right now was herself.

"In and out. She should be back soon. She keeps telling me I'm doing great. Sadie was amazing. She's been rubbing my back."

I nodded. And when the next contraction hit, I massaged her lower back until it subsided. For over an hour, we did the same thing. Talking quietly between contractions when Bianca felt up to it. Her moaning and swaying seeming to be the way she felt most comfortable. After a while, though, the contractions grew closer together, and Bianca stopped talking in between.

A midwife came in an checked her, then announced she was getting the doctor. "The baby's head is almost ready to crown," she said to me with a smile and calmly left the room.

And I stared after her dumbfounded. Why wasn't anyone rushing around? Why wasn't there a team of doctors here, ready to catch this baby?

The midwife returned a moment later with a young female doctor, and the midwife put her hand on Bianca's shoulder. "Are you comfortable there, Bianca?"

Bianca nodded once, and the midwife grabbed a stool.

"Then you go ahead and push whenever you feel the need. I'll be here to catch the baby."

I looked around confused. "Shouldn't she be on the bed?"

The midwife smiled gently. "She should be wherever she wants to be. And since she got here, that's the position she's favoured. It's very natural. Lots of women deliver standing up or on their knees."

Bianca let out a low, guttural groan, silencing me. Then gazed up at me, her eyes wide with fear. She grasped my fingers tight.

"Hurts," she choked out. "Can't do—"

Another contraction cut her off, and I squeezed her fingers back.

"You can," I said firmly in her ear. "You're already doing it."

Her head turned to me, and our eyes locked for a moment. Then something steeled in hers before her eyelids closed and she gripped my hand harder.

"Need to push," she moaned.

The midwife was saying encouraging things to her, but the words all became a blur as I focussed in on the woman I loved. Her body tensed with each contraction, her low moans piercing my heart. I wished like hell I could take her pain away. Because I would. In a heartbeat.

"I love you," I whispered in her ear, holding her tight, while her legs shook.

And then her head dropped back on her shoulders, relief replacing the pain that had etched lines across her beautiful face. And a long, loud cry pierced the air around us. I stared down in shock at the midwife holding a tiny, pink baby.

"Bianca, lean back a little. I'm going to put her up on the bed in front of you."

"Her?" Bianca choked out the question.

And then the baby was lying on the bed, between Bianca's arms, her thick cord still attached to her mother. While I just stared at her in amazement, too frozen to the spot to do or say anything as my heart doubled in size to make room for our daughter. Bianca ran her fingers over the tiny baby's features as if in awe and then looked over at me with tears streaming down her face.

"It's a girl."

I had to fight back the lump in my throat before I leant in and kissed her lips so softly. "She's perfect. And so are you."

She let out a sob against my mouth, then leaned her forehead to mine. And that was how we stood, the baby between us, a new beginning I never thought I'd have.

"Thank you," I whispered, burying my face in her neck.

"Would you like to cut the cord?" the midwife interrupted gently. "It's stopped pulsing, so the baby has everything she needs."

I nodded, relishing these little tasks I hadn't gotten to do with Sadie. The midwife and I helped Bianca and the baby onto the bed, settling our little girl on her mother's chest and covering them both with a blanket.

I moved a chair close to them, and for a long time, neither of us said anything. There was nothing to say. Everything was exactly as it was supposed to be.

44

BIANCA

A timid knock at the door interrupted the bubble of insta-love I'd been floating in ever since my daughter had been placed in my arms. I almost wanted to tell whoever it was to go away. I wasn't ready to share her with the world just yet. But when Sadie's cautious face peered around the door, I gave her a warm smile and beckoned her in. She tiptoed over to the side of my bed and stared at the tiny, blanket-wrapped baby in my arms.

Riley slung his arm around his eldest daughter. "Sadie. Meet your little sister." The pure pride in his voice was clear as day.

Sadie's eyes widened. "It's a girl?"

"Yep."

"What's her name?"

Riley squeezed my hand. "Well, we were pretty sure she was a boy. We didn't actually discuss a girl's name. So she doesn't have one yet."

Sadie elbowed her dad. "How bummed are you that you're stuck with another female?" she asked, laughing.

But he just kissed the top of my head. "I couldn't be happier. All the best things in my life are female."

Another knock at the door sounded, this one louder, and when Riley called out, a man I didn't recognise stuck his head around the door. He took two cautious steps into the room, giving me an apologetic nod.

"Ethan, come in," Riley called.

Riley held out a hand to him, and I watched in confusion as Sadie flipped her hair, giving the man a smile that was nothing short of flirtatious. Whoa.

He grinned back at her, but thankfully, it was the grin of a protective older brother rather than a man who found her attractive. He had to be close to the same age as Riley and me, but I couldn't blame Sadie for trying her hand at flirting. The man was gorgeous. His leather jacket bore an MC emblem, and I wondered where the hell this biker had come from, what he was doing in my room, and how my boyfriend knew him.

"B, this is Ethan. He pulled me out of my car wreck and—"

"What!" I choked. "What car wreck?"

Ethan looked between Riley and me in amusement, and Riley turned to me sheepishly.

"I didn't have a chance to tell you yet. The jeep is a write-off."

"Oh my god. The cut on your head! I was so wrapped up in the baby..." I grasped his hand and pulled him close to me so I could examine him. "Are you okay?"

"Fine," he assured me. "Thanks to Ethan. He was the first on scene. Patched me up so I could be here with you."

Riley was making out it was no big deal, but I was doubtful. How bad was his accident if the entire jeep was scrap metal?

Riley squeezed my thigh gently through the blankets covering me. "Seriously, B. I'm fine. It was no big deal."

"He was lucky," Ethan confirmed. "But I really need him to get some scans done and make sure he doesn't have a concussion. I know you've only just had a baby, but..."

"I'll stay with her," Sadie said, and when Riley gave me a questioning glance, I nodded.

"Go. We're fine. We'll be here when you get back."

Riley kissed all three of us before he followed Ethan out the door.

"See you around, Ethan!" Sadie called after them, then flopped onto the end of my bed dramatically once the door had closed.

I stifled a laugh but didn't comment on her obvious, school-girl crush. I remembered what it felt like to be fifteen. You fell in love at the drop of a hat. It was harmless. And we had other, more important things to discuss.

"Sadie, can we talk?

The girl took her arm off her face and turned her head.

"You're a bit amazing, you know that?" I told her.

She shook her head as she sat up. "You're the one who had a baby!"

I reached out and took her hand. "You kept your cool and called the ambulance. And you obviously knew about your dad's accident but you kept it to yourself to protect me while I was in labour. Thank you."

She shrugged, then stared down at her hands. "I'm sorry I've been such a brat."

It was my turn to shrug. She had been a brat, but Riley and I hadn't made very good decisions either. "I know your dad has been on you to accept me, but I get it. I really uprooted your life and put you in the spotlight. I know my lifestyle isn't normal and it's not easy to get used to. I'm sorry you keep getting caught in the crossfire."

She nodded, then stood, moving to my side to give me a one-armed hug. She ran a finger down the sleeping baby's nose. "Thank you for my sister. I always wanted one. I'm glad she's not a boy."

I laughed and hugged her back. "Me, too. We're going to have a ball dressing her up."

Silence settled over us as we both watched the baby sleep.

Then I said quietly, "You know there are advantages to having me in your life. I can introduce you to Tate. I saw his posters all over your walls."

"Eh." Sadie sighed. "I don't think I'm into him anymore. He's such a...boy."

She gazed longingly towards the door Ethan had walked out of earlier, and I stifled a laugh. Sadie wandered off, no doubt to see if Ethan was still lurking around, and I placed our still nameless baby in the bassinet beside my bed. It almost broke my heart to do so. The moment I put her down, I wanted to pick her straight back up again. She was so beautiful she took my breath away, with her tiny button nose and rosebud lips. My heart seemed to have tripled in size in the past twenty-four hours—letting in not just the baby, but Sadie, too. They joined Riley who had held my heart for years.

I laid back on the bed and closed my eyes, the first waves of exhaustion washing over me. I'd been riding high since I'd gone into labour, but I was suddenly aware of aches and pains in muscles I didn't know I had. And I was tired. So very tired. I reached out a hand, grasping the side of my daughter's bassinet and pulling her as close to me as I could get her. She didn't stir, and I let sleep take me.

I awoke sometime later to the sound of the door creaking open and a hushed argument. Riley slept in the chair beside my bed, his hand resting on top of mine, both of us still holding the bassinet where our little miss slept soundly. I turned to the door and saw four heads poking around it.

"Sorry," Low whispered. "But we couldn't wait to come meet the newest edition to the gang."

I laughed and beckoned Elodie, Jamison, Reese, and Low into the room.

The guys held back, standing at the end of the bed. Elodie came to my side and hugged me gently, while Reese went straight for the bassinet.

"Ohhhhhhhh," she gasped, covering her mouth with her hand. Then she burst into tears.

"Hey." I laughed, touching her hand.

She wrapped her fingers around mine and squeezed as she shook her head. "I'm so sorry. I can't help it. She's just so beautiful."

Low went to her side and peered into the bassinet. A slow smile spread across his face. He put his arm around his wife and pulled her to his side, dropping a kiss to her hair. He whispered something in her ear, and the smile she gave him in return was blinding.

Riley finally woke up, and rounds of congratulations and back slapping continued while he grinned like the cat that got the canary. Flowers were thrust into my arms along with gifts, and I opened them all, cooing over how sweet they were. The baby woke up and was passed around like the world's most precious football, while I grinned from ear to ear. Reese cried again when the baby was placed into her arms.

"What the hell is going on with you? PMS?" I asked, unable to hold back my laughter. She had black mascara tracks running down both cheeks.

She shook her head and gave Low a questioning look.

He shrugged, then said, "Up to you."

They had the attention of the room now, and Reese turned back to us. "I didn't want to say anything..." she said to me with pleading eyes. "I didn't want to steal your thunder..."

I waved my hand around in the air. "No thunder to be stolen. Spill your guts, woman."

I watched her closely as she nodded, then rummaged through her handbag. She came up triumphant with a blurry black-and-white photo that I immediately recognised as an ultrasound picture. God knew, I'd had enough of those recently. I could spot one a mile away. My eyes bulged.

"We're having a baby!" she shouted.

And then it was my turn to cry. Emotion caught hold of me so quickly that a sob burst from my chest before I could control it. The guys all looked over at me, startled by my weeping, but I motioned for Reese to come forward and wrapped my arms around her. I knew exactly how much she'd wanted a baby and how worried she'd been that it might not happen for her. In the background, Elodie assured the guys my reaction was completely normal. Hormones and all that. Reese and I were both full of them, and we hugged and sobbed, and then eventually, laughed at exactly how ridiculous we were being.

She pulled away, but I didn't let go of her hand. I called Elodie into the little circle.

"We'll all have babies the same age," I practically sang. "We can go to mummy and me classes together and take them to the park, and they'll grow up to be best friends."

Tears were threatening my eyes again, but I didn't want to cry anymore. This was the happiest day of my life. I couldn't imagine anything topping it.

EPILOGUE
RILEY

*B*ianca's blonde hair fell through my fingers like golden strands of silk. I smoothed it back off her face, so beautiful and relaxed with sleep. We'd had a rough few hours after our friends had left the hospital. The baby had been unsettled for most of the evening. Probably protesting the fact she still had no name. Bianca had fed her, multiple times, then handed her to me to burp and settle. It was strange to have this new little person we didn't yet know, but already loved so much, in our lives. We weren't sure what made her happy, and neither of us had any experience with babies, so it was all trial and error. We were both exhausted by the time she finally fell into a deep sleep and I was able to crawl into bed with Bianca. She'd immediately curled into my chest and gone to sleep. But, despite my exhaustion, I hadn't been able to nod off. The private hospital room was dimly lit and quiet. Cosy really. But something tugged at me.

Bianca's eyelids fluttered open, and then she smiled up at me. But the smile quickly fell from her face, and she sat up a little straighter.

"What? What's wrong?"

Her gaze sought out our daughter, who still slept soundly, and I shook my head.

"She's fine," I whispered, placing a kiss to Bianca's temple. "I've been watching her this whole time."

Bianca relaxed a little but frowned. "You need to sleep, too."

"I know, it's just..." I knew what I wanted to say. I wanted to ask her to marry me. Again. She was already my partner, my lover, and the mother of my child. But I wanted more. I wanted her to be my wife. I wanted to stand up in front of all our friends and family and tell the world that she was mine and I was hers. Because that was how it always should have been. We'd wasted so much time. I didn't want to waste a second more. But she'd already turned me down, more than once, and I didn't want to ruin this amazing day with the memory of another failed marriage proposal. So instead, I changed the subject.

"She still needs a name, B." I trailed my fingers along her bare arm, just enjoying the feel of her skin. "We haven't even spoken about one."

"I know. Got any ideas?"

"Brittany. After your sister."

Bianca leant in and brushed her lips over mine. "You're beautiful for even suggesting that. And I would really like for Brittany to be her middle name. But I think she deserves her own first name. Something that's just hers."

"Chloe? Amelia? Isabelle?"

She shook her head.

"Lily? Summer? Skye?"

She pulled a face, and I sighed.

"Work with me here, B. Give me some sort of feedback at least so I know if I'm on the right track."

She looked over at our sleeping bundle for a long moment. Then she turned back and said slowly, "What about Billie?"

I quirked an eyebrow. "Billie?"

She nodded. "You wanted William for a boy. Billie is kind of the feminine version."

"Billie." A grin spread across my face. "I love it. But it's not the pretty, girly name I thought you'd want."

"Oh, you better believe I'll still be buying her all the adorable dresses. But I think this little miss is going to have a lot of her daddy in her, too. I can already see her kicking ass on a football field somewhere."

I laughed. "Damn straight. Billie Brittany Clarke." Her full name made me smile. "She'll be BB, just like her mum."

I pulled Bianca back against me, and when she lifted her face, I couldn't help but press my mouth against hers. I hadn't expected more than a brief brush of lips, but Bianca held me to her, opening her mouth, her tongue finding mine. We kissed for a long time. Slow and sweet and so full of feeling I had a lump in my throat by the time we broke away. I pressed my forehead to hers.

"You're everything, B. You, and our girls. You know that, right?" I whispered.

She nodded, unshed tears shining in her eyes. I knew why. I felt it, too.

"Ask me now," she whispered.

My heart leapt, and I pulled back to study her face, checking to make sure she was saying what I thought she was saying.

"Go on," she encouraged with a laugh as she took in my stunned expression.

I found her fingers and threaded mine in between, then brought them to my lips. I kissed each one in turn. "I've loved you for longer than I can even remember, Bianca. You've given me everything, now I want to do the same for you. I want to spend every day for the rest of my life, making you as happy as I am right this very minute."

A tear spilled over and ran down her cheek. I brushed it away with my thumb.

"Let me try, B. Let me try to be the man who makes you happy for the rest of your life. Let me be the one to wake up beside you every morning. Let me be the last person you see each night. I want it all. And I want it with you."

I needed to wrap it up because my words were becoming hoarse and I didn't want to cry in the middle. "Bianca James, will you please marry me?"

Even though she'd asked for this, my heartbeat still faltered in the momentary silence that followed.

"Yes," she cried loudly.

Billie let out a startled cry, and we both froze.

Bianca clapped a hand over her mouth and frantically rocked the baby's bed. "No, no, no. Go back to sleep, baby girl."

Billie scrunched her tiny features, but her eyes fluttered closed again, and Bianca and I both let out a relieved sigh. She turned back to me.

"Yes," she said again, in a much quieter voice.

I laughed as I wrapped her in my arms, finding her lips once more. My chest swelled with pride. I had everything I'd always wanted.

And this was only the beginning.

THE END

Want a free Only You series bonus book? Only the Lies is free when you join my reader family newsletter! Join for free here -> www.ellethorpe.com/newsletter

Or keep reading for a sneak peek of my hot new series of dirty talking, small town cowboys.

SNEAK PEEK OF TALK DIRTY, COWBOY

BOOK ONE IN THE DIRTY COWBOY SERIES

CHAPTER 1

PAISLEY

*T*he scratched kitchen table was covered in dirty dishes, cutlery, and food scraps. A plastic cup lay on its side, liquid slowly trickling out of it. Ugh. It looked like animals had eaten dinner there, not two small children. A long sigh fell from my lips as I watched the spilled drink drip into a puddle on the floor. At least it was just water, I supposed, as I fished around the sink for a sponge. At least it wasn't something sticky, and at least it wasn't dripping onto the carpet.

I made a mental note to check the state of the kitchen *before* sending Lily upstairs for a bath next time. If she hadn't been neck-deep in bubbles, I would have had her clean the mess up. I could hear her little girl voice belting out a *Moana* song from down here, and I smiled despite my annoyance that neither of my children seemed to know where the dishwasher was. Her singing warmed my heart. She took after me like that. I sang a lot too. Especially in, but not limited to, the shower.

Shoving aside the electricity bill that was two weeks overdue, I unearthed my phone and pulled up the Spotify app, scrolling until I found my favourite cleaning playlist. As Sir Mix-a-Lot's classic nineties hit, "Baby Got Back", poured through the speakers, I let the bass roll through me. I stacked the pile of dirty plates and danced them to the dishwasher. I couldn't help it. That damn song was infectious.

By the second chorus I was singing along at the top of my lungs, with my butt shakin' as I dropped forks into the cutlery holder and filled the sink with soapy water to attack the pots and pans. I attempted a quick little twerk, which went horribly wrong and I vowed to leave that one to the teenagers. Yikes.

"Muuuuuuum! Would you please stop that! Ugh! You're so embarrassing!"

I spun around, expecting to see my eldest child standing in the doorway with his regular preteen scowl on his face, but there was no one there. So I bumped and grinded the air as I danced towards the adjoining living room, wiping my hands on the back of my jeans as I went.

In the living room, Aiden was staring at the TV like a mind-less zombie, his fingers flying over a controller while he played some game that looked suspiciously like a rip-off of *The Hunger Games*.

"You know, you should never tell someone to stop singing, Aiden. Singing means they're happy. Sad people don't sing."

"Unless you're Adele," Aiden muttered.

He had a point.

"Henry! Go to Sandman's Curse!"

I jumped at his sudden change in volume, then rolled my eyes, realising he had an earpiece in. A microphone dangled on a cord by the far side of his face. The kid was obsessed with this game lately. If I didn't physically remove it from his hands some days, he'd do nothing else.

"Henry! No, back me up. I'm going in!"

On the screen, animated figures moved around, locating supplies and shooting at their enemies.

"Who are you playing with?" I asked curiously.

It always slightly concerned me when he played online video games, what with all the cyber dangers. He mostly played with a few school friends, but occasionally a name I didn't know popped up and when that happened, I liked to check out the situation and make sure he actually wasn't playing with some sicko making out to be a ten-year-old boy. This Henry kid's name had come up a few times in the past weeks and I hadn't had the chance to decide if this online friendship they'd developed was appropriate.

"Henry. You know, my bestie."

I raised an eyebrow. "I thought Simon Herringdale was your best friend?"

Aiden shrugged. "He is. He's my school bestie. Henry is my gaming bestie."

I was surprised when he didn't add a "duh."

"Rightio then. Tell Henry I said hi." I made a note to thoroughly check out this kid.

Aiden shot me a dirty look and covered his microphone with his hand. "I'm not telling him that!"

I raised an eyebrow. "Right, of course not. Sorry to be so uncool."

He rolled his eyes and went back to his game. Oh boy. He was only ten and already I was dreading the teenage years if this was where this attitude was heading.

I jogged up the stairs as a Celine Dion song came on and sang *extra* loudly, just so Aiden wouldn't miss out on the off-key, high-pitched bits that I was *super* good at. I hadn't been blessed with much of a singing voice, and it was the true bane of my existence. I would have loved to front a cover band or something. But unlike most of the *American Idol* wannabes, I knew I was bad. So the only people who got to hear me sing were my two poor, unfortunate children. God save their little ears.

I busted in on Lily and her bathtub full of horses and

scooped the giggling five-year-old up into a threadbare towel that really needed to be replaced. I hid my sigh while I dried her off and got her into her pajamas. I deliberately picked out a cute little onesie that made her look younger than she really was and wondered if she'd let me do her hair in pigtails tomorrow. She was getting big and was already in kindergarten. It made me sad sometimes. I missed her and Aiden being babies.

But then I shook my head. I might have missed them being babies, but I didn't miss the way my life had been back then. Full of stress and always lonely because my husband was a workaholic asshole who cared more about building his business than he did about his wife and children. I'd never sung back then. So now that I was asshole husband free, I made an effort to sing every day. Because he might have walked out of our lives with almost everything I owned and left me with nothing but my children, but it had really been the best thing that had ever happened to me. It gave me the kick up the butt I needed to get myself together. I'd let a man rule my life and left myself vulnerable in the process. I knew better now. Knew myself and what I wanted better too.

I lifted the horse quilt cover and motioned for Lily to jump in. She wiggled beneath the thick, warm blankets and I lay down beside her, reading her a story then waiting until she fell asleep.

I tiptoed back downstairs and crossed my arms over my chest when I noticed Aiden was still engrossed in his video game. "Bed, kiddo."

I held my hand up in a stop motion before he could even get his complaints out. He rolled his eyes, tossed the controller onto the coffee table, and huffed up the stairs in a funk of mumbled whining.

I pretended not to hear and called goodnight to him as sweetly as I could. Sinking down on the lounge, I let the pile of cushions envelop me in their fluffiness. I loved those kids to pieces, but I was always exhausted by the time they went to bed. I was looking forward to a night of watching Netflix and drinking wine.

But first, I had to clean the bathroom. I picked up a pillow and groaned loudly into it. Oh boy. Was my life ever exciting.

On the TV, Aiden's video game was still going, his computerized man standing still now that there was no little boy controlling him. "Ugh! Aiden!" I muttered. He was always doing this. Just leaving his stuff turned on for the battery to die. Or leaving his stuff on the stairs. Or basically anywhere but where it was supposed to go. I picked up his headset, looking for the power switch to turn the Bluetooth headphones off, and jumped a mile when a deep voice said, "Hello?"

I glanced at the screen. In the corner, a pop-up window showed a grainy webcam video of a man wearing a headset. My eyes widened. Where had that come from? I checked who Aiden was playing against, with dread rising in my gut—HenryAceiii. Oh no. No. No. No. This guy—no, this *man*—was not the Henry that Aiden had been playing with for the past few weeks.

And worse, the man was smiling, like me standing there gaping amused him.

Wait, *could* he see me?

Fury raged through me and I yanked the headphones over my ears. "You have got to be kidding me, you creep! How dare you start an online friendship with a ten-year-old boy! What kind of perverted animal are you?"

The smile immediately dropped from the jerk's face and he put down the controller he'd been holding. He raised his hands slowly in mock surrender, which only made my blood boil hotter.

"Woah, woah." He leant forward towards his camera. "Back the truck up. You're Aiden's mum, right?"

"I am, *Henry*. If that's even your name." I folded my arms across my chest.

"It's not."

I barked out a laugh. At least he was an honest sicko. "Of course it's not. Don't think I'm not reporting this. I will be—"

He laughed. The sound deep and rumbling. It made me want to reach through the TV and strangle him.

"Wait. Before you call the police, let me explain. I'm Henry's dad. You're the singer?"

I paused. "What?"

"You like to sing, yeah?"

His country accent reeked of small-town manners and long days on cattle stations. One I might have found attractive. But not when he was preying on my child and getting off on listening to me sing. Ew! Creep. Dirty, filthy creep. "I—no," I lied, unable to stomach the thought he might have been...oh god no. I couldn't let myself go there.

"Yeah, you do. I hear you singing it every day. The big butts song?"

My face flamed red and I suddenly hoped that our webcam was as grainy as his. The thought that he'd been listening to me sing, maybe for weeks now, was downright embarrassing. I'd never considered that anybody could hear what was going on in our house whilst Aiden was gaming. That was naïve of me.

I studied the man's laid-back body language. He was relaxed on a lounge not that different to my own. He wore a checked shirt, with the sleeves rolled to the elbows, the buttons loose around his neck. His skin was tan, his eyes friendly. He didn't look like a pervert. But it's not like being handsome got him off the hook completely. After all, Ted Bundy was a handsome man as well.

"You really heard that?" I asked, a little of the fire going out of me. If he was Henry's dad, that possibly made sense.

He chuckled, the sound deep and rich. "I did. I've heard many of your, uh, performances while Henry plays. You're good."

I frowned. Well, that was a red flag. The man was a liar. Nobody enjoyed my singing. Except me.

"Do you really have a son? You're not trying to groom my child?"

He choked on the word "groom". "I assure you, I have a kid. I have the messy bedroom and a load of foul-smelling socks to prove it. And here, look." The camera fuzzed out for a moment, before focusing again on a photo of the man with a child that looked to be Aiden's age.

It was really a very sweet picture. And I could relate to the dirty socks. That was for sure. Deciding to give the man the benefit of the doubt, I stood up again. "Well, thank you for the singing compliments. I am sorry you had to endure that. I'll turn this off now."

I reached for the headphones.

"Wait!"

My hands paused in midair while I waited for him to elaborate.

"Do you want to play?"

I frowned, looking down at the controller in my hands like it was some sort of UFO. "Video games?" Please, oh please let him mean video games. If *play* meant something else, I'd be shutting down Aiden's gaming account quicker than you could blink.

On the video, Henry's dad held up the controller. "Of course," he said with a puzzled expression.

I let out a sigh of relief. "I can't. I've housework to do. Plus, I don't...game."

He scrunched up his face. "Me neither. But do you really want to do housework? I've got a load of dirty dishes to wash and

I'm avoiding them. You'd be doing me a favour by keeping me from them. One game?"

I thought about the toilets that needed scrubbing. Then focused on the image of the handsome man with the cute accent on my screen. "One game," I agreed.

*K*eep reading here!

ACKNOWLEDGMENTS

First of all, a huge thanks to you guys, my amazing readers. I seem to gather a few more of you with each book, so if you're new, make sure you come find me on social media or drop me an email sometime! I love hearing from you! Thank you for spending your book money on my drama-filled, angst-ridden stories. I hope you love them. Please come join my readers group on Facebook for fun and games and general drama llama goodness. www.facebook.com/groups/ellethorpesdramallamas

And a special thank you to a couple of my drama llama readers...Julie Dickerson, who came up with the title Only the Beginning. And to Sarah Barton from A Book Obsessed Brit, and Stef from There, Their and They're who both typo hunted for me.

To my editor, Emmy, from www.studioenp.com. Thank you for all your hard work, and for getting this book in at the last minute. To all the Instagrammers, book bloggers and reviewers who make up my promo team. I'm so incredibly grateful for you all. Your support means everything. I don't have a cover designer to thank this time, because I designed this cover through my own graphic design business, Images for Authors.

To my author besties, Jolie Vines and Zoe Ashwood. I don't even know what to say to you two anymore. It would be like missing limb if I didn't have you two in my life. You two keep me sane. Thank you both for your amazing critiques and proofreads.

To my beta readers Shellie Maddison, Ally Murphy, Alisa Cavanaugh, Tamara McCall, Shannan Percival, and Karen Crompton. You're all incredibly helpful in different ways. The six of you together are like a some sort of beta reading super team. Thank you for always jumping to read my work whenever I send it to your kindles.

To Jira. Meeting you was my beginning of everything. And I'm forever grateful for the incredible, supportive man you are.

And to Tombliboo, Flicky-J and Heidi-Bug. I love your guts.

ALSO BY ELLE THORPE

The Only You series (complete)

*Only the Positive (Only You, #1) - Reese and Low.

*Only the Perfect (Only You, #2) - Jamison.

*Only the Truth - (Only You, bonus novella) - Bree.

*Only the Lies - (FREE Only You, bonus novella) - Cleo.

*Only the Negatives (Only You, #3) - Gemma.

*Only the Beginning (Only You, #4) - Bianca and Riley.

*Only You boxset

Dirty Cowboy series (complete)

*Talk Dirty, Cowboy (Dirty Cowboy, #1)

*Ride Dirty, Cowboy (Dirty Cowboy, #2)

*Sexy Dirty Cowboy (Dirty Cowboy, #3)

*25 Reasons to Hate Christmas and Cowboys (a Dirty Cowboy bonus novella, set before Talk Dirty, Cowboy but can be read as a standalone, holiday romance)

Buck Cowboys series (Spin off from the Dirty Cowboy series)

*Buck Cowboys (Buck Cowboys, #1)

*Buck You! (Buck Cowboys, #2)

Saint View High series (Reverse Harem, Bully Romance)

*Devious Little Liars (Saint View High, #1)

*Dangerous Little Secrets (Saint View High, #2)

*Twisted Little Truths (Saint View High, #3)

Saint View Prison - (Reverse Harem, Romantic Suspense)

Book 1: Locked Up Liars (Saint View Prison, #1)

Book 2: Solitary Sinners (Saint View Prison, #2)

Book 3: Fatal Felons (Saint View Prison, #3)

Add your email address here to be the first to know when new books are available!

www.ellethorpe.com/newsletter

Join Elle Thorpe's readers group on Facebook!

www.facebook.com/groups/ellethorpesdramallamas

ABOUT THE AUTHOR

Elle Thorpe lives on the sunny east coast of Australia. When she's not writing stories full of kissing, she's a wife and mummy to three tiny humans. She's also official ball thrower to one slobbery dog named Rollo. Yes, she named a female dog after a dirty hot character on Vikings. Don't judge her. Elle is a complete and utter fangirl at heart, obsessing over The Walking Dead and Outlander to an unhealthy degree. But she wouldn't change a thing.

You can find her on Facebook or Instagram(@ellethorpebooks or hit the links below!) or at her website www.ellethorpe.com. If you love Elle's work, please consider joining her Facebook fan group, Elle Thorpe's Drama Llamas

- facebook.com/ellethorpebooks
- twitter.com/ellethorpebooks
- instagram.com/ellethorpebooks
- goodreads.com/ellethorpe
- pinterest.com/ellethorpebooks